UNDER A CLOUD-SOFT SKY

Also by Elizabeth Gill

Far From My Father's House
The Singing Winds

UNDER A CLOUD-SOFT SKY

Elizabeth Gill

Hodder & Stoughton

First published in Great Britain in 1996
by Hodder and Stoughton
A division of Hodder Headline PLC

A CIP Catalogue record for this title is available from the British Library.

ISBN 0 340 66620 X

Typeset by Avon Dataset Ltd, Bidford-on-Avon, Warks

Printed and bound in Great Britain by
Mackays of Chatham PLC, Chatham, Kent

Hodder and Stoughton
A division of Hodder Headline PLC
338 Euston Road
London NW1 3BH

In memory of my father, Frank Gill, who was born at the Golden Lion and owned and ran the steelworks in Tow Law for many years.

And for my sister, Julia, who remembers our childhood and the places that I write about with such affection.

A great many people helped me with the research for this book. I would like to thank them. Phil and Sue Gates, who put me in touch with Arthur Wilkinson who told me about life in a steelworks; Kevin Leary of Lanchester History Society, who found Billy Hobson who told me about sharp sand quarries; John Smith of Durham University who got me some information on the Irish in Tow Law; the Tow Law History Society – my schoolfriend Jennifer Anderson, Ailsa Hanlon, Ronnie Storey, Ken Clarke, Arthur Marley and Madge Coughtrey; Brian Liddell of Printability Publishing Ltd of Hartlepool, who gave me the idea of sending my characters on holiday to Seaton Carew; Tommy Moore of Derwentdale History Society; the librarians at Durham City Library, the Town Hall library at Bishop Auckland and most especially those at Crook library, who have not only helped me with my work for years but always make me feel cheerful when I go to see them; and my good friends Billy and Una Horne for all the help and support. Una even thought of the title for the book.

Here is no pomp –
No storied building high:
Only the moor's dark rim
Shoulders the cloud-soft sky.

From the poem 'Weardale' taken from the collection *Rhymes of a Weardale Lad* by George Leslie Lister, published in 1969 by G. Bailes & Sons Ltd of Durham. Permission to quote was kindly given by Mrs Isobel Lister.

Prologue

At first Dennes used to think that he remembered the house where his mother had been born but as he grew older he realised that it was her talking about it that he remembered, and her talking about it altered as things changed, so that in his mind the house could be anything he wanted and he could people it with kindness. He only knew that it was near a river, that she had lived there with her parents and that it had been his fault they had had to leave. When the gin was sweet on her breath she blamed him for his being a baby, for his being there at all, for her losing her home and her parents because they had been ashamed and had put her out.

For a long time there was only the two of them in the house in Wesley Street. They lived in a small town called Deerness Law up on the moors of north-west Durham. He remembered stealing things for her, he thought he remembered that right from the start, her laughter, her seeming delight when he brought home whatever food he could take from the shops, her pretty teeth biting into the cake, and his reward was being pulled into her arms, against her body, the smell of gin.

'The only thing I'm glad about is that you aren't a girl,' she would say. 'You won't grow up, will you, Dennes, you'll be my little boy.'

He didn't want to stay her little boy, he wanted to grow, to grow up and be older, he willed himself there because he soon realised that the men who went upstairs with her gave her money and she didn't like going upstairs with them, she only pretended to them that she did because there was no money. He needed to be big enough and old enough to make money so that she wouldn't have to go upstairs with men any more.

For some reason the people in the village didn't like his mother. People didn't talk to them and they were not invited into other houses for a cup of tea.

He had come in one day out of the light, out of the street and he had said, 'Where's my dad? Why don't I ever see him?'

She had looked at him. Her lovely golden hair was thin and lank by then, her blue eyes dull.

'Your dad was a soldier, he went away and didn't come back. I expect he got killed. Aren't I enough for you? I'm enough for most. Don't you think I'm pretty, Dennes?'

Dennes pressed her about his father as he got older. What had he been like and when had he been killed and in which war, but her answers were short and vague and he learned nothing, and there was a small part of him which feared that he had had no dad at all.

When Joseph was little she kept on saying how glad she was that she had two boys, but all Dennes could think about was whether there would be enough to eat when Joseph grew and needed more bread, and he got work where he could so that there would be coppers to bring home to her.

Gradually she changed. She laughed less, she stopped cooking food for them, she stopped cleaning the house. She was not pretty any more by then and there was no comfort except sometimes when she was drunk and the men had gone. She tried not to get drunk before they arrived but she always did after they had gone. She didn't sleep and she didn't eat, she sat by the window and drank and she would think about the house then.

'I used to play the piano and we had a lawn and I could dance. I used to dance with men.' She laughed and put the cracked cup briefly to her lips as though she was drinking tea, taking tiny sips from it.

2

'I danced too often, Dennes, that's how I got you.'

Dennes grew and Joseph was her little boy. Dennes was not little any longer. He thought it was alarming how he grew. He was taller and bigger than the other boys and it meant that he could get work and make money when they couldn't – all you had to do was lie and sometimes you didn't even have to do that as long as you were cheap. Making money was like throwing it over the edge of the old whinstone quarry because it was such a small amount compared to what they needed. Dennes tried to make sure that he bought food for himself and Joseph before he went home. She rarely ate, but if there was not enough for gin she used to cry, and the sight of his mother crying was more than he could stand.

In the house daily there were men. Sometimes they stayed and he and Joseph slept on the rug by the fire, and when he awoke in the night there were sounds from above, laughter, the bed creaking, a man's voice low and her voice taking on the note that Dennes hated, the almost pretty, almost childlike voice, pleading. He knew somehow that that was what they wanted, that it was what all men wanted, for her to be almost a child, for her to pretend that she didn't want them to touch her so that they could be big, so that they could be powerful, so that they could win and be important. She never used that voice when the men weren't there. Dennes wanted to kill them.

The women in the village hurried past him. The back street was his territory, keeping an eye on Joseph until he got old enough to fend for himself, watching other children go to school.

'Can I go to school?'

'Not today. Run down to the Golden Lion and fetch some beer.'

From somewhere was the desperate desire to read and write, going to school occasionally – she didn't notice – struggling there at first because children younger than he was knew more and then the realisation that it was just another trick after all, except that reading turned more tricks for you if you let it. It let you run away in your head. It was another kind of pleasure and you could learn to control it, you could blot out the darkness and make it open at your will.

He was her big boy now, he was bigger than she was, as though not

3

only was he getting bigger but she was getting smaller. Sometimes he was in the way and it frightened him. Men frowned at him, sometimes more; he kept Joseph out of the road of their hands and their belts, away from the clouts and the kickings.

One

It seemed to Grace Hemingway, by the time she was fourteen, that there was no other place on earth which mattered but the small town of Deerness Law and its surrounding moors. She went to other places, it was true; her parents were concerned for her, they even talked of sending her away to school though it came to nothing and she was glad of that. She had been to Durham and Darlington and Bishop Auckland. She had seen the Tyne and the Tees and she knew that in the future she would see the Thames, because her mother had a sister in London and when she was older Grace would go there, but as far as she was concerned the real world was here where the bitter winds swept the fell, the people worked at her father's steelworks, and on a clear day when she had managed to escape from the house and its grounds there was beyond the town the clearest purest air that God saw fit to grace the earth. To grace it. Was that how her mother saw her? Something high and pure like the air upon the fell? Grace had seen the sea and to her that was what the fell was like, another sea where the wind reigned with its strange noises, the grouse flew low over the purple heather in the early autumn and as far as you could see there was nothing but that rich colour. She thought of God there. She never thought of God when she was in church but when she didn't believe in him she only had to go to the fell. It was better than any cathedral, better even than the rose window and the special knocker on the door at Durham Cathedral. It was the most wonderful place in the whole world and she lived here.

From here high up ran the water which turned into the River Wear. She had leaned over Framwellgate Bridge at Durham and seen the castle and the cathedral and the Wear in its wide way on to Sunderland, but here was where it all began, on the edge of the Durham coalfield and from the dale, the high fells and the moors where it started its journey running among the heather, where the curlew cried and the sheep fed and people had lived for hundreds of years.

People hadn't lived in her pit town for a long time like that. The village itself was less than fifty years old. Her father and his partner, Nicholas Barmouth, had come here twenty years before, in 1870, because of the mines and the raw materials to make iron and steel, and they had stayed.

It was winter here now and there were no bees buzzing in the heather. Everything was dark. The light had begun to fade from the short November afternoon and she would get into trouble when she reached home for staying out like this by herself.

She walked up past the Lizzie pit which stood on the outskirts of the village and then down the Front Street and off to the right, past the Co-operative store, the draper and the grocer and the shoeshop on the corner, down past the butcher's shop and the baker's, past the few houses and the Mechanics' Institute and then into her own short road where the doctor had his surgery, and there further along, standing quite alone, was her house.

Grace loved it like she thought she would never love a house again. It was a big square stone building with its own driveway which went around to the back, with carriage-houses and stables and a big yard with a hen house and a wash house and the back kitchen where Mrs Jackson, the cook, and Ruth, the maid, spent most of their time. Through from there was the kitchen and the pantry and the big place under the stairs where they kept crockery and jugs and vases and all manner of glassware. There was a little window under the stairs which you could see from the yard. It had looked to her when she was small like a shop with the different coloured glassware glinting through the window in the sunlight.

Through double doors there was the main part of the house where she lived with her parents, the dining-room and the sitting-room which overlooked the garden, and her father's study and the big dog-leg staircase which led to the bedrooms and from which a big arched window overlooked the yard. From her bedroom on a clear day she could see to Yorkshire. From the back bedrooms you could see the yard and the fields which belonged to the house and the backs of the houses on the main street. Further over was a pitheap past which you couldn't see anything, though there were more houses, and at the very top of the view were the graveyard and some trees. When she had been small Grace was happy that she did not sleep at the back of the house like Ruth did. She didn't like the idea of the graveyard even though it was nowhere near the house, a good field away.

The lights were on both at the front and the back. She went in by the side entrance which led from the back hall down past the front kitchen and through the front hall and the double doors. She could hear her mother, Dorothy, playing the piano. Mr and Mrs Barmouth were there for the evening and had come early. The piano playing stopped as she went in and her mother greeted her and scolded her a little, and then Mrs Jackson came in with the tea. There was fresh teacake and strawberry jam.

Alexandra Covington, Grace's friend, arrived shortly afterwards with her father. He owned three pits in the Deerness valley and they lived on the edge of the town towards the fell. Grace and Alexandra were both fourteen and had been friends for as long as Grace could remember. There were few girls in the village other than the doctor's daughter and the vicar's daughter who had anything in common with them, and Alexandra considered them both too stuffy. Alexandra was anything but stuffy, Grace thought now, as her guest arrived. She was a big dark girl who liked her food, had run her father's house for the last five years since her mother died and read all the books she could get her hands on.

They went up to Grace's bedroom to discuss the book they were

7

both reading and ended up talking about dresses and their hair until Ruth came to help them to dress for dinner.

'We don't need any help, Ruth,' Grace said, 'we can help each other.'

'Mrs Jackson said I had to come up so here I am,' Ruth said simply.

'Have a sweet,' Grace insisted, opening the box which Nicholas Barmouth had presented her with over tea. Ruth stared into the box and gingerly reached out. 'Have two,' Grace said.

'Thanks, Miss Grace.' Ruth stuffed them into her apron pocket. 'Don't want chocolate all over your dresses. I'll eat them later if you don't mind.'

They spent as long as they could changing for dinner to keep out of the way of the adults and finally went down only when they had to. Mrs Barmouth, Grace thought casually, didn't look well but then she was never well, and Mr Barmouth, although he was always polite to her, usually looked as though he would have been glad either to have been somewhere else or to have come without her. Sometimes he did come without her. She was pale and though the dinner was the best that Mrs Jackson and Ruth could prepare and therefore was good she ate virtually nothing.

Later Grace and Alexandra escaped again to her room and there Grace said, 'Mrs Barmouth didn't eat much, did she?'

'My father says she's dying.'

'Dying?'

Grace had never met anyone who had died except Alexandra's mother and that seemed such a long time ago now. She did not really believe that anybody died. She did not believe that she would ever die and leave the fell. But Alexandra's father was probably right. Mrs Barmouth had looked bad for a long time now. Because he had nobody else to talk to, Mr Covington talked to Alexandra like she was a grown-up, so they usually found out everything that went on, even though Grace's parents told her little. When she came into the room they usually stopped talking or changed the subject, which would have been very frustrating had she not had Alexandra to consult about important matters. If Alexandra mentioned them to her father Grace got to know

8

what she wanted. All she wanted now was for her small world not to change, for Mr Barmouth and Mrs Barmouth and her mother and father and Alexandra and Mr Covington and Ruth and Mrs Jackson just to stay as they were and for this Christmas to be the best ever. She hugged the thought to herself. Christmases were always good.

When the guests had gone Grace went to bed. She wasn't tired but she knew that her parents liked to have some time to themselves. Sometimes Alexandra stayed and Grace didn't feel lonely. Now Ruth helped her to undress and brushed out her hair and Grace chattered so that Ruth would stay a little longer, but in the end she let her go. Ruth had to get up early to light the kitchen fire; it wasn't right to keep her too late.

'Do you think we'll have snow for Christmas, Ruth?' she said as Ruth reached the door.

'I just hope it stays warm enough for that,' Ruth said with a shiver as she went out.

Grace went and stood by the fire for a few minutes after Ruth had gone and thought how lucky she was. She and Alexandra had arranged to go riding the next morning. She loved these mornings – the valleys ghostly with mist, the odd leaf glistening on a branch, the dawns dark red and slow and the stars paling slowly into light. She took a last peep through the curtains at the fields beyond the house, but it was too dark to see anything, and then she climbed into her warm bed and was soon fast asleep.

Two

It was just another journey as far as Nat was concerned. Ever since he could remember they had been leaving places. He longed to stay in one place for more than a short time. It seemed to him that they were forever packing. At one time his mother had done so cheerfully, but now she was tired of the continual shifting and longed for somewhere to call home. She never said anything and it would have done no good because they always had to leave. His father was always quarrelling, always causing trouble of some kind and being put out of work. Nat felt guilty for minding. Thomas Seymour was a good honest man and he tried for better conditions for the men wherever he went, but his family were the ones who suffered. Sometimes Nat wished that his father had not been quite so keen on trying to get things right. His father called himself a socialist and was proud of having read a book by a man called Karl Marx which his father said would change the world and make men equal.

Sometimes they went by cart, sometimes by train. He did not like the cart journeys but he did like trains until he began to associate trains with leaving, and after that there was no pleasure in them. Taylor, who was two years younger than he was, still got excited and Dolly who was the youngest at nine did whatever her mother told her.

Their mother would enliven the journeys by telling them tales of the old days when their grandparents were small children and there had been no trains. Nat could not imagine a world where you could not move around freely but he thought that from their point of view it might have been an advantage, at least his father would have had to stay in the same place more or less.

They had been a lot of places by the time Nat was thirteen. He had attended a lot of schools. That was awful too, having to prove yourself in the school playground and be jeered at for your accent because it was different. Everywhere you went people sounded different and they were always the ones at home. You were always the foreigner. In the end he complained about school, about going.

'Plenty of lads my age don't go at all.'

'Well, they should,' his father said and he turned Nat to him in the serious way that Nat hated. 'Education is power, Nat, don't forget. Education and sobriety are the ways to win.'

And so another train and another place but this time it was to the edge of the Durham coalfield, to Deerness Law, a town so small and windswept that after living near the mighty goings-on around the River Tees Nat felt a superiority the moment he arrived.

'It's not much of a place,' he said to Taylor.

Taylor sniffed.

'I'm hungry,' he said.

Taylor was always hungry. His stomach was the most important thing in the world to him, that was why he was so podgy. He had a round face and bright, happy eyes and as long as there was food within sight and reach he didn't care for anything else.

The house was a foundryman's house in a street not far away from the railway. It didn't impress Nat. The wind blew in at the back door and out at the front and he was sure that he could smell the sheep in the nearby fields.

'It's nice here,' Dolly said, coming into the room with bedding.

From the window Nat looked out over the back yard.

'It's not nice, it's just another place.'

'Don't be like that, our Nat,' she said, and he turned and smiled and thought, who could resist her? She was so small for her age that he could pick her up and carry her upstairs or on to a cart or up the steps of a train. She and Taylor fought but, perhaps because of the distance of years between them, she never fought with Nat and when Taylor fought with her Nat always bettered him for her within seconds. Taylor knew better than to go crying to his parents over this and Nat taught him how to play draughts, and to fish when they had lived over at the coast near Middlesbrough.

There were two bedrooms in the house. He and Taylor and Dolly would sleep in one and his parents in the other. He could hear voices downstairs, new voices.

'It's the woman from next door,' Dolly said. Dolly always knew everything. She had lugs like an elephant, Taylor said. 'She's called Mrs Boylen. She's made tea and soda bread.' Dolly wrinkled her nose as she spoke, she hated soda bread, but Taylor had heard the word food mentioned and made his way off downstairs, clattering as he moved too fast.

Dolly came over to the window.

''Tisn't much of a view,' Nat said.

'You're always complaining, our Nat. There's nothing wrong with it. Anyroad, Mrs Boylen said my dad'll get taken on at the foundry no bother.'

'Yes, but for how long?' Nat said.

'Will you help me with this?'

This was the bedding which was too big for her to manage by herself.

'No.'

'I'll tell Mam.'

'Tell her then,' Nat said and he sauntered off downstairs and out of the door before anybody had a chance to stop him.

The main street went on and on. Nat thought it was the most dismal-looking place he had ever seen. It wound down from one slight hill to the bottom where there were railway gates and then up at the other side. There was the odd shop but he cared nothing for shops. As he walked snow began to fall. He pushed his hands into his pockets and watched as the streets turned white and his booted feet made imprints, and he kept his head down against the way that the snow was beginning to blow hard into his face. He kept going until there were no more houses and no more shops and no habitation of any kind, until he reached the fell.

Sheep huddled in against the stone walls. A narrow road trailed out of the town and the fell itself had nothing growing on it; it was vast and the wind howled across it and drove the snow relentlessly as far as he could see. What sort of place had his dad brought them to now?

When he got back his mother, Gwen, had a bright fire burning in the kitchen, the table and chairs were in place, the better stuff was in the front room and he didn't doubt that his dad and the man next door would have taken the beds upstairs. As Nat came through the door his mother looked up from where she was dealing with pans on the fire. She was a slight, pretty woman, dark-haired with soft blue eyes, heavily lashed.

'And just where have you been?' she said.

'Out.'

She looked hard at him.

'I needed you here to help. You had no right to go and leave our Dolly with everything to do upstairs. She's just a bairn.'

'Where's my dad?'

'He's gone to see about work and before you ask, no, you cannot go. It's school for you tomorrow.'

'I'm not going to no school,' Nat said. Nat could have left school by now, he was thirteen, but his dad believed in as much schooling as you could get. The minute the words were out he knew them for a mistake, he was even sorry. His mam had had her fill already that day, she didn't need him to cheek her. She didn't generally lose her temper, she was too nice for that, and he was already sorry.

'Get upstairs,' she said.

Nat quietly called himself names. She was tired now. He wondered whether saying that he was sorry would make a difference and decided not so he went up the shadowed stairs and into the bedroom. The beds were made up and Taylor and Dolly were sitting there. It was cold and snow blew hard at the window.

14

Gwen called the other two children from the bottom of the stairs. Taylor looked at Nat and Dolly pulled a face.

'Have you cheeked my mam again? You're not nice to know,' she said and went out.

Taylor said nothing before he went.

Nat lay down on the bed, regarded the ceiling and listened to voices below. Some other neighbour calling, probably with a cake for tea. He went on lying there and the smell of freshly baked cake wafted through the ceiling. The snow stopped, the wind died and he could hear the sounds of Dolly and Taylor playing in the yard. They would be building a snowman. The room got colder. It was funny, he thought, how when it wasn't snowing it got colder. It was quite dark now. He leaned over and lit a candle and watched the shadows flickering on the walls through the draught from the window. Eventually he heard his mother's footsteps light on the stairs and she came into the room.

'I forgot about you,' she said, 'somebody came in. Are you frozen?' Nat felt awful. She sat down on the bed. 'We will find a place to stay some day,' she said. 'Come down and have some cake.'

'I'm sorry,' Nat said.

'You're a bad lad,' she said and kissed him. Nat loved being close to her, she smelled of tea and milk and cake crumbs. She was small and skinny but there was a softness about her and instinctively he knew that women always had that softness. Dolly had it, and the lass he had kissed at a party, and they smelled just wonderful.

She got up and Nat went with her, vowing never to make her cross again. Taylor was wolfing cake in the kitchen and Dolly was playing by the fire. His mother gave him a big mug of tea and some fruit cake which was fresh and moist, and then his father came in. He was smiling which meant that he had work, so there would be meat at the weekend and plenty on the table. His dad was always taken on because he was a skilled man, a moulder.

His mother didn't tell his dad of him like most would have, but that was not because he was forgiven, it was because his dad wouldn't have done anything about it anyway. His father wasn't capable of telling anybody off, which was funny if you thought about it because his father was as determined and stubborn as anybody Nat knew. He was not a weak man, he just had different ideas than other people had. He wouldn't hit a child and he wouldn't let any other man do it. Nat had seen him get hold of a man who was thrashing a horse and frighten the man so much that he ran away. His father didn't have to use violence. In his presence they rarely fought or argued and when he was younger Nat had cried hard over just a word from his dad. Now he didn't, but now he was more careful not to cross him. His dad wanted to be proud of him and Nat was ashamed that he didn't seem able to be anything that his dad wanted him to be. He didn't like school. All he wanted to do was leave and have a job so that they might be able to stay longer in one place, but his father wouldn't hear of it and when Nat did badly he just shook his head. Taylor and Dolly did well at school. Nat wished that his dad could be pleased with what he did but there was never any reason for him to be.

The next day was their first at school. At one end of the building it said 'Boys. Woodwork' above the door and at the other end 'Girls. Cookery'. Dolly didn't want to go in on her own. Nat didn't want to be seen going in under the 'Girls. Cookery' entrance but he had no choice. She would cry if he left her. Some of the boys in the yard nudged one another and winked and Nat knew that come playtime they would call him names. School was the same no matter where you went. All that altered was the view from the window.

In the mid-morning playtime he couldn't even see whether Dolly was all right because the boys had a separate yard from the girls. Taylor was playing football. Nat wished he could join in like that and be accepted. He propped up the classroom wall. There was a biting cold wind but Taylor looked warm, running about.

Nobody spoke to Nat but nobody bothered him either and he went back inside, grateful. The teacher was a pretty young woman with fair hair and a neat figure. She smelled of lavender water.

Nat took Dolly home for dinner. Taylor had gone off somewhere and came in when they were almost finished the meal, full of tales about a stream not far from the village. He ate his dinner quickly, twice as much as anybody else, and then ran back to school. It was not quite time for the bell. Two boys came up to Nat and began jeering at him for being with Dolly, and Nat thought it prudent to make short work of them because there wasn't much time. The result was bleeding noses, tears from them and being caned hard over the hands for fighting. So much for the smell of lavender water, Nat thought, as he went back to his desk. His father wasn't pleased with him either. That night he called to Nat as the others went to bed and Nat knew what was coming. He went back to the kitchen fire.

'I heard you were fighting again today.'

Like it didn't always happen, Nat thought savagely.

'Fighting doesn't get anybody anywhere, Nat. Don't you know that by now? History teaches us that. If we want to make anything of ourselves and our lives we have to use our brains.'

'I haven't got any brains,' Nat said.

'Of course you have. You just choose to use your fists because you're a big lad.'

'It's the only way I know. Can I go to bed now?'

'You might as well,' his father said, with a sigh.

His mother had put hot bricks in the beds but the room was bitterly cold. Dolly had her own small bed but was in with Taylor for warmth. When Nat slid in beside her and blew out the candle she turned to him and whispered, 'Are you all right, our Nat?'

'I'm fine. Did you like school?'

'I'd rather stay at home with my mam. Taylor likes it. He's promised to take me to see the stream tomorrow.'

'That's nice,' Nat said.

The stream was a good two miles from the village. There was a bridge which Taylor and his new friends spent some time trying to block with stones. Nat could have told them that they were wasting their time but he didn't. He could remember being younger and enjoying doing just the same thing, wading backwards and forwards with big stones while the river ran through the cracks, regardless. He supposed that was a child's idea of power and wondered what his father would think of it.

17

The snow had gone and the sun sat in a clear sky. Dolly sat beside him on a big stone on the bank, content to watch Taylor trying to change the world, and Nat thought suddenly that he didn't want her to grow up, that he would like her to stay exactly as she was; and then he knew that was a parent's view of things, he knew it was daft in somebody his age and he smiled.

'What's up with you?' she said.

'Do you ever wish you were grown up?'

She frowned.

'And have to do all the things my mam does? No. Grown ups have to have babies.'

This was a dangerous area. Nat said nothing more. Taylor splashed in the stream and issued orders. Nobody would ever think he was the newcomer, Nat thought. The funny thing about it was that the other lads seemed to accept that Taylor should tell them what to do and Taylor didn't seem to realise that he was doing it. He just went on, straining to move a rock which was much too big. In desperation he turned to Nat.

'Give us a hand, then.'

'What, get all wet just for that?' Nat said scornfully.

Taylor looked hard at him.

'You never do owt, our Nat.'

'I came here with you, didn't I?'

'Yes, to sit on the bank like a lass.'

Nat considered whether he should clip Taylor's lugs and then decided against it. He had caused his mother enough problems for one week.

'I don't care,' he said so Taylor, denied a fight, turned back to what he was doing and succeeded in dragging the stone into the middle of the stream with the help of a smaller boy.

It was almost dark when they trudged back up the hills to their new home. Nat gave Dolly a piggy-back because she was tired by then, and when they got there he could see the flames from the big kitchen fire through the window, and when he opened the door his mother and father were sitting there together. It was a homecoming which Nat did not forget, their smiles, the slight anxiety leaving his mother's face, his father getting up to take Dolly from him; and then they all sat down at the table together and had broth, thick with vegetables, and ham and pease pudding and he went to bed later, replete and happy. Saturday nights were the best times. He lay awake for a while, watching the other two sleep and listening to his parents talking below. The smooth sound of their voices sang him to sleep.

Three

Louisa Barmouth died before Christmas. Grace could not help but blame her for doing so. It didn't exactly blight their lives but as well as being her father's partner Mr Barmouth was his friend, and so there was quite a lot of upset at a time when Grace could have done without it. She didn't say anything or let any of them know about how selfishly she felt but it niggled at her.

First there was the funeral. She was required to go because her parents always dragged her to everything that wasn't interesting. The parish church was at the far end of a very muddy lane and on a day like that when the rain didn't know how to stop it was the last place anybody would have wanted to be. Dorothy cried and Alexandra, who always had colds in the winter, had a continual drip on her nose and the church was colder than the day and dark and gloomy. Grace thought longingly of fires and hot tea and was only grateful to leave poor Mrs Barmouth in the icy ground and make her way to Esh House, the Barmouths' home near the bottom end of the village where the funeral tea was being held.

'Don't funerals make you hungry?' Alexandra said as she bit into a thick ham sandwich.

Grace sipped her tea thankfully and stood as near to the fire as she could get.

'I'm frozen,' she said.

'It was a mite inconsiderate of her to die at this time of the year,' Alexandra said. 'You would think she could have held on until we could have had fine weather for the funeral.'

Grace smiled. She knew Alexandra so well, and that Alexandra was aware of what she was thinking.

'I don't see why people have to die at Christmas.'

'It's so uncivilised of them,' Alexandra agreed and they grinned at each other and hid their faces in case anybody should see their disrespect.

Esh House was the same kind of house as her own, Grace thought. Built at the same time about thirty years ago, they were solid Victorian affairs, square and large-stoned and pleasing with fireplaces in every room and plenty of space around them. There was no way apart from her obvious absence that you could tell the mistress of the house was dead. Florrie Appleby, the cook, had put on a good spread for those coming back from the funeral and as far as Grace could see they had made sure that nobody would be able to fault the house; it was shining clean, the brasses bright, the smell of polish everywhere.

She could hear Mr Barmouth talking to her father; they were discussing business and she had overheard her parents the night before saying that work would be the saving of him. Her father always maintained that work would be the saving of every man. What he thought would be the saving of every woman she wasn't quite sure.

Grace felt better after she had warmed up and had some tea.

'The best coking coal in the world here,' her father was saying to Mr Barmouth, though it was something they both knew and she herself had heard a thousand times. They kept on saying it as though to reassure themselves that everything was all right, that Louisa was not really dead, that things would go on just as they had done.

After the funeral her father and mother suggested to Mr Barmouth that he should go home with them, and though he refused at first they managed to persuade him. That was difficult too, everyone being very bright and cheerful, and the short winter day already getting dark. They would be obliged to stay in the sitting-room for hours trying to make

22

conversation. Alexandra was not there, she had gone home with her father, and Grace felt excluded from the three adults. In the end she went off to the kitchen where Mrs Jackson and Ruth were drinking tea by the fire. They both looked up when she came in but Mrs Jackson only smiled. Grace often found her way there when she was short of company. They poured tea for her and she sat down with them. The kitchen fire was comforting, black and shiny, being well looked after, and every time the blaze got down it had a huge bucket of coal thrown at it so there was always the most wonderful brightness and warmth. It made Grace want to curl up like a cat and purr with contentment.

'Do you think Mr Barmouth will marry again?' Mrs Jackson asked.

'His wife's only been dead a few days,' Ruth said.

'Men marry again and quickly,' Mrs Jackson said and Grace thought that Mrs Jackson knew all about these things, being widowed herself.

'And where would he find a lady around these parts?' Ruth said. 'There's nothing here but foundries, pits and muck.'

'Don't you like living here, Ruth?' Grace asked in astonishment.

'Not me,' Ruth said, 'I'd like the city, Newcastle or even better than that, London.'

'Horrible dirty places,' Mrs Jackson said.

'I have an aunt who lives in London,' Grace said.

'Have you ever been?'

'Not yet, but I shall go when I get older. I don't particularly want to. I like living here.'

'You'll soon hanker after other places,' Ruth said.

'That's where Mr Barmouth will have to go if he's to find another wife,' said Mrs Jackson and she sat back in her rocking chair and cradled her cup in her hands.

Four

When he awoke Nat groaned and turned over. It was Sunday, the worst day of all. He knew it shouldn't be like that but it was, in spite of the big dinner. He had to get done up in his best clothes, all of which were too tight, and go to chapel and then he had to go to Sunday School. He had tried in vain to tell his dad that he was too old to go to Sunday School but his dad wouldn't listen.

Nat tried to be honest with himself. He quite liked the chapel here, it was painted in different colours and the minister was a friendly sort who didn't seem to mind if you talked before the service began. That Sunday a baby was being christened and he brought it around and showed it to everybody because he said it was a new member of their church. Then they all got up and trudged through the little tunnel. Half of them, the older ones, went into a small room, the younger ones into the big room which had the stage. With the door shut the older ones read the Bible until it was time to go.

Nat liked coming home. The January day was fine. Back at the house there was soon the tantalising smell of meat and vegetables and then they all sat down together. His mother made big Yorkshire puddings with onion gravy. After that his father fell asleep by the fire in the front room, Dolly helped his mother to clear up and Taylor disappeared beyond the yard.

25

Nat wandered up the back street. There hadn't been a fine Sunday for some weeks since he moved in. This made a nice change. It was bitterly cold but the sun shone. Small children were out. The girls were playing skipping games. Further along a boy just older and bigger than him was standing against the back wall. He called out and Nat stopped.

'You haven't been here long, have you?' the boy said.

'Haven't seen you at school,' Nat said.

'Don't go. I'm a foundryman. School's for lasses.'

He took Nat into the house. The yard was untidy as if they had lived there for a long time. There was a half-dismantled pram which somebody was making into a bogey, and bits and pieces of various things which could have fascinated Nat for hours but the boy went into the house and he followed.

It was dark in there, the curtains were almost closed, but it was dark in a different way too. The fire was low; there was a smell of unwashed bodies and dust. There had been no cooking done that day. It was damp. Dirty dishes littered the table and the windows were rain-spattered. As Nat stood there a younger boy came in. He grinned at Nat.

'This is him. He fettled Angus Simon and Willie Smith the first day. Don't you remember, Dennes, I told you.' He looked admiringly at Nat. 'Got in your road, did they?'

'Summat like that,' Nat said.

The older boy went into the pantry and came back with a big jug of beer.

Nat had never tasted beer, his father wouldn't allow it in the house, but they seemed to assume that he would have some and poured a big mugful and passed it to him. When he first tasted it he didn't like the flavour, it seemed so thin and bitter and yellow without a head which Nat felt sure it should have had, but it would not have been nice to refuse. They sat down in the cold grubby kitchen. From time to time there were sounds from upstairs.

'My mam,' the older boy said and explained no further.

Nat drank and the more he drank the easier it became to get down and the better the taste got and in no time at all he had finished the whole mugful. It was instantly refilled. Nat was particularly glad of that. He felt happier now than he had felt since arriving. In fact he felt happier than he had done in a long time and even the almost dead fire and the dark dirty room did not dim that happiness. It seemed as though he could be clever and funny – he could even sing, which he had never been able to before. By the third mugful the good feelings had worn off and there came over Nat a sudden desire to go home. He felt decidedly ill. He said his goodbyes or at least he tried, but the words would not come out in the right order though it didn't seem to matter. The younger boy had gone to sleep, the older one was laughing at everything he said.

Nat got as far as the back lane before he threw up and threw up and went on throwing up, not just the beer but all the dinner he had eaten. Afterwards he felt better but weak and tearful and empty. There was no one about, the children had gone in, dusk was beginning to fall. He walked on a little way, taking in the crisp air until he thought that his mother would not know what had happened and then he went back home.

The tea was set out in the kitchen, egg and bacon pie, custard tarts, tea and butter and jam. It made him feel sick again. His mother wanted him to sit down with them and eat but even though his stomach was empty the very thought of food made him want to retch. He said that he didn't feel well and went off to the bedroom. She came after him.

'You look so pale, I hope you're not getting anything,' she said.

Nat hid his face against the pillows thinking that she might be able to smell the beer on his breath. When she had gone he lay there, in the gathering darkness and the quietness, listening to the voices of them as they ate tea and he smiled to himself. He soon felt better and within the hour was downstairs drinking a big mug of tea and eating bread and jam. It tasted so good. He resolved not to drink again but he remembered how he had felt while he was doing it, how wonderful like never before and then he thought of how he would have felt if he had been sick at home and had to confess that he had been drinking, how upset his parents would have been. His father would have been disappointed in him again. People said that his father was a man of vision. Nat didn't know what they meant by that, visions were things people in the Bible had. His father, keen on bibles and chapel as he was, had certainly never had a vision of that type. Nat thought of the dirt in that house. His mother would have called it 'hacky'. He was glad that his house was not like that but in some ways he envied the other boy.

His father was restless that spring and summer. Usually when they moved that restlessness did not come upon him for some time but it was as though it had never gone away, as if they had not moved over from Middlesbrough where the rest of the family had been happy. Nat knew that they could not go back, that his father's name was on some kind of blacklist there, he would not be taken on. He thought often of Middlesbrough which he had known well where the ships came in and went out, of the different kinds of people, strange tongues and coloured skins and the excitement of it all. It was so busy. It was busy here too but in a different way that had everything to do with steel and nothing to do with anything else. He knew that his father grew tired of it, he grew tired of it himself. There was nothing but school and home and chapel and Sunday School. He would have liked to have gone out at night with Dennes Eliot, the boy from the dirty house, but his mother did not like the family and would not let him go. As the evenings lengthened Nat became restless, knowing that Dennes worked in the steel foundry as an apprentice moulder, had freedom and did what he wanted. Nat even took to playing football with Taylor and some of the other boys though he cared nothing for football and wasn't very good. Taylor was good and laughed at his attempts to score a goal. Taylor had lots of friends by this time. Nat wished for that ability. People didn't come to him and he didn't know how to go to them. Dolly had a particular friend called Alice and seemed happy with the one person. They played at houses together and rarely went beyond the yard.

Nat watched his father's restlessness, dreaded it, even grew used to the howling gales and sleet that went by the name of spring here. The odd daisy showed in the grass. It wasn't that he wanted to stay here, he just didn't want to move on to yet another place, and he wasn't the only one. He watched his mother watching his father and knew that she sensed it too. Hadn't she seen it a dozen times and more? They began to live frugally. She saved and the pennies went into the little tin box on the mantelpiece which Nat thought might have been a tea caddy in a former life. They lived during the week as simply as she could manage. Only on Sundays did she splurge on meat and even then sometimes it was not good meat. A kind neighbour gave them rabbits which his ferrets had caught. Nat hated rabbit. It smelled sweet and looked like what it was and it was so bony. There were pigeon pies too. The meat was grey.

Nat thought it was strange how people were. As long as his father and mother had been happy here he had not wanted to stay or even to have been here in the first place, but now that his father showed signs of wanting to leave he wanted to stay as though he had been born here and had happy memories of the place. Instead of which it was just a dirty little town on the edge of the Durham coalfield where they had nothing but a house perched so that the wind blew straight through it. He thought that he could learn to love the house if his father should want to move. He dreamt that he was hanging on to the outside door and his father was urging him away. It was nothing new, it was nothing to do with the grubby little place. He felt that way about everywhere they went as soon as he knew that his father would make them leave. It was just a matter of time and not a very long time at that.

One day he and the others came in from school to find their parents sitting over the fire. It was a cold bright day and ordinarily he and Taylor would have gone straight back outside again to play football with some of the others; it had become an established thing after school and even Nat liked getting outside and putting school at some distance from him. He was doing worse and worse there because he wanted to leave. He sensed that there was something wrong as soon as he reached the doorway. Normally his mother would have had tea and cake ready for the children as they came in but the table was bare and they both looked up and neither of them smiled. Taylor and Dolly came in after him and there was an unnatural silence in the room until their mother said steadily, 'Your father's going away.'

29

Nat's first reaction was one of anger. Had his father really made a mess of things already? They hadn't been there five minutes.

'I don't have to go,' his father said, seeing his face. 'I mean, I haven't been asked to leave or anything but there's an opportunity . . .'

Opportunity was his father's favourite word. Everything, even the hardest things in life, were opportunities.

'I'm going to South Africa.'

Not Sunderland or Durham or Yorkshire. Somewhere so far away that it was past thinking about.

'There's work there, good work, digging gold,' and his father set off, talking like he usually did. Nat had heard it all before. His father's ship was about to come in, the end of the rainbow was about to unfold. He watched his mother's face. Could she have agreed to this? Could she have put up the money? Was that what she had been saving for? He thought not. The money that she had so carefully saved for as long as he could remember was for hard times, not for dreams. He wondered what fool had put such notions into his father's head. His mother said nothing. She kept looking down and it was no wonder, Nat thought, to be left here with three children and no man. When his father had finally finished telling them what a wonderful opportunity this was and how good it would be Nat said shortly, 'I'm fourteen soon. I'll go to work.'

'You will not,' his father said but for once Nat defied him. He looked straight into his father's guileless blue eyes. 'Who's going to keep us in the meantime with you gone?'

'I'll not be gone long.'

Nat looked scornfully at him and turned and walked out of the house.

That night when his father had finally gone to bed and the children were asleep he sat by the fire with his mother.

'You mustn't blame him,' she said. 'He can't help it. People can't help what they are.'

'Or their dreams?'

'He wants to do well for us, that's all he ever wanted. He's a good man and your father and you should respect him.'

'How did he get the money?'

'He borrowed it. Fifty pounds.'

She looked ashamed, as well she might, Nat thought. Fifty pounds was a fortune. His father would never be able to repay it. It was typical of him to persuade somebody to lend him the money; his father had a tongue like silver and now he was going to dig for gold. Well, he had finally got what he wanted, Nat thought. He could go and chase his dream and his wife and children would have to survive as best they might.

Nat went to bed. Once there all he wanted to do was sleep. He wanted to blot out the nightmare that his father's desires had provoked in him. He knew now why he had not wanted to care about this house or this place or any other place, because the moment that he did so his father would destroy any feeling they had of belonging, in some way he would spoil it. Nat hated him so keenly just at that moment that he felt hot. He tried to bury himself in the bedclothes but to do that would have meant disturbing Taylor. Taylor and Dolly were guilelessly sound asleep, like the children they both were. He had never felt so grown up and he knew that when his father left he would leave school and go to work and support them. He would take that concerned look out of his mother's eyes for good.

He thought of the boy from the dirty house, Dennes, of his mother who was mucky and went to bed with men for money and he wondered if parents were ever any use.

Nat had looked forward to the day that his father would leave. He had thought that he would feel like a man, so strong and capable, but when it happened, when his father's train was out of sight and they had turned and gone home again he felt helpless and sick like a small child and wished things differently. He didn't want anything to eat, though his mother made the tea just as if nothing had happened. Taylor and Dolly went out to play. It was a warm summer afternoon. Nat was to start work the following day. He was going, like Dennes and like his dad had done, to be a moulder. His dad had spoken up for him and

Nat was proud but school had never looked such a cheerful prospect. He wandered down the back lane until he saw Dennes who grinned at him.

'You needn't worry,' Dennes said, with the confidence of somebody much older than his fifteen or so years. 'I'll look after you.'

'Will I need looking after?' Nat said, feeling worse.

'Naw.' Dennes put an arm around his shoulders. 'But I'll look after you anyways.'

Nat smiled back at him and followed him into the house. There was nobody around. Lately there had been a miner staying in Dennes' house.

'Your dad on shift?'

'He's gone.'

'Gone where?'

'Dunno. Like yours.'

'I know where mine's gone.'

Dennes flashed him a knowing look.

'Africa's a big place. Anyroad, he wasn't my real dad.'

'Where's your real dad?'

'Dunno. Never knew him. Don't think she does neither.'

There were sounds coming from above them. Nat glanced at the ceiling.

'Who's up there then?'

'Dunno,' Dennes said, and grinned.

The first day at work was a bit of a shock to Nat but it was better than school. His mam put him first, she treated him like she had always treated his dad. He got his meals first, he got her attention first, he was earning money.

The foundry was rather frightening in a way because it was all new, the heat and the cold, the brightness of the metal, red hot, the various workmen busy about their tasks. The noise was tremendous, the dirt and dust were thick. Dennes knew everybody and they seemed to like him. Nobody tried to hurt Nat or bother him and gradually that first day his fear went and his confidence grew, and Nat could not understand why his father had wanted to leave. It was the most fascinating place that he had ever been to, it was exciting, being part of something which was all men, where everybody knew everybody, where everybody's job made up a part of the whole, and to know that what they made went on to do such important things, to keep the railways going and to make the ships what they were. It made Nat feel so very important even though he was just starting here and had no skills. The men smiled on him, some of them even spoke to him and Mr Barmouth actually came into the works several times that day and was there much of the time, talking and sometimes frowning and sometimes smiling, joking with the men and going to watch the different processes. He wasn't clean and aloof like posh people might be, Nat thought, he had foundry dust all over his suit and especially all over his hat which looked as though it had seen many a day in the foundry.

For the first time Nat felt like a man. He felt as though he was doing something worthwhile.

When they stopped, which they did more than once because the hot work made everybody tired and thirsty, Dennes laughed with the others. Nat couldn't understand how he could be so cheerful with such an awful home to go back to. On the way home Nat said, 'Come back with me and have some tea. My mam won't mind.'

'She would mind all right, she doesn't like me.'

'She's never said so.'

'No, well.'

Dennes wouldn't be persuaded so Nat went home by himself. It being a Monday and washing day he had thought there would be little of substance for him to eat, but when he got home his mother had prepared broth and there were big chunks of ham and pease pudding with bread.

'You had such a lot to do today,' he said in appreciation.

'We have to keep the workers fed,' she said, smiling.

'Could Dennes come to our house?' Nat asked, when he had eaten.

His mother frowned. 'I don't think I want that lad here,' she said.

'He helped me such a lot today. His dad's gone and his mam . . . he works hard and he never gets anything to eat.'

'I can see that but he's dirty, Nat.'

'He's never been looked after. His dad's gone off somewhere and his mam's—'

'Yes, I know what his mam's like.'

Nat didn't ask again and his mother didn't mention Dennes. A week later Dennes, dirtier and more cheerful than ever, declined to walk home.

'I don't live there no more,' he said. 'My mam's gone off with some man and she's taken our Joseph with her.'

'Where are you living then?'

'Oh, around.'

Nat had by then learned that Dennes' cheerfulness was no indicator of how he was feeling.

'I'll lodge with somebody,' he said.

Nat trudged home to find his mother contrite.

'Has nobody taken that lad in?' she said.

'I don't think they have.'

'People think he's a bad lot.'

'He isn't,' Nat shot back. 'Just because his mam went with men for money . . .' His mother's face was so shocked that Nat said nothing for a few moments. 'Well, she did.'

'I know she did,' his mother said softly, 'there but for the grace of God go all of us. You can bring him back with you but he doesn't sit down in my house or eat until he's had a bath and I've checked him for whatever he might have.'

'A bath?'

'You tell him,' she said.

Dennes was round-eyed at the idea of a bath.

'I can't go washing all of me,' he said, 'it weakens your back to have it washed.'

'My mam says,' Nat said.

The kitchen was tactfully empty when they got home. Nat watched his friend looking around what was probably the cleanest house he had ever seen. The brasses shone in the firelight. The tin bath stood in front

34

of the fire and steam rose from it and his mother put the clothes horse covered with old sheets draped around it for privacy. Dennes didn't hesitate and could soon be heard inside the clothes horse, singing loudly and sloshing water on to the floor. Nat's mother insisted on throwing out his clothes despite his protestations that they were all he had.

'They're fit for nothing,' she said, 'dropping off your back.'

'But Mrs Seymour, what will I wear?'

She insisted on washing Dennes' hair in something which smelled awful in case he 'had anything' as she called it, and going through his hair carefully with a fine comb. Some time later a shiny clean Dennes emerged, dressed in Nat's father's clothing which fitted him fairly well, Dennes being tall and big for his age, and then a surprise. He had pale golden hair.

'Only lasses have hair this colour,' he said ruefully.

'Not any more,' Nat said. 'You don't half look bonny.'

'Shut up,' Dennes responded.

'Leave him alone, Nat,' Gwen said and the colour of Dennes' hair was forgotten when she set before them the most wonderful pot pie in the history of the world. It smelled like the best thing this side of heaven. It oozed a thick dark gravy and neat pieces of beef. The onions were shiny, the potatoes were soft and creamy, the suet was light. Steam rose reassuringly as she piled their plates high and the top of it soaked up the gravy. For once Dennes said nothing. He ate, and when he had eaten she put another plateful in front of him. When that was gone, and three cups of tea thick with sugar, he sat back, smiling at her.

'I'll work hard,' he said.

Dolly was not very happy that Dennes would have her bed and she had to sleep with her mother.

'I'll miss our Nat. He tells me stories in bed.'

'I'll come and tell you stories when you go up.'

'That's not the same,' Dolly said, huffily.

Five

One fine Sunday that summer Dennes and Nat went for a walk. They left the village and took the road up over the fell. Smoke rose from the odd farmhouse and there was no one about for some time, so they saw the two girls long before they reached them across the flat expanse of fell. The slight, fair girl was sitting down and the bigger darker girl was standing over her, and neither of them looked happy. The dark girl looked over when she saw them and called to Dennes and Nat when they were close enough to hear her, but Nat also heard the other girl trying to stop her. They went across and the big dark girl looked straight at him from a pair of large brown eyes.

'Am I glad to see you,' she said.

Nat had not expected that a well-bred female would talk so freely. Dennes evidently liked it and grinned at her.

'What's up, flower?' he said.

'Grace is hurt.'

Grace was the most beautiful girl Nat had ever seen. She had dark blonde hair, darker than Dennes', and bright blue eyes and she was small-boned, fragile-looking with a pale skin and a full pink mouth.

'I'm not injured,' she protested.

'Ankle, is it?' Dennes said, getting down beside her.

'Everything hurts,' she said softly.

'All right, put your arms around my neck.'

She looked at him and blushed.

'I can't,' she said.

'Don't be soft, do it,' Dennes said matter-of-factly. 'I can't lift you from there if you don't.'

She went scarlet in the face but did as he told her and Dennes lifted her into his arms and up.

'It's a good thing it wasn't the other one,' he said softly to Nat before he lifted her. 'She's a grand big lass.'

The other girl came back from collecting Grace's hat which had fallen off, probably when she fell.

Nat looked critically at her. She was what his father would have called handsome, fresh-faced, clear-skinned, bigger built. He liked the way that she looked straight at you and the way she talked. Her hair was wavy and untidy and her dress wasn't nearly as pretty as the other girl's, and Nat didn't dare to look at her figure which was generous in every direction.

'It's a good thing it wasn't me,' she said. 'I weigh a lot.'

'You're just a greedy man's armful, that's all, pet,' Dennes said.

Nat stared at him but to his astonishment the girl tried to look shocked and only succeeded in smiling.

'You're very rude,' she said.

'I'm too heavy,' Grace said.

'I'll let you know when you are.'

It was a long way back to the village. Nobody said anything. The dark girl strode out confidently. Three-quarters of the way back Dennes stopped.

'Here, Nat, take hold of her, will you?' he said.

So it was Nat who arrived on the doorstep with Grace in his arms. He was so confused he couldn't think of anything to say. He hadn't known until she directed him that she was Anthony Hemingway's daughter. Mr Hemingway and Mr Barmouth owned the foundry where he and Dennes worked. He wasn't prepared either for the way that Mr and Mrs Hemingway invited them in and said how grateful they were. Mrs Hemingway fussed and took the girls away but Mr Hemingway invited Nat and Dennes into his sitting-room, a big comfortable room which overlooked a garden with glasshouses and lawns and flowerbeds. There were armchairs in the room and mirrors and tall vases of summer flowers and square leather seats at either side of the fireplace with boxes for coal and wood.

Mr Hemingway asked Nat his name, and when he told him said, 'I'm very grateful to you, Nat.'

'It was Dennes mostly.'

'Then I'm very grateful to you both. The girls shouldn't walk as far as that. I can't think what they would have done.'

'The fell's nothing to be frightened of,' Dennes said.

'It's not the fell, it's some of the people there are about nowadays. Would you like some tea? Mrs Jackson has just made apple pie.'

After Mrs Hemingway stopped fussing the girls were left alone in Grace's room with the window open over the porch roof.

'You can stop thinking about him right now,' Alexandra said, and Grace started.

'What?'

'Dennes Eliot.'

'I wasn't thinking about him. How could I be?'

'How couldn't you be?' Alexandra said, sitting down on the bed. 'I've a good mind to go out that way next Sunday and turn my ankle, except that he could never carry me all that way. I could turn it nearer to home, of course.'

'He's awful,' Grace said. 'Common and badly spoken and . . . Have you seen his eyes, like the velvet cushions in my mother's sitting-room? Have you ever seen a boy with fair hair and green eyes before? He carried me all that way.'

'What else could he do?'

'Didn't you like him?'

'Nobody in their right mind could like him. I wouldn't mind kissing him though,' Alexandra said and they went off into a fit of giggles.

Dennes and Nat put away two helpings each of apple pie and cream

39

and two cups of tea before they went home. Mrs Hemingway thanked them profusely and saw them out of the front door with the porch at the side of the garden. It was all stained-glass windows and plants. She walked them up the garden path to the gate.

'So,' Dennes asked slowly as they went home, 'what did you think of little Miss Hemingway, Nat?'

'I thought she was bonny, but I liked the other lass better.'

'Yes, I thought you did. You're just muck under her shoe. Don't forget it.'

Nat looked at him.

'Didn't you like Grace Hemingway?'

'I wish I could have made her walk home. She's never lifted a finger in her life.'

'What about the other one?'

'That's more like a lass. Can you imagine getting your hands on that?' Dennes grinned dirtily to himself. 'They'll be sent off to marry rich men. They won't stay here among the likes of you and me, just watch. That's me finished walking on Sunday afternoons. What a waste of time. I could have been asleep,' Dennes said.

The summer went on and Thomas Seymour, Nat's father, did not come home, but with Nat and Dennes working they managed well. It was a long warm summer and working in the heat of the foundry made Nat appreciate the time off that he had. He wished sometimes that they were still living over at the coast and that he could have bathed in the sea, but here the moor turned purple with heather in August and the sun beat down on the hillsides. They plodged in the burn and threw water at one another and it made him feel like a child again. Having Dennes to lodge was much more interesting than being the only breadwinner and Dennes made him laugh. Dolly and Taylor were not so close to him now. They didn't understand about work, how it was nice to come home and talk about the men and the foundry and the goings-on. When Nat handed his pay to his mother he was proud.

Right into October and the beginning of November the weather continued warm and though the nights drew in the children played outside until dark. It was only when it was almost December that the darkness and the cold came together and drove people indoors.

A whole year went by. Taylor was working too by then, they had good money coming in, but it was taking them all the time to pay off the fifty pounds which their father owed and keep themselves.

There had not been many letters and there had never been any money. Nat had wished at first that his father would come home but he had stopped thinking that now. They didn't need him any more. What he wanted to hear less than anything was that his father could not afford to pay his passage home. There was no possible way that they could raise any more money. Nat and Dennes came home on an early December day to find a visitor. As Nat stepped into the house he knew that something was wrong. His mother was sitting huddled by the fire and their visitor, a man of about his father's age, looked across at him without smiling. Nat's mother introduced them.

'This is my son, Nathaniel and my lodger, Dennes Eliot. Nat, Dennes, this is William Daniels.' She stopped there as though she would have gone on but couldn't remember what to say.

The man was interesting to look at, Nat thought, not especially tall but with fine eyes and a slender face.

'I bring bad news, I'm afraid. It's your father. He's been killed in a mining explosion.'

He had such a funny accent, as though he came from the south, and he got hold of their mother's hand in a way in which Nat couldn't like. It was typical of their father, he couldn't just stay here and be killed in an explosion like anybody else, he had to go thousands of miles to do it.

Later, when Nat had gone upstairs into the cold darkness, Dennes followed him there. Dennes shut the bedroom door and then he said hesitantly, 'I don't like him.'

'What does that have to do with owt?'

'He's got a face like a weasel. You don't think he mebbe killed your dad, do you?'

'What for, his money?' Nat moved restlessly over to the window even though there wasn't a blind thing to see.

41

'If your dad had made it rich—'

Nat laughed. 'He wouldn't have.'

'What for?'

'Because he couldn't see the nose in front of his face.'

'You aren't very nice about him.'

'He always thought that things were going to be better, but he was never no good at making them better,' Nat said.

'He was your dad. Aren't you sorry?'

But that night in the late darkness it was different. He tried not to remember how his dad had been, he tried not to think about the good things but they would keep coming back, even though he reminded himself of all the things his dad had not done and not been. All he could remember was that his dad had believed that people should be treated fairly, given good wages for what they did and respected. Somehow, Nat thought, it was difficult to better that.

Long after the others slept Dennes lay awake, waiting for Gwen to come upstairs, but she didn't. In the end he slipped on his clothes as quietly as he could in the darkness and went downstairs. She was sitting over the fire, not crying as he had thought she might be, just sitting there with the firelight winking around her by a small light which cast her shadow big in the room. She turned when she heard him and even smiled.

'I thought you were asleep long since,' she said.

Dennes stood in the middle of the room, feeling like a fool.

'What does William Daniels do?'

'Do?'

'Is he a foundryman or a pitman?'

'I don't know, Dennes, I didn't ask him. I expect so, just like everybody else.' She came over and ruffled his hair, something which women had taken to doing since they had discovered its colour and shine. Dennes usually anticipated the move and backed off first, but this time he didn't. 'Go to bed,' she said, 'it's late.'

That irritated him too, like he wasn't a man, earning a wage and much taller and bigger than she was.

'I'm not tired.'

'Haven't you worked all week?'

'Aren't you going to bed?'

'I couldn't sleep. I keep thinking about things.'

'What kind of things?' Dennes was near to her now. She was not like his mother had been and yet she was more than how mothers should be. Yes, she made good dinners and provided clean beds and clothes, but she had pretty hair and neat ears and a creamy skin. His mother had smelled of gin and sometimes of other things, sharp and sour, but the look and the smell of Gwen made him want to reach out like never before. Nobody had ever touched him or held him that he could remember except his mother, and he denied the need now by stuffing his hands into his pockets.

'I keep thinking of things I don't have any more and how I'll manage without a man.' Her voice wobbled. Dennes didn't know what to say. 'He was my children's father. You can't get that again.'

'You have Nat and me.'

She looked at him. She had blue eyes, soft and clear.

'You're a great comfort to me, Dennes,' and she leaned over and kissed him on the cheek.

Dennes had never been kissed before like that. It felt strange, and afterwards he could not help moving close. She gathered him into her arms and took him against her and her hair smelled of soap. It was the best moment of Dennes' life. He closed his eyes and prayed to God that nobody should move so that if it never happened again he would remember and be grateful. He made a vow to himself, that he would never let any harm come to her who had taken him in and treated him better than he had ever thought to be treated in his life. She put her fingers into his hair and stroked his head.

'It's all right,' she said, 'don't worry.'

'Nat and me, we'll look after you,' Dennes said roughly.

And then she drew away and smiled into his face all warm and kind.

'I know you will, Dennes,' she said.

He went back upstairs and lay in bed staring up into the blackness and he heard her come to bed. Nat turned over, awakened.

'Have you not been to sleep yet?'

'No,' Dennes said blissfully.

'You'll be no good in the morning,' Nat prophesied and turned back over and began to snore very softly.

William Daniels was nice to the children, that was what their mother thought, Nat knew. He brought presents for them when he came, a new football for Taylor and a pretty necklace for Dolly. He brought books for Dennes and Nat. Nat was surprised when the moment they were alone Dennes threw the book across the bedroom.

'You'll damage the spine doing that,' he observed.

'Since when have you cared?'

Nat went over and picked up the book. It was about birds and had illustrations.

'All he wants is to get his hands under your mother's skirts,' Dennes said savagely.

'That's not a very nice thing to say.'

Dennes looked straight at him.

'You think I'm wrong?'

'No . . .'

'But?'

'There's no reason why she shouldn't marry again.'

'If he wants to marry her.'

'Why shouldn't he?'

'Why should he if he can get what he wants without?'

Nat sat down on the edge of the bed where Dennes had flung himself full length.

'What makes you think that?'

'Men like that can buy women, they don't have to marry them.'

'He won't be able to buy my mother.'

Unlike their father, William Daniels liked a drink. One night when he came back to their house early and Nat was sitting in front of the fire, he sat down there, rather bright of eye and smiled.

'I like your shoes,' Nat said.

William smiled even more.

'I keep them well-polished.'

'They look as though they cost a lot of money.'

'I know. They didn't. I bought them cheap from a woman whose husband had just died.'

When Nat and Dennes went to bed that night Nat said, 'He isn't rich.'

'How do you know?'

'He bought his shoes secondhand. Do you think that's a good sign or a bad one?'

'I'm not sure yet,' Dennes said. 'I think we were right to suspect him. So he isn't even rich,' and Dennes sat down on his bed. 'He was more interesting when I thought he had money. What has this gained us? He's just another dull person.'

'It proves one thing,' Nat said, climbing into bed. 'My mother only likes one kind of man – dreamers. We have to stop her from marrying him.'

'How are we going to do that?'

'I wish you two would go to sleep,' Taylor murmured from the bedcovers.

They waited until his breathing was even again before Nat said in a whisper, 'My father was a dreamer but he was a good man.'

'I don't think William Daniels is good *or* clever,' Dennes said and turned over.

All day long Gwen sang and it was not especially tuneful. It was almost Christmas and she was forever starting up *The Holly and the Ivy*, of which she knew every verse, and there were too many, Nat thought. He suspected that William Daniels would appear with gifts some time before Christmas Day but he did not. Instead he came over one Sunday morning and persuaded her out of the house even though she said that she was trying to make the dinner.

'Dolly can manage for half an hour, can't you, Dolly?'

'She's only a bairn,' Dennes protested darkly.

'You can help then, can't you?' William said.

Dennes swore but only under his breath so that Dolly couldn't hear and only when the door had closed after them.

'Do you think Mr Daniels has presents for us?' Dolly asked.

'Shouldn't think so,' Dennes said.

'I like Mr Daniels,' Taylor said.

'That just goes to show how much you know,' Dennes said.

Six

It was the meanest house that Nat had ever come across. He couldn't understand why it seemed like that. They had lived in tiny pit hovels without even a tap, with just one room up and one down where the icy winds blew from the Durham moors. They had even camped outside when they got thrown out of their house once during a strike, but there was something about this place which made his insides feel cold.

His mother did not feel that way, he could see. She liked moving into the posh part of the village and Nat had thought that he would like it because she was so pleased.

On one side of the street the houses had small front gardens but on their side the houses opened straight on to the road. Theirs was the corner house at the top and before it reached the road it had a fence where a straggly lilac tree grew. There was a gate, and even to one side a tiny lawn where no one would ever sit because the sun didn't reach it, and then another step down into the yard.

At the bottom of the yard was the wash house and at the top end the back door which led into a long narrow kitchen and a pantry. From the kitchen there were two steps up, the staircase on one side and the doors leading into the dining-room and the sitting-room. Beyond them was a half-glassed door leading to the outside. In any other house it

47

would have been a front door but because it was the corner house the front door was at the side.

Upstairs were three bedrooms. His mother clapped her hands and declared that any woman would be happy here. One of the bedrooms was big, his mother had that; one was big enough for Nat, Dennes and Taylor. Dolly had the tiny back bedroom to herself.

From his window Nat could see the back lane and the beginnings of the steelworks. From the front bedroom there was nothing but the houses across the road. Further over was the doctor's house and then along the lane the house where Grace Hemingway lived so that he would see her sometimes on her horse or out walking or with her parents. Alexandra's house was further over on the edge of the village.

Nat had tried to talk to his mother at first, to tell her that they couldn't afford such a house out of his and Dennes' pay, but she only laughed.

'William— Mr Daniels will help,' she said.

'Do we want to be beholden to him?'

She smiled. 'He's asked me to marry him,' she said.

That night when Taylor was asleep and Dennes lounged by their bedroom window with his hands in his pockets, Nat got up from where he had been reading on the bed and went to him there.

'Did you know he'd asked her to marry him?'

Dennes leaned back against the sill and looked narrowly at him.

'I didn't think he was doing it out of the kindness of his heart.'

Nat said nothing and Dennes moved impatiently.

'We've got to do something.'

'There isn't much we can do. She likes him. After all, he got her this place.'

That Christmas was the worst of Nat's life. William Daniels spent so much time with them and it seemed to Nat that his mother's laughter had taken on a coarse note. William brought Dolly numerous presents until she waited for his arrival.

One Sunday that winter when Nat and Dennes had been for a walk after dinner they came home to a row. In the sitting-room Nat could hear his mother, and William Daniels and Taylor. By the time he opened the door William Daniels had hold of Taylor and was undoing the belt from around his waist. Nat could see that Dennes' first reaction was to wade in, and he caught hold of Dennes firmly by the arm until Dennes stopped trying to go forward.

'Don't do that,' Nat said softly to William Daniels.

His mother stared at him and William Daniels scowled.

'He swore at me and more.'

'I never,' Taylor gulped.

'This is nothing to do with you, Nat,' his mother said.

Nat ignored her.

'You're not his father. You have no right to hit him.'

William Daniels' dark eyes narrowed.

'Maybe you'd like to be next,' he said.

Nat put his fingers on Dennes' arm again in warning as he felt him tense.

'My father never laid hands on us and you're not going to do it now. Let him go. Tell him you're sorry, Taylor.'

Nat saw William glance across at him and at Dennes and then slowly he released Taylor. The boy's eyes were huge with fear and as William Daniels let go of him he trembled.

'I didn't— I didn't mean to be rude. I— I'm sorry.' He bolted out of the room, his feet clattering on the stairs. Nat imagined him bursting into tears when he reached the bedroom.

'He wouldn't mean to be rude, Mr Daniels, he isn't like that, really,' Nat said. 'I'm sorry.'

'You will be,' William Daniels said and he walked out of the house.

The outside door had barely closed before Gwen went over to Nat and she slapped him so hard across the face that his hair went into his eyes.

'How dared you do that?' she said. 'How dare you flout my authority like that and interfere?'

He said nothing.

'Go upstairs and stay there.'

Nat went. Dennes followed, saying softly on the stairs, 'That's the egg-and-ham pie done for. Pity, I was looking forward to it.'

49

Dolly and Taylor were sitting together in the boys' room. Dolly got up and ran to Nat. He put his arms around her.

'Mr Daniels was awful to Taylor. I don't like him any more.'

Dennes sat down on the bed with Taylor.

'You all right?' he said. The boy's face was streaked with tears but he nodded.

'I didn't cheek him, honest I didn't, Nat, but you told me not to leave Mam on her own with him and he sent Dolly up here and then he tried to get rid of me and he's been on the beer. I could smell it. You were gone such a long time,' and Taylor shuddered.

They stayed up there because Gwen didn't shout them down and it became colder and colder. Dolly got into bed and went to sleep. There was only one candle.

'I'm starving,' Dennes announced finally, and made for the door.

'Careful,' Nat said.

'Don't worry. I don't want no smack in the gob.'

Gwen was in the front room, drinking tea by a big fire. Dennes hovered in the doorway.

'Shut the door then,' she said loudly and made him jump. 'There's a draught.'

'Can I come in?'

'Nobody asked you to stay out, or are you and our Nat joined at the hip? Thick as thieves. I saw you, don't think I didn't.'

'You saw me what?'

She turned and looked clearly at him.

'If you hadn't been there things would have been different.'

Dennes thought for a second.

'If I hadn't been there Nat would have done something else. He's like that.'

'He's a rude, disrespectful boy. The trouble was that Thomas never thrashed him.'

'Well why don't you thrash him now? He's not likely to stop you, is he? Mr Lovett probably has a decent garden cane in his shed—'

'Oh, be quiet, Dennes.'

'It's awfully cold upstairs,' Dennes said.

Gwen got up and went to the foot of the stairs and called, 'Taylor! Dolly! You can come down.'

The children came running down the stairs.

'You're not really going to let him go to bed with nothing to eat, are you?' Dennes said.

'You're the lodger, Dennes. That's all you are. Don't forget it,' and she fairly swept out of the room.

'Shite,' Dennes said softly to himself.

Taylor and Dolly bounced back into the front room after tea. Dennes went through into the kitchen. Gwen was washing up.

'If you want something to eat you'd better get it now,' she said.

'What's that?' Dennes said, catching sight of the glint on her finger.

She stopped and stretched out her left hand. Above her wedding ring was a ring with three dark red stones set in gold.

'It was a present from William. Don't you think it's pretty?' she said.

'Are they rubies?'

'No, garnets. Thomas couldn't afford to give me anything like this. If you aren't going to sit down and eat you can go to bed. You have to be up.'

Dennes looked at the table. The egg-and-ham pie was half-eaten.

'You wouldn't let me—'

'No, I wouldn't, and when you go upstairs you can tell Nat that I don't wish to see him again until I have a full apology and until William has an apology too.'

Dennes trudged back upstairs. The candle had gone out, the evening was full dark now. They sat by the window. The wind howled through.

'We could always leave,' he said.

'I couldn't leave the bairns.'

'When she marries him, something tells me you will. He gave her a ring, three stones, garnets.'

'God,' Nat said.

'Fancy being pleased with garnets.'

'What's wrong with them?'

'They're not real stones, not like rubies. If I had a woman I'd give her sapphires or emeralds. He could have given her a lump of coal and

51

been more to the point. A black diamond. He could have given her jet.'

'Jet's for funerals,' Nat pointed out.

'Your mother wants an apology and for him.'

'I told him I was sorry.'

'I don't fancy your chances against three garnets, Nat. If you don't knuckle under you, me and him are going to end up knocking each other's teeth out and either way you lose your mother and your Dolly and Taylor. Not having any family is . . . well, it's not up to much.'

'Tonight?' Nat said hopefully.

'No, I don't think you're in with a chance over the egg-and-ham pie. You might stand a chance tomorrow. Of course there is always the alternative. You can just go down and take what you want.'

'She's my mother. She's done everything for me.'

'In that case I think we should talk about something other than food,' and Dennes went and lay on the bed out of the draught. 'Did you see Grace Hemingway this morning when she came by on her horse? Nice backside.'

'Dennes!'

'What?' Dennes said and laughed.

Nat left the window and lay down with his hands behind his head.

'The horse wasn't bad either. It had a nice backside too,' Dennes said and they both laughed.

Seven

Nat apologised profusely to his mother the next day and to William Daniels rather less profusely when they met again, but Dennes lay in bed at night and wondered what the future would be like when neither he nor Nat had a home. It wasn't a prospect to look forward to with glee, and now for the first time he really believed that Nat's mother would marry this man and he could see that William Daniels didn't care for the children at all. He had stopped pretending. When he came now it was to invite Gwen to church socials or to friends and that was a relief. Having the house to themselves they could sit over the kitchen fire on these winter evenings and play games and talk. Dennes tried not to think about how things would be later because he had the feeling that no matter how bad it got, Nat would not leave Dolly and Taylor with a new father such as he thought this man might be, and when that happened Dennes would not be able to stay, he would probably not be allowed to stay. He had seen how William Daniels disliked him.

William never again raised his hand to any of them but that was because when the man did come to the house Nat made sure he was always there. When the marriage took place Dennes knew that he would have to come to a decision, and it wouldn't be an easy one because if he left, if Nat had no backup, William Daniels would try to subdue him and Nat wasn't big enough or old enough to take him on by himself. It was an impossible decision and Dennes could see himself sucked in, living as unhappily as before with people who were continually at war with one another. He tried to think of himself far away but he couldn't see where it was or where to go, and he would be alone in a way in which he had never been. He didn't know whether he could stand that.

There was another problem too. Gwen had not forgiven Nat for challenging William Daniels. She was cold with him and under her continual displeasure Nat became quiet. Everything he did was wrong for his mother. He couldn't even bring a bucket of coals in but he was making a mess, if he didn't speak he was sullen, if he did speak he was rude. If he didn't sit with them he was unsociable, if he did he was in the way. Finally one Saturday night that spring, when the children were in bed and William Daniels had been expected and had not arrived, Nat was putting coal on the fire and a hot piece was dislodged, dropping straight on to the rug which Gwen had just finished making the week before. She bounced up out of her chair, walloped him hard over the face and shouted at him. Nat backed away, and when she would have followed, yelling, Dennes grabbed hold of her. Nat walked out. Gwen protested, tried to hit Dennes and couldn't because he held her arms, and when he shook her she burst into tears.

'You do know what you're doing, don't you?' he said insistently. 'You're driving him away. Is that what you want? You want rid of Nat? He doesn't have to stay here. He wasn't wrong in the first place. You know that very well. Don't you? Don't you?' He shook her again. She twisted away, crying.

'He's my son,' she said. 'He treated me like a fool.'

'So you wanted William Daniels to mistreat Taylor?'

'No.'

'You were going to let him.'

'I didn't mean to let him, it was just . . . it was because of Nat. I knew that it was.'

'You can't have William and Nat.'

'I don't see why not. If Nat would only . . .'

'If Nat would only what? William doesn't like him, he doesn't like anybody who challenges his authority. Nat's too old for another father, one like that anyway.'

She turned around, looked at him from wet eyes.

'How old are you?'

'I don't know exactly. Sixteen, maybe.'

'Yes. Well, you and Nat needn't worry. I don't think William is coming back.' She would have made an exit then except that Dennes held her.

'Tell me.'

'I can't tell you, Dennes, you're just a boy, however . . . however old you seem.'

'Tell me.'

'We had an argument.' Dennes let go of her. 'He wanted to . . . he tried to . . . I'm not a girl any more. I wanted to marry him because . . . so that he would be a father. I wanted a father for Dolly and Taylor. Maybe Nat doesn't need anybody, though I think he could do with somebody clever enough to keep him a boy a little longer. Since Thomas went away, no, even before that, long before that he wasn't a father to Nat, not the kind of father that Nat would have wanted. I think Nat despised him.'

'I'm sure he didn't.'

'I wanted to provide somebody for them who would be better than that, somebody strong, but William, he sees me differently. He sees me as I was and I'm not like that now. I have three children, I married young. I like going out with him, yes, I like having a new dress and a garnet ring and being with him so that we can be a couple – not being a couple is very hard, nobody asks you anywhere, but . . . I'm not sure I want to marry him. I'm not sure I want to marry anybody. Last time I was married I was about as old as you. I'm twice that old now. I'm thirty-two. I don't think I want . . . to be that close to him, or anybody.'

'He's the wrong man then, isn't he?'

'As though there were so many to choose from,' Gwen said with a bitter smile. 'I don't want to lose Nat, I do love him, it's just that I feel there should be somebody to blame because it started there, the thinking that I didn't want to marry the man, that I had been deluding myself . . .' She gazed down at the garnets on her finger.

'Why don't you give Mr Daniels the ring back if you don't want him?' Dennes suggested.

'How can I? He got us this house, he pays the rent—'

'It's only a house,' Dennes said. 'Why don't you give the ring back to him?'

He could hear his own voice so soft and persuasive and made himself stop.

'I want to make it up with Nat,' Gwen said.

Dennes went off upstairs but the children were asleep and Nat's side of the bed was empty.

'He's gone,' he said.

She began to cry.

'Where would he go?'

'I don't know. Don't worry, he couldn't do owt wrong, he doesn't know how to. He's got a halo around his head the size of a dinner plate. I'll go and look for him.'

Dennes took his jacket from behind the outside door and left the house. He couldn't think where Nat might be either. He was hardly likely to go to a pub. Everybody knew how old he was, he wouldn't get in there. It was bitterly cold. Dennes went off down the road and into the main street. Nobody was standing around and it was not surprising, he thought. A bitter wind howled across the wide road and up the pavements. Past the railway gates he paused outside the Golden Lion, listening to the sound of talk inside. He would have liked to stop off there but he didn't. Up past the foundry gates of the steelworks and up past the Variety theatre and on up to the crossroads where the Presbyterian church stood out and the lights were on in the Black Horse Inn. There was nobody about on Bridge Street either. Dennes walked back down the main street and up the bank and towards the end of the village, and was just about to turn back when he saw somebody quite tall – Nat had grown considerably lately – in against the wall for warmth. You could just see Covington's house from there.

'I've been all over the place looking for you,' he accused Nat mildly.

'I've made up my mind,' Nat said. 'I'm leaving.'

Dennes followed his gaze. Some of the windows were lit in the big house. You couldn't see much, it was far off on its own and there were trees.

'What about Alexandra?'

'I'm glad you think it's funny.'

'I don't think it's funny, Nat.'

'My mother likes William Daniels better than me.'

'I don't think there's going to be a problem. I think your mother has decided that she'd rather have you safe in your little bed than William Daniels in hers.'

'Then why does she treat me like this?'

'Because it's your fault she's given the old bastard the heave-ho.'

They walked slowly up the bank. When they got back Gwen actually threw herself at Nat. Dennes stood a little apart with his hands in his pockets and watched them.

'I'm sorry,' she said. 'I didn't mean to hit you, really I didn't.'

'Make the best of it,' Dennes said, 'while you can still reach.'

She laughed, and traced her fingers along Nat's face and kissed him.

'I shall give William his garnets back and we'll be like we were.'

When Nat and Dennes went upstairs to bed Nat was silent.

'You don't seem very pleased,' Dennes said, 'for somebody who won.'

'You make it sound like some kind of contest. It wasn't like that. If he had been a decent kind of a man it would have been different. My mother's not old, you know. It isn't very nice for her going to a cold bed every night.'

Dennes laughed.

'And here's me thinking you were still a bairn,' he said.

Eight

Nat felt guilty over William Daniels. It didn't matter how much he did, he couldn't make up to his mother for the loss of his father. He couldn't be his father and now he felt as though he had deprived her of grown-up company, and it was not easy on his conscience. He had wished when William Daniels was around so much that his mother was not so pretty, he wished her plain and pasty-faced and fat and now he was sorry. He tried to ease things for her but nothing helped. She no longer wore the garnet ring and Dennes had assured him that William Daniels had come to the house and that the ring had officially been given back. He knew also that she had been to see Mr Hemingway's manager to see if there was a house for them but nothing had happened yet. Houses, it seemed, were in short supply and Nat felt bad about that too. She had loved the lilac house, as they thought of it, she had sung on wash day and she had worn pretty dresses and gone out. She sang no more that spring even when the weather softened, and he could see that she took no pleasure in the work. She never went out and although she was always clean and tidy she didn't change her dress because there was nobody to change it for. The children went back to their old ways, Taylor to play football and Dolly to her toys on the scrubby piece of lawn beside the house.

The house was always spotless, there were always clean ironed clothes, there was good food and polished furniture but Gwen worked all the time and would not even go for a walk on Sunday afternoons when Nat suggested it. He realised after a little while that they could not go back to what had been before, you could never go back because his father's death and William Daniels' absence had changed everything.

That Easter, Dolly was still child enough to want pace eggs. Gwen boiled them in onion skins and Nat and Dennes took Dolly and Taylor to the first field on a hill they could find to roll them. Taylor stood watching scornfully at first and then joined in, shouting and shrieking.

When they got back Gwen was done up in a pale yellow frock with wide sleeves and tight cuffs and a new hat.

'I'm trying it on, that's all,' she said but they encouraged her to go to chapel that Sunday evening just so that she could 'air her bonnet' as Dennes called it.

Nat was taking Dolly and Taylor to a special Sunday School outing that day. It was the first fine picnic of the year, and because they would be back late, and Gwen had gone to chapel with coffee and cake afterwards, Dennes left the house and found some of his friends in the Black Horse at the top of the main street. He wanted to sit down and have a few drinks and talk about work, and at first he was quite happy to do so. The girl who served the drinks, Lily Hodgson, was pretty and she talked to him, the fire was big because the night was cool and the first beer went down well, and then suddenly he didn't want to be there. He didn't understand it. He stayed, made himself stay, he had another drink, listened to the talk but his mind was no longer on the conversation and the beer didn't taste right. He left amid protests and walked slowly back down the High Street, wondering whether he was getting a bad cold or something. He was usually sociable, at ease there the few times he could afford to go, and he was rather irritated with himself because he didn't often go for a drink and he couldn't afford not to enjoy himself.

He let himself quietly into the house. There was nobody about in the kitchen, and no sounds of the children upstairs, but he could hear something. He opened the door which led into the hall and listened, and sure enough there was a strange noise coming from the front room, though the door was closed and (this not being an ordinary foundryman's house) the walls were not thin, but he could hear it, a desperate kind of sound like a hurt animal. Dennes hesitated. His instinct told him to to hurl himself into the room, but he remembered last time there had been a crisis and Nat had held him back. He wished that Nat was there now. He tiptoed along the hall and soundlessly turned the doorknob and the noise became louder, a kind of rhythmic whimpering with a sob through it. Dennes didn't see at first what he was meant to be seeing, his mind gave him scenes from his childhood which he thought he had cleaned from his mind, his mother beneath a man with her legs apart and her breasts bare, on a bed, on the floor, on the kitchen table, against a wall and in other ways too which he closed his mind over for sanity's sake, forced it all out of his mind a second after the images placed themselves there, because this woman was not his mother. Her clothes were torn and her body showed creamily in the light. She was crying as though she had been crying for a long time, her voice was hoarse as though she had screamed, her face was shiny with tears, her distress was a sad song. The resistance was gone from her though the room showed signs of it, something broken in pieces on the floor, the furniture all pushed back, and down on the rug which she had made that winter – though it had never been the same since Nat dropped live coal on it – a man was very slowly raping her. He was holding her down, though Dennes wouldn't have said it was necessary any more. His body moved in deep enjoyment and he was smiling and talking very softly to her.

It was only seconds. Dennes even considered what to do. He tried to be rational, he tried to see something to hit the man with, and then she saw him and the man realised, and in that moment Dennes knew he had to act because William Daniels was stronger and older than him. All Dennes had was suprise, so he took what advantage he could, prayed that Nat would come back, and then that he wouldn't because the children were with him, and as Daniels eased out of her Dennes threw himself at him. To his horror, instead of retreating and crying and getting out of the way like any sensible woman who had just been assaulted in an awful way, she seemed to think that he was Nat and that she couldn't let William Daniels hurt him. In some complicated way it was as though she had carried him, nurtured him and had to save him.

'Get out the way, Gwen,' he yelled, shoving her. He couldn't help reflecting, though, that William Daniels was very likely going to kill him, not just because he had stopped him but because Dennes had seen him do this thing. The look on William's face was murderous. They went down heavily among the furniture. Dennes had never thought that furniture had such angles to it, it seemed all points and hard edges as you were slammed against it, and William Daniels was slamming him now, like somebody with half a dozen fists. It was the first time in his life that Dennes had ever been glad for the kind of upbringing which would have turned most people's stomachs. His mother had always seemed to go for the kind of men who considered constant beatings as mandatory for child-raising. Survival was a case of learning to evade fists, of knowing how to gain advantage over people who were three times as big as you. William Daniels was not much bigger than him, that was a pleasant surprise. He was wider certainly but that was definitely, Dennes thought, landing a bunched fist in it, a disadvantage when it was your stomach. His fist sank well in and Daniels lost his wind.

Gwen came back and tried to hit William Daniels with her best vase, but she missed and it buried itself in the wallpaper before crashing to the floor. No aim, that was the trouble with women, Dennes thought idly as William banged his head on the floor. He managed to land a neat clout on William's ear. It spurted blood immediately and enabled him to roll clear and get to his feet.

'He'll kill you, Dennes, stop it!' she shrieked from the far wall. 'Run!'

Dennes had no intention of doing anything of the kind. He was beginning to enjoy himself. It was the first time he had realised that he was almost a man in height and strength. He was hot with the desire for revenge. He gazed at his opponent and thought that it was not just now he had wanted to hurt this man, he had always wanted to do it, right from the beginning, right from the very moment that William Daniels had set eyes on this woman and thought that she was some kind of present, a prize, a victim. And he had been right. This man had never wanted Nat's mother in an honest way, he had wanted her subdued, submissive, as a slave for whatever disgusting needs he had. It was not going to be, any more than it had already been, Dennes decided, and it had already been far too much. As William Daniels gathered his strength, as he got to his feet, raised himself up from the floor, he was to Dennes like all those men who had done such things to women and to boys, who had enjoyed their pain and their distress and he saw his own actions almost as a spectator would, firstly a good mouthful of fist to halt William Daniels, and then another in the stomach to cripple him and finally a third in the face to knock him down. He seemed to go down almost in slow motion. He went down and down heavily, with his arms flailing to try and save himself, with his face bloody and his thinning hair not quite plastered to his head, with his clothes askew and his feet twisted and all the wind and all the resistance knocked out of him. He went down, and when he hit the floor it was to Dennes as though the whole room took the impact of the sound and absorbed it, hugged it. And then there was silence.

Gwen didn't say anything. He thought that she would, he thought that she would say something quite normal somehow, but she didn't. She was standing back against the wall just as she had been. Her pretty dark hair was half down, her face was bruised and there was blood on her mouth. Her arms were across her front to hide her body, her clothes were ripped and she was shaking, but she was watching William Daniels as though he was some enormous stinging insect.

'He's going to get up,' she said finally.

Dennes looked critically at the man.

'I don't think he is.'

'He's going to get up from there, Dennes, and kill you.' The tears began again.

Dennes went on looking at him, watching carefully in case she was right and William had some devious move planned, but nothing happened. The seconds went by and he didn't get up. He was quite still. Dennes' knuckles ached, and when he glanced at them they were covered in blood, and he was hurt too. He wiped his face with the palm of his hand and there was more blood and he ached desperately everywhere.

He heard the back door, and she straightened, so she had heard it too. He could hear Dolly's excited tones and Taylor calling for his mother. Dennes stood against the door and shouted to Nat. Taylor tried to get into the room but Dennes just leaned on the door until Nat was outside. He was very tired now, leaning was a relief.

'What?' Nat said and Dennes smiled. Trust Nat not to make a fuss.

'Can you send Taylor and Dolly upstairs?'

'Why does he want us to do that?' Taylor complained but Nat didn't ask any questions.

He ushered the complaining Taylor and Dolly whining 'but I'm hungry, Nat' up the stairs, and then Dennes opened the door just as much as was necessary to let Nat into the room. Gwen's eyes flooded with relief when she saw him but she didn't move. Nat looked at her and at Dennes and then at the still figure of William Daniels. He got down and looked harder and touched him and then he said, 'He's dead, Dennes.'

'He can't be,' Gwen said, the words quivering.

'I think he is. I can't feel any breath.'

'You might be wrong. How can you be sure?'

Dennes got down and felt for a pulse but there was nothing.

'He can't be dead,' Gwen protested. 'Dennes only hit him.'

There was blood on the back of his head.

'You'd better get the police,' Dennes said, feeling sick.

Nat looked across William Daniels' body at him.

'No,' he said.

'But Nat, we have to,' Gwen said.

'And have Dennes hang for a bastard like that?'

'We can't go on as if it didn't happen,' Dennes said, 'it did and I did it.'

'He banged his head on the hearth when he fell. That wasn't your fault and anyway . . .' Nat glanced at his mother and then at Dennes.

'The police aren't going to care. You did it as far as they are concerned and he's a respectable man. Nobody could call you respectable. You won't get off with it, Dennes.'

Nat got up and went to the door.

'Where are you going?' Dennes said.

'I'm going to see if Mr Lovett's left his wheelbarrow in the garden.'

It was a dark night. They were pleased about that. Nat and Dennes carried William's body outside, and in the back lane they stuffed it into the wheelbarrow and wheeled him away down the lane and out of the village.

It felt like a long way to the old whinstone quarry. It was the one place where children were not allowed to go. Suicides went there. It was a long drop over the side and into the water. They unloaded his body from the wheelbarrow and tipped it over the side. There was a gap in time and then a reassuring splash.

They saw no one on the way back. Nat replaced the wheelbarrow in Mr Lovett's front garden across the road. Gwen was sitting over the kitchen fire. She was clean and tidy by then with her hair up, wearing a nightdress and a big cardigan. As Nat got down beside her she began to cry, but she wouldn't let him touch her. She got up and insisted on bathing Dennes' hands and face. Then she went to bed. Nat offered to stay in the room with her, but she refused. She even shut the door after her. Nat went back downstairs to where Dennes was sitting over the kitchen fire.

'Are you all right?' Nat said.

'How can I be all right? I just killed a man.'

'He was a bastard,' Nat said.

'That doesn't make it right.'

'It was an accident, and it was his own fault anyway.'

Dennes said nothing.

'He was raping my mother, Dennes. What were you supposed to do, ask him to stop?'

'I just wish you'd been here, that's all,' Dennes said, voice shaking dangerously.

65

'I would have done the same thing and you would have helped me get rid of him. You never liked him and you were right. One of these days my mother's going to find a man who isn't a fool.'

'Your mother's probably never going to want a man to touch her again in her whole life.'

'What can we do?'

'Not much.'

'You stopped him.'

'It was too late by then, Nat, he'd . . . he'd— I could kill him again!' He looked up. 'What if they find out?'

'I don't think they will. Who cares about him? He has no family, and his friends were only through my mother. Nobody really liked him.'

'When they find the body they'll want to know.'

'Dennes, they won't find him, not there, and even if we were seen nobody will tell the police. People around here look after their own, and he wasn't one of us. Nobody in the world will miss him.'

They went to bed, though neither of them slept much. In the dawn Dennes fell into an uneasy doze where he relived the dark walk to the quarry edge.

Nine

The next day was washing day. Nat's mother always got up especially early on washing days but today she didn't. Dennes wasn't inclined to go to work. His hands were bad and he was sore. Nat went to work, though he didn't want to, just to keep Taylor company. Dolly had school holidays and went across the road to play with a friend. Gwen sat by the fire. Dennes stayed in bed until mid-morning but when he went downstairs she was still in her nightdress. She started when he walked into the kitchen and clutched her cardigan around her. Dennes got down beside her.

'It's all right. It's over.'

'Things like that . . . you don't get over them.'

'I know.'

'I thought he was going to hurt you. I was so frightened. I would never have forgiven myself, never. It was my own stupid fault. I let him walk me back here because he insisted and then I let him into the house because he was so polite. He said that he wanted to talk and then . . .'

'It wasn't your fault. How could you have known?'

'I keep thinking, he might have hurt one of you, you or Nat. I was so frightened.'

'You are the one he hurt.'

Gwen put both hands over her face. Dennes drew her out of her chair and to her feet and into his arms while she protested but once in his arms she buried her face against his shoulder.

'You're so tall now,' she said from the safety of his shirt. 'Boys don't stay boys very long,' and she shuddered.

Dennes held her tight. She didn't object; he rather thought she shut her eyes. She thought he was too young to be a threat and there was no reason why she shouldn't go on thinking that, but in a strange way Dennes didn't feel like a boy any more. Killing a man was like a horrible rite of passage somehow. You couldn't be young any more when you'd killed, even if it wasn't intentional, and then he realised coldly that if William Daniels hadn't died like that he would have tried to kill him anyway because of what he had done. It was not a comfortable thought but it was a powerful one, and as he went on holding Gwen there he started to feel differently about her, as though in some basic way she belonged to him because he had killed the man who was hurting her. Part of Dennes wanted to let go and run away, but he didn't, he just thought how small she was, how her body felt soft and warm through his shirt. He was sorry, he had wanted to protect her from the smallest hurt and now she had been hurt so badly that she might never recover and he had not been there to prevent it. When she drew back he let go of her.

'I can't stay here any longer,' she said. 'We must have another house. I had to go into the front room to clear up but I can't go in there again. To think how much I loved it here.'

When Nat came home they sat around the table and talked about what they could do.

'There aren't any foundrymen's houses,' Dennes said.

'There is an alternative,' Nat said.

'What's that?'

Nat looked at his mother.

'I hear that Matt Smith's mother is coming out of the Golden Lion.'

She stared at him for a moment or two.

'You're suggesting that we should go and live in a public house?' she said. 'Your father hated drink, Nat.'

'I'm not saying that we should drink any of it but it's a much bigger better house than most and what with three of us working and the money it would bring in . . . Maybe you should think about it.'

Gwen drank the rest of her tea.

'We could take people, people who are travelling, if it's a big enough house.'

'Mr Barmouth owns it,' Nat said.

'It'd be dear.'

'It might not. I could make some enquiries.'

'There'll be plenty after it once word gets round,' his mother said.

That evening Nat and Dennes walked to Esh House. It had big gates and a long drive. Nat didn't know whether to walk up to the front door or go round the back, but Dennes marched up and knocked on the door. A pretty maid answered the door. She looked up into Dennes' eyes and blushed and after that Nat didn't worry about whether they would get inside.

'I'm Dennes Eliot and this is Nat Seymour. We'd like to see Mr Barmouth. Is he at home?'

She ushered them into the hall and said that she would enquire. Moments later Nat followed Dennes into the most interesting room he had ever seen. From floor to ceiling the walls were covered in books. Nicholas Barmouth got up from the desk where he had been working and looked levelly at the two boys.

'Well now,' he said, 'and what can I do for you?'

Nat looked at Dennes, and when he saw that Dennes was inclined to let him do the talking he said, 'It's about the Golden Lion, sir. We need a house and my mother needs an occupation, and we were wondering if you might be inclined to think of us when you're deciding who to take in there.'

'Your mother is . . . ?'

'Gwen Seymour, sir. My father died—'

'Yes, I think I recollect. South Africa, wasn't it?'

'I have a sister and a brother and . . . we need a house badly and we can all work to run the public side of it.'

Nat watched Nicholas Barmouth carefully. He was not an old man,

69

not nearly as old as Mr Hemingway, and he was a clever man, too. The Golden Lion was essentially a foundrymen's pub so he needed foundry people in it. The foundrymen went in in their dirt after their shift to send some beer down among the dust.

'If there's a chance of us having the Golden Lion, my mother would be glad to come and see you herself,' Nat offered.

'I think that might be a good idea,' Mr Barmouth agreed.

When they got back outside again, nobody said anything as they walked down the drive until they reached the gates, and then Dennes said, 'I think you ought to come with her.'

'I thought maybe you would.'

'You did all the talking.'

'You're bigger and older than me.'

'You're her son.'

'We could both come.'

'It would be too many.'

'I'd like to be like Mr Barmouth,' Nat said.

'He doesn't look very happy.'

'I meant rich like him, to own a foundry and know how things run.'

'He was a foundryman, a fettler.'

'Was he?'

'That's what everybody says.'

'He's not that old yet either. Maybe we'll end up like that.'

Dennes smiled ruefully.

'Not me,' he said. 'Wait until they find William Daniel's body. I'm dead.'

Nat put an arm around his shoulders.

'They won't find him, Dennes, and even if they did they wouldn't know how to connect you with it. Don't worry.'

'I have nightmares about it.'

'He deserved to die. Nobody has the right to do such a thing.'

'The thing is, Nat . . . I didn't intend to kill him, but I think I would have anyway.'

'I would have, too – at least, I would have tried. And I helped, don't forget.'

'I'm glad you did.'

'So am I.'

'I hear that Mrs Seymour is charming,' her father was saying as Grace walked into the room.

'She is,' Nicholas Barmouth said, and he frowned. 'I can't quite see her running a foundrymen's pub.'

'Or as a foundryman's wife?'

'I was a foundryman.'

'You were a skilled man, one of the best, and you weren't foolish enough to go digging for gold,' Anthony Hemingway said.

Her mother was sitting by the window, sewing. Grace went to her.

'I want to talk to you,' she said.

'Is she to have the public house, then?' Anthony was saying.

'I'm trying to arrange it.'

'What about?' Dorothy said now.

'About London. I don't want to go.'

Her mother stared.

'Not go? Grace, every girl in her right mind wants to go to London for the season. There'll be parties and dances. You'll have new dresses. Your aunt will take you everywhere—'

'I don't care about things like that. I don't want to go.'

'Whyever not?'

'I won't see the heather,' Grace said. 'If I go in June and stay the whole summer, I'll miss everything here.'

'There is nothing happening here,' her mother said. 'That was the reason we wanted you to go.'

'I don't want to go.'

Her mother said nothing, and since they were speaking softly the men in the other part of the room didn't hear them.

'I don't ever want to go and live anywhere else. I don't want to leave here.'

'There's nothing here for you, Grace.'

'Everything's here,' Grace said, voice thickening. 'Everything.'

'We live here because of your father's work, not out of choice. I

71

don't want a life like that for you, I want you to see society, I want culture for you, nice people—'

'And what about what I want?'

'You will want those things, in time. Your going to London is just to give you a taste of what you can have. I want you to have a good summer, a good time. Is there something wrong with that?'

'I can have a good time here.'

'Doing what? Running wild on the moors and giggling with Alexandra? It isn't suitable for a young lady, Grace.'

'Then I don't want to be a young lady. I don't want to leave Alexandra or here.'

'You're only going away for a short time and there will be parties and dances and people your own age who are like you. You can't get that here. Your aunt hasn't seen you in years and she is dying to show you off. You've grown so very pretty, Grace, you have no idea how lovely you are.'

Her mother was always telling her how pretty she was. Grace hated it. She was sixteen. Her prettiness felt like nothing to do with her, it was somehow as though she was pretty in spite of who she was. People didn't listen to what she said or want to know what she thought. Either they stared – that was mostly men, and other girls' mothers, enviously and resentfully – or they backed away or turned away, thinking that she would not want anything to do with them because they were not similarly blessed with such looks. Grace did not consider it a blessing. She knew it for a curse. One of the reasons she got on so well with Alexandra was because the other girl cared nothing for anybody's looks. Grace was also beginning to look around her when she went out for sight of Dennes Eliot, who appeared to be similarly unimpressed. She liked that. Her mother said that being pretty was the most important thing a young lady could be. That was why Alexandra would never marry, nobody would ever want her because she was outspoken and immodest and big. She would be an old maid. Maybe, Grace thought angrily now, they could be old maids together and keep house up on the moors and be eccentric and gather herbs like old Mrs Wicks who cured folk in the village. It would be like being a doctor.

72

Grace didn't argue any more; she had behaved very badly to begin with. She could see from the tightness of her mother's mouth that Dorothy was most unhappy with her. She supposed it was hardly surprising. Her mother had never been further than Durham for years, she wished for all the things that she meant to provide for Grace, it must be very hard for her to realise that Grace did not want them. In fact she could see by her mother's face that she could not believe it.

'May I go and see Alexandra now?'

'It's late, Grace.'

Grace said nothing more. Did her mother not understand that she needed to talk to somebody? She agreed and said goodnight, said a polite goodnight to Mr Barmouth, kissed her father and then went off upstairs, dissuading Ruth from following her, just as she did so many evenings that Ruth gave in immediately. Neither of them told her mother that Ruth didn't undress her, brush out her hair, do all the things that young ladies had maids for. Ruth knew by now that Grace liked to be left alone. What she didn't know was that Grace got out of the back bedroom window – Ruth's room, but Grace was always back before Ruth went to bed – climbed over the henhouse roof, slid along the back wall a little way to the gate, clambered down over the gate, out of the yard and then around the back and through the houses and away.

Alexandra was never in bed until very late. Her father was always by the study fire and she would be alone in the kitchen with a book, once Mrs Vinny the cook had gone to her own cottage with her husband who looked after the grounds.

Alexandra was sitting by the big kitchen range; the kitchen was in their house the cosiest room. Alexandra was quite a good hand in there; her cooking and baking were excellent, and when Grace arrived she made tea and gave her a scone which was the lightest Grace had ever tasted.

'I made them this afternoon,' she said.

Grace ate the scone and enjoyed it even though she wasn't hungry.

'I told my mother I didn't want to go to London.'

'And what did she say?'

'I think she thought I'd lost my mind.'

'She's probably right.'

Grace stopped in mid-bite. 'You really think I should go?'

'I'd love to go.'

'I wish you could come with me. The idea of spending the summer with my aunt gives me the shivers. My mother, of course, is dying to go. I know that I'll be bored silly within two days.'

'What would you be doing if you stayed here?'

'Nothing. It's what I'm best at.'

Alexandra laughed. 'You're so idle,' she said.

'We could paddle in the stream up on the fell, lie in the heather, read books, sunbathe and talk about Dennes Eliot's beautiful green eyes. What more could anybody want?'

'New dresses, boys who can dance, chocolate pudding . . .'

'I'd give it all for one kiss.'

'Ruth thinks he's common,' Alexandra said.

'Oh, Ruth would. She's like that. She thinks that the height of sophistication is the doctor's son, Peter Clifford, because he reads poetry. Poetry. I ask you. News, Alex.'

'What?'

'They're moving to the Golden Lion. I heard Mr Barmouth and my father talking. Mrs Seymour has been to see him and they're going to live in the pub.'

'We won't see them.'

'We never see them now. You like Nat Seymour, don't you?'

'I think he's very nice – for a common boy.' Alexandra stopped and considered. 'No,' she said finally. 'I think he's very nice.'

Ten

Gwen was determined from the first that it would not just be a foundrymen's pub, and she set aside another room so that those who were washed and dressed would not have to mix with those who were not. Nat was dubious at first about this practice, but after a slow beginning it started to work. The foundrymen came because they had always come there, because they considered her one of them, other workmen in the village came into the other room to meet, and even the Methodists came since it was in the Golden Lion that the union meetings were held. His mother decided that she would also take in passing travellers because the building was bigger than most and had two spare bedrooms.

When the first of these travellers arrived that summer they needed food as well as drink and a bed, and after that it seemed that Gwen was always working. Dolly was almost twelve and she was good in the kitchen, cooking, baking and bread-making, and she helped to serve the meals and make up the beds. She liked seeing to those who stayed and Gwen looked after the men in the bars.

Nat found it difficult to reconcile the woman who served beer, laughed and chatted and told jokes, with the one who had gone to chapel with his father though her family had been Church of England. She no longer went to chapel and wouldn't think of going to church, and since no one in the house was young enough for Sunday School any more, Nat enjoyed his Sunday mornings lying in bed with nothing to look forward to but a big dinner and the peace and quiet.

The only stipulation Gwen had made was that the boys were not to go into the bar and not to drink. Dennes sometimes went sneaking off to the Black Horse and on occasion, now that Nat was sixteen, took him with him.

The girl who helped at the Black Horse, Lily, was a married girl whose husband, Mick, worked away. She was pretty with bright yellow hair, blue eyes and a pink complexion. The men said that she had Viking blood and vied with one another asking her out but Lily, although she was content to talk to them, joke with them, serve them beer and receive their compliments lightly, would have nothing to do with anybody. Nat and Dennes were happy enough just to go there and sit with their beer and listen to the talk and the laughter and watch Lily, so pretty, smiling and taking the money.

Nat liked being part of the talk. He knew the men who went there and the ones they talked about. He also knew Mr Hemingway and Mr Barmouth, the men who owned the steelworks. They were deemed on the whole to be fair, though Anthony Hemingway was not liked as much as Mr Barmouth because Barmouth had not forgotten that he had been a foundryman himself, though Hemingway had provided the Mechanics' Institute where the men went to read and talk and play billiards.

One night that summer when Gwen was locking up and Dennes was still about, she said to him as he would have gone upstairs, 'I want a word with you.'

'What?'

'In here.'

The big kitchen at the back was the only room they had to themselves downstairs. It had comfortable chairs by the fire and a big table. The fire was banked down for the night. She turned around and folded her arms and looked severely at him.

'Shut the door.'

Dennes put one heel against the door.

'You took Nat to a pub. Don't bother to deny it, I could smell the beer on his breath when he came back.'

'We live in a pub.'

'I told you not to.'

'I'm not a bairn, you know.'

'You're living under my roof—'

'It's my roof too. I pay my way.'

'You had no right to introduce Nat to beer. His father hated things like that—'

'We're making a living out of it—'

'Don't argue with me! I won't have it and that's final. I won't have you teaching Nat bad habits.'

Dennes looked steadily at her.

'This is all to do with what I came from, isn't it? I don't have any bad habits. I don't think an occasional drink is bad—'

'Nat is my son. He'll do as I say.'

'I wouldn't count on that, not for much longer, and you have no right to expect it either from him or from me. He's sixteen and I'm at least a year older. We bring men's wages into this house. You have no right to tell us what to do other than the right that we give you—'

She clouted him over the face just as though he was Nat. Dennes had never in his life let anyone hit him without retaliating, and his instincts got to him before his reason. He didn't hit her, but he got hold of her and put her back against the wall with the breath knocked out of her, one hand at her throat. She gave a small shocked cry.

'Don't you treat me like a child,' Dennes said softly. Then he let go of her and walked out.

He walked the streets until he was in control of his temper. It took quite a long time. He expected that when he got back she would be in bed and the house would be in darkness, but a light was burning in the kitchen. When he walked in she looked up from where she was sitting by the fire and said instantly, 'I'm sorry.'

Dennes went in and shut the door.

'No, it was my fault. I shouldn't have taken Nat with me and I

77

shouldn't have done that to you, not after . . . not after . . .' Dennes absurdly wanted to cry like the child that he wasn't. 'I swore to myself that I'd never let anybody hurt you, and not only did he but now I've done it myself.'

'It wasn't you.' She got up from the fire and went to him. 'It was me and my awful temper.' She kissed him where she had hit him, just to the side of his mouth, and Dennes laughed and said she could hit him any time she liked if she was going to be that nice to him afterwards.

'I won't. I won't ever do it again.'

'What, kiss me?'

'No, hit you. You seem like a child to me.'

'A bad child.'

'Yes, but you're not, not at all. If it hadn't been for you . . .'

'It's all right.' Dennes took her into his arms and stroked her hair.

'He hated me.'

'He isn't worth your tears.'

'I didn't mean to make him think . . .'

'You didn't do anything. He was an evil man.'

'I keep thinking that I must have done something, that it must have been at least partly my fault—'

'Whatever for?'

'Because I'm a woman. It was the way I did my hair or wore my dress—'

'It was nothing to do with you.'

'I don't think I'm ever going to want to be near a man again as long as I live,' Gwen said, hanging on to him. 'When I'm in the bar and I see them . . .'

'They're not him. Most of them, they're all right. They wouldn't hurt you.'

Gwen drew away. Dennes let go of her. She smiled at him.

'It's very comforting having you and Nat.'

'I won't take him to the Black Horse any more.'

'I thought you both particularly liked Lily.'

'We do,' Dennes admitted, and Gwen went off to bed, smiling.

* * *

78

That was the happiest summer of Dennes' life. He and Nat did go to the Black Horse occasionally, but mostly they helped Gwen in the bar. It was a long hot summer. There was a garden to one side of the yard at the Golden Lion, and here they ate their meals when the weather was fine. Between the three of them working at the foundry and the pub itself they made good money. They ate well, they had new clothes, there was enough to spare for the odd trip into Durham or Bishop Auckland. They had a day trip into Weardale and when the main holidays came Gwen got somebody in to look after the pub and they spent a few days at the seaside.

Dennes knew that Nat longed for the sea. They had lived over there when they were young and Nat had never stopped talking about it, so that summer they decided to go to Hartlepool. They found a comfortable boarding house in Seaton Carew where they could get bed, breakfast and a meal in the evening and they spent a few days lying on the sand and paddling in the water which was the closest Gwen would go to a bathing machine though they tried to persuade her. They walked on the promenade, visited the park and saw the shops in Lynn Street in West Hartlepool. Late on the long summer evenings Dennes and Gwen would lean on the rail at Seaton and watch the fishing boats come home. It was the first time that he had ever seen the North Sea, and it was not a disappointment. He wanted to live there, to have a big, bay-windowed house which looked out over the sea, to be near enough to watch the winter waves come roaring up the beach as Nat had described them, to watch the children in the summer having donkey and pony rides, to see people throwing sticks for their dogs, young couples walking hand in hand. The water was icy, the sand was warm, the food at the house was good and the beds were comfortable. It seemed to Dennes like paradise. Gwen was like a young girl then, laughing, pointing to the boats as they came into sight, talking with warmth in her voice, and he wanted to spend every moment with her. Taylor went off on his own and Nat would take Dolly about with him, so Dennes went everywhere with Gwen. He had never seen her so lively. Her face and hands turned a pale brown with the sunshine, her eyes soon cleared of worry, and the second-to-last evening when they were walking on the sands down by the water's edge, he stopped and drew her into his arms and kissed her.

He didn't intend to do it, he hadn't thought about it, it was almost as though somebody else had done it, or somebody else had shoved him into it somehow. He wasn't pleased with himself at all, but it was like jumping into a pool of warm water: once you had begun you couldn't stop yourself. He felt her hesitate in his arms, begin to kiss him back, and then she stopped. She pushed back out of his arms hurriedly and looked at him from shocked eyes.

'I'm sorry,' he said at once, 'I didn't mean to do it.'

'That's not the way to kiss me, Dennes.'

'I know. I'm sorry,' Dennes said again, and then he couldn't bear the look on her face and he bolted.

He didn't go back to the boarding house for the meal that evening, and when it was very late he stood outside against the sea rail. She must have been watching for him because she came out and approached him and said, 'It was my fault.'

Dennes was irritated.

'Why does everything have to be your fault all the time?' he demanded, turning to look at her as he had sworn to himself he never would again.

'You're just a boy.'

'No, I'm not!'

'And I'm like your mother—'

'You were never like my mother, thank God.'

'I took you into my house—'

'Are you trying to make this worse than it is?'

That silenced her. And then she retreated into domesticity.

'Aren't you hungry, Dennes?'

'Will you stop being somebody's mother just for a minute?'

'I daren't.'

Dennes watched her. He had imagined that love would be perfect when it arrived. He wondered, considering his life this far, how he had got that idea, where it had come from. This was far from perfect, this was the most uncomfortable thing which had ever happened to him. It

80

was like a betrayal not only of himself and of her, but of Nat too. He wanted to deny that love, to pretend that it had never come into being. He could imagine Nat's hurt, shocked reaction.

You could look at her without love and see a woman almost of his mother's age. Her body had given away its secrets long ago. Lines were appearing around her eyes, her chin wasn't quite as firm as it should have been, her eyes were world-weary. And under that neat dress her breasts were not high like a girl's, they had fed three children, her stomach would not be flat, her arms and legs not youthful and slender. It made no difference to anything. He loved Gwen Seymour entirely and appallingly. He tried not to but he loved her, for her laughter and her conversation and the shine which appeared in her eyes when he made her laugh.

'How long is it since I took you into my house?'

'Gwen—'

'How long?'

Dennes didn't reply. He couldn't think of anything to say.

'Your mother walked away and left you,' she said. 'You had nowhere to go, nobody would have you, you were penniless and dirty and ignorant—'

'I know that!'

'Well, then,' she said quietly, and turned and walked back into the boarding house.

They were going home the next day. Dennes was glad of it. He hadn't slept. He felt as if he didn't want to see the hateful place ever again, and when they went home the happy summer was over. Gwen treated him as though he had done something unforgivable, her manner cool. She rarely spoke to him. Dennes was miserable. He thought about leaving.

One evening, a few days after they had come home, he was sitting outside. It was very late. He thought that everybody had gone to bed. The pub had long been shut. It was a warm windy September night, too good a night for sleeping. There was an old bench in the garden. At one time it had been a respectable oak pew, but it had been there when they arrived at the pub (and no doubt for some years previously) and the wind and rain had done their work on it. It was rotten. He sat there and the lights went out upstairs, and then the back door opened. It was Nat. Dennes had a great inclination to get up and make an excuse and go to bed. Nat looked at him in the way that Dennes dreaded, like he had looked at William Daniels when he was about to hit Taylor, cold and straight.

'What have you done to upset my mother?' he said.

Dennes sighed. He would have given a lot to have put one over on Nat some time.

'You're too sharp, you know.'

'I know that you've quarrelled. She doesn't do that unless there's a good reason for it. So, what have you done?'

'Nothing. I wouldn't do anything to hurt her. You know I wouldn't.'

'So you haven't quarrelled?'

'It was just a – a disagreement.'

'What about?'

'You're like a dog with a bloody bone, aren't you?' Dennes said becoming angry. 'Just leave it.'

'She's my mother.'

'She's also a person, Nat, entitled to some privacy, and so am I.'

'Why don't you just tell me it's none of my business?' Dennes didn't answer him. 'Are you going to leave?'

'I'm thinking about it.'

Nat swore under his breath.

'I knew you were,' he said. 'Can't you sort it out with her?'

'I'm trying to.'

Nicholas Barmouth came to the Golden Lion that week. At first Dennes didn't think anything about it, it was his pub, but he stayed for quite a long time, chatting to Gwen and drinking his beer and Dennes could see Gwen smiling. He called in again the following week and he stayed for even longer that time.

Dennes helped Gwen to clear up in the bar.

'What did Mr Barmouth want?'

'This is a public house, Dennes. Men come here to drink beer.'

'Not the foundry owner.'

'There's no law that says the foundry owner can't come in. He does own this place as well.'

Two nights later Nicholas Barmouth came back. Dennes was in the bar when he arrived and saw him start to talk to Gwen. He saw how her face changed, he saw how she paled and the nervous look in her eyes.

It was a warm night and they were not busy. Later Dennes retreated outside. It wasn't much of a view from the garden, just houses and the big buildings of the steelworks, but at least you could see the stars. Nat came out of the house.

'Did you hear about Mr Barmouth?'

'What about him?'

'He's asked my mother to go to the Variety with him.'

Dennes said nothing.

'Maybe we should encourage her,' Nat said. 'She hasn't been anywhere since William Daniels. Or do you think it's dangerous?'

Dennes turned around.

'What do you mean?'

'I'm not sure I want Mr Barmouth for a father.'

Dennes went out the following evening despite knowing that it was most unlikely Mr Barmouth would come to the pub. That week Dennes went to the Black Horse three times, until Gwen complained that he was never there to help and Lily Hodgson smiled so warmly on him that he left hastily.

The following night Nicholas Barmouth came to the Golden Lion. Dennes wanted to lift him off his feet and throw him, preferably out of the window, but he couldn't so he went off and left Gwen to cope with the customers.

Later she came to him in the kitchen. She closed the door softly behind her.

'Nice suit Mr Barmouth was wearing,' Dennes said without looking at her.

'I expect he has them tailored in Newcastle.'

'Or Sunderland maybe.'

'Maybe.'

'He wears old suits in the foundry, you know, and a dirty old hat. Keeps the sparks off, a hat.'

'I don't want you to go.'

'What am I supposed to do, stay here and watch you marry him?' She shook her head.

'It's just a— a fancy you have.'

Dennes laughed.

'Is that what you think? Are we back to "Dennes, you're just a boy" again?'

She didn't say anything for a few moments and she didn't come any closer to him.

'People can't go back,' she said finally. 'They can't relive what they've already had and where you are now that part of my life is over. If sometimes I want it back very much that doesn't make any difference. You can't get that part of my life back for me and I wouldn't ask you to do it. You have your whole life in front of you. Don't spoil it.'

'Spoil it? What a very strange way of looking at things. What do you think my life is, something innocent and pure?'

'You're not much more than a child.'

'I was never a child.'

Dennes went to her. She had unthinkingly made it so easy for him. All he did was draw close. She was already nearly back against the wall. She had nowhere to go. She pushed at him with her hands while her mouth betrayed her with its softness. He moved her arms up around his neck and gently assaulted her lips and then kissed her hard and long, and thought of what it would be like to have her so that she cried out her pleasure. He didn't think that she had ever known that, but at least she wasn't thinking about William Daniels, that was something. That would now be the memory behind this one, it would be coloured and smudged and part-healed because she was in safe arms being kissed the way that she wanted to be kissed. She pushed harder at him and he let go. She put her fingers up to her mouth and sobbed.

'Mr Barmouth has asked me to go to the theatre with him and I have said yes.'

'No—'

'And you will never do that again. Promise me.'

'No!'

'There are . . . there are more important things in life than passion. You don't understand that yet.'

'It isn't just passion. I love you.'

'Not like that—'

'Yes, like that! I can't help it. You can pretend that it isn't so if you want—'

'Never again, never. Promise me, Dennes.'

'No!'

'Dennes!'

This because he ran, out of the kitchen, through the passage, beyond the back door in the gloom and finally to the street. He could hear her calling his name into the street, and even there he thought he could still hear it, on and on like an echo across the road, when it was only his ears aching for the sound of her voice. It was quiet, only the odd person in the main street, not many lights in the houses, lights still on at the Cattle Mart Hotel across the road and past the railway gates. He began to walk slowly up the main street, away from the Golden Lion, away from her.

Eleven

Grace's uncle and aunt, although not rich fashionable people, were kind and introduced her to a good many people she would have been happy to know if they had lived near her beloved fells.

She became impatient at her unhappiness that summer. She longed to get away from London. She knew from meeting other people that to them her life in a small mining town on the edge of the Durham coalfield was the worst possible situation for any girl with looks and sensibility. She would never find a husband there.

Her aunt was careful in her selection of friends and Grace found herself getting to know the kind of young men who had never worked. She found them boring and stupid. Having been brought up in a home where the Puritan work ethic was adhered to like breathing, Grace found herself wanting to say offensive things, but she didn't.

She was occasionally invited to fashionable parties in the squares of Belgravia and Mayfair where the rich lived. She would not have upset her aunt by saying so, but Grace liked these times least of all. The people lived off money made in mines and factories and mills, but they knew nothing of the misery they inflicted, and had they known, she suspected, they would not have cared. Grace had gathered from her parents that the upper classes did not think of their workmen as people, that they never went there, they left the running of their mills and mines to other people, and here in London she had glimpsed people sleeping under the arches of the Thames' bridges, children in bare feet begging on the streets. The poor people who had housing lived in cramped rows of terraces built among the docks and factories in the east, and through her few excursions to different areas Grace remembered well the smell of bone-crushing and candle-making and human waste which pervaded these places.

In the west end of London rich people lived on land which had been fields not long since. Her aunt and uncle were not rich, but they lived in a charming villa which needed more servants than Grace had ever seen just to keep it going, and the villa was nothing compared to the places she sometimes went to dance that summer.

To her dismay a very rich young man had discovered a liking for her, and although Grace was a modest girl she had looked into her mirror and understood why. These men cared nothing for the person she was, only that she was beautiful. It was her looks that gained her the attention of the rich.

There was nothing wrong with him, she told herself, he was fair and slender and amusing. It was only when she finally escaped from him one hot July evening into his parents' London garden which was full of white roses that she reached the truth. The only reason she had looked on him with favour was because he reminded her dimly of Dennes Eliot.

She started to laugh against herself. If Dennes had been brought up here he would have been barefoot on the streets as a child, possibly dead by now. She shivered. She could not forget him even here, and she was angry with herself.

Grace wondered what it was like to be a child without a father, with a mother who took men into her bed for money because she knew no other way of survival, to have that mother leave, to be abandoned, to have no family. She thought of Dennes picking her up so carefully that day on the fell and carrying her so far, and not because he liked her. It had been one of the humiliations of her life to discover that, having admitted to herself that she liked Dennes too much, he did not like her. He did not even what the girls in the village called 'fancy her'. Grace knew instinctively that he did not, and it upset her very much. She knew how much she appealed to men, how they fought to be near, to dance with her, how they did their best to amuse and entertain, and some of them were very far above her socially, whereas Dennes was as far below her as he could be. She argued with herself that she would not have wanted to appeal to somebody like Dennes, but it wasn't true. She wished him sleepless nights because of her. He had not then picked her up into his arms on that day for any motive other than the altruistic, and in her heart she knew it and liked him the better for it.

'There you are.'

She turned, her thoughts interrupted. He was almost Dennes. To her further shame she had pretended that he was Dennes when they danced, since it was most unlikely that she would ever dance with Dennes. But he was not Dennes. He was a gentleman. She doubted he would ever drink too much beer or carry a stupid girl miles home over a Durham fell or call her 'flower'. He had doting parents, plenty of money, an education, a country house. He was called Henry Ellingthorpe, and his world was one of pleasure. Her aunt was very proud of the fact that she had gained and kept his attention, had probably even written to Grace's mother to tell her of such a triumph, of her hopes for the future.

'You're meant to be dancing with me,' he said.

If this had been earlier in the season, Grace, still impressed because of his wealth and Oxford education, would have gone with him, but now she merely glanced at him.

'I don't want to dance.'

'Ee by gum,' he said, and earlier that would have made her feel obliged to laugh. Her London friends mocked her for what was a northern accent, and since the only northern accent these people recognised was Yorkshire they imitated that as best they might. He dropped the accent and came over.

'Why don't you want to dance, Grace?'

He was so very fine. Grace wished with all her heart that she might love him.

'I want to go home.'

'Do you have a headache?'

A headache, Grace had discovered, was a useful female standby.

'No,' she said.

Her aunt came out to her and Henry retreated.

'Is there something the matter, Grace?' she said, and Grace burst into tears.

Henry sent her armfuls of white roses. The smell made her want to be sick. She sat by the window in her bedroom the next day. The view was of a park. She thought of how the heather would bloom purple on the moors above the village soon. It was the middle of the afternoon when her aunt came to her.

'Are you feeling better now?' she said.

Grace said that she was. Her aunt sat down beside her at the window.

'You don't look better. What is it, Grace, what's the matter?'

'I can't tell you.'

'You must. It's obviously making you very unhappy, and since I'm looking after you here, I have to know.'

Grace didn't know what to say.

'Has Henry done something he shouldn't, tried to kiss you perhaps?'

Grace wanted to laugh. Here in London things like this were of major importance. Henry had in fact kissed her several times. It was very pleasant but it didn't make her want to throw herself at him.

'Come along, Grace, do tell me.'

'I've fallen in love with a very unsuitable man.'

'Haven't we all,' her aunt said.

Grace went over to the bed and sat down.

'Tell me about him,' her aunt said.

'He doesn't even like me.'

'And is that why you've fallen in love with him?'

Grace smiled. Even just talking about Dennes was a relief. To actually be able to say his name aloud would be exciting.

'No. At least I don't think so.'

'You don't care for Henry Ellingthorpe?'

90

'I like him.'

'Worse and worse. Of course you couldn't care for Henry.'

'Why not?' Grace looked at her.

'He's handsome, rich, genial and wants to marry you, I suspect. Life is never that simple.'

'Do you think he will?'

'I'm expecting him here any day.'

'Do you think my parents would be pleased if I said I'd marry him?'

'I should think they'd be very upset indeed if it was for the wrong reasons, though to be honest every mother dreams of her daughter making a brilliant marriage, if only to boast to her friends.'

'My mother never boasts.'

'Has she ever had the opportunity?'

'I think a rich marriage is exactly what my mother wants for me. It was what she never had.'

'So who's the man?'

'I couldn't even begin to talk about him.'

'I think you ought to. Is he your father's gardener?'

'Worse than that.'

'Worse than a man whose world is full of turnips? Goodness.'

Grace smiled.

'He can't be so very bad, or is that why you like him?'

'Perhaps it is,' Grace said thoughtfully, 'though if that was the reason surely it would be because I wanted to hurt my parents and I don't. I'd hate to think that they even imagined I might think about him.'

'I won't say a word. I promise.'

'He's very very good-looking.'

'Better than Henry?'

'Whole oceans better. He doesn't talk about stupid things like Henry does.'

'Does he talk to you at all?'

'He's not interested in me.'

'I may come to be glad of that. Do you see him?'

'Not often. A long time ago when I hurt myself up on the fell he carried me most of the way home, and it was a very long way.'

'That was very gentlemanly.'

'I think it's the only gentlemanly thing he's ever done in his life.'

'Does he have a profession?'

'He has nothing. He never went to school. He has no father. His mother went off and left him. He works at the foundry. He's one of my father's men. His name is Dennes Eliot.'

'Grace—'

'I know. I do know. I shouldn't ever think about him and I have tried and I know that my parents would be very worried if they knew and I shall probably never ever even speak to him again. I know that people in the village would say that he's not fit to breathe the same air as me. I can't help what I think, only what I do. I just know that I couldn't marry Henry Ellingthorpe if he was the last man on earth.'

Her aunt said nothing for a minute or two and then she said,

'You would be very foolish to turn him down. Passion doesn't last like money and high position, Grace. That may seem very callous to you, but it's true. Your mother and father have spent a great deal of money on you, and it seems to me that you are about to have the chance of a brilliant marriage. It would be worse than foolish of you to refuse. Your parents already know that Henry is likely to make you an offer. If you have a modicum of sense left in your head, you won't turn him down.'

Twelve

Alexandra was going to Durham that summer to spend a few days with her uncle, aunt and cousins. A visit away from home was more than she had had in years. In fact it was enough to make her worry about the clothes she didn't have, and to go quietly to a dressmaker in the village, and there to feel angry about the fact that she was not tall and slender.

She was to go to Durham by train and stay for three whole nights and go to a dance. Her dancing was very rusty. She tried humming a tune and dancing around the sitting room, but she couldn't see herself, and since she had never had a partner, except Grace who couldn't lead, she always led, so she didn't know what it was like to dance as a girl.

She had had made a pretty pale lemon dress with a trailing skirt, and she thought she looked as good in that as she had ever looked in anything. She was so excited that she could not sleep for two nights before she left. She was so guilty at leaving her father that she would have given anything for him to tell her to have a good time, but he didn't seem to notice. She knew that he would be content to sit as usual by the window with his brandy.

Alexandra walked to the station, feeling nervous and lonely, but she enjoyed the journey, especially when the train pulled into Durham station and she saw the castle and the cathedral and the neat roads with their shops and houses. She wished that she had been lucky enough to live there. Her cousins were there to meet her, Arthur and his wife, Jean. They lived in the city itself.

They had no garden. Their house had a yard at the back and opened out on to the street at the front, and was so noisy. Alexandra threw open her window wide because she enjoyed the noises of the city.

They had four children, two girls and two boys. The boys were younger and spent a lot of time laughing and fighting on the stairs and in the hall, and the girls who were twins of about her age giggled and didn't say much to her. Sometimes she heard whispers of 'Fatty' in the hall.

It was difficult for Alexandra to do what other people wanted, she was not used to it. She would have liked to go into the tiny bookshop at the end of the road, but this was frowned upon. She would have liked to have a picnic on the banks of the Wear. Instead of that, they visited shops, and since Alexandra had little money this was of no interest.

During the evenings various neighbours dropped in and they sang around the piano. The neighbours were not the kind of people whom Alexandra had much in common with. They did not read, they did not talk to her. They talked about one another and the people they knew, and since Alexandra knew none of them she found the time dragging.

On the Saturday night she went to a dance with them. It was not far away so they walked to the big hall some streets from them, but it was not as she had dreamt dances might be. The musicians were not very good, the violinist made her want to cringe, and throughout the evening she stood with her back to the wall trying to smile while nobody asked her to dance. It was the longest evening of Alexandra's life. She watched her two slender cousins dancing past, this way and that, with young men they knew. She watched them laughing and talking. Nobody talked to her or noticed her. She had never been so glad to go to bed. She had never been so glad to get on the train and go home. It was such a relief to go back to the house on the fell with only her father for company. At least there she could do what she wanted. There was the peace and quiet. She was so grateful that she didn't have to listen to the boys calling her names from beyond her reach, or her cousins' giggles, and most of all she didn't have to stand watching other people dance, knowing how fat and plain she was. She cried a good deal the first night that she was at home, but the window was open and the fell looked so friendly. Only the sky was empty.

Thirteen

On the train home, Grace considered how she should have had 'dis' in front of her name. Henry Ellingthorpe had proposed, she had refused, her aunt had tried and tried to talk to her, Henry Ellingthorpe had proposed again, Grace had turned him down, her aunt had written to her parents, her parents had written to her aunt, and she was on her way home.

She was worried because her parents were upset, but the nearer she got to home the more excited she was. As she drew nearer she almost forgot the reason that she had been sent back before the season ended, and when her father and mother met her at the station with grave faces she wanted to laugh and hug them and be glad. Then she remembered.

All the way home nobody spoke to her, and when they finally reached the house it was no better. Dinner was a silent meal. Grace went to bed as soon as she could and wept.

She was not allowed away from the house. Her mother gave her dull sewing to do, and when she appealed to her mother that she might go out one day because it was lovely, her mother refused and Grace turned to her in despair.

'Am I to be punished because I couldn't love him?'

Her mother looked at her.

'Love had nothing to do with it, Grace. It was your duty that

97

mattered, and you would have nothing to do with that.'

'You wanted me to marry Henry Ellingthorpe even though I cared nothing for him?'

'When I married your father I scarcely knew him. Love is not a passion, Grace, it is a quiet thing which grows during a marriage with time and with perseverance. You had the chance to make a brilliant marriage and you refused. Why did you think your father and I spent all that money sending you to London, buying you finery, seeing that you met all the best people? Did you really think that was so you could come back here like this? Where do you think we will find you even a reasonably suitable husband now?'

'I don't want a husband.'

'Don't you? And what else do you think your life has fitted you for?'

'Nothing! And whose fault is that?'

Her mother's face turned pale.

'I think you had better go to your room,' she said.

Grace flung down her sewing. 'Gladly,' she said.

During the evening Ruth came upstairs with her dinner on a tray.

'I don't want it,' Grace said.

'I didn't suppose you did. Not as good-looking as Dennes Eliot, was he?'

Grace looked quickly at Ruth. 'You think I'm stupid and childish. If I could have helped it, Ruth, I would. Henry was everything every woman wants, kind, generous, educated, rich, charming.'

'You didn't like him?'

'I liked him a lot. That was the trouble. I felt so awful saying no, so guilty as though I had encouraged him, and I didn't. At least I didn't think so. I didn't mean to. My parents seem to think I've broken every commandment there is. I'm not eighteen yet, Ruth, and now . . .'

Grace got up agitatedly and went to the window and then she began to cry, openly, hard. Ruth went across and put an arm around her.

'It isn't all bad. Dennes Eliot is still up for grabs. Mind you, you'd probably be killed in the rush.'

'I wish I didn't like him so much. I don't understand why I feel like this. My mother says that I ought to have done my duty and married Henry and I know she's right, I know she is, but I just . . . I just couldn't.' She turned to Ruth and began to sob against her shoulder.

'Sh, sh,' Ruth soothed. 'Henry wasn't the only lad in the world. There'll be another.'

'There won't, not like Dennes.'

'Let's hope not.'

'I know. I know that he's awful. It doesn't make any difference.'

'If it's any consolation, you're not the only one—'

'But why? Why do women like men who aren't good for them?'

'Because it's more interesting, I expect, or maybe they think that he'll love them and they'll be the one to change him.'

'He's never loved anybody in his life,' Grace said harshly. 'He's low and horrible and I hate him.'

'There are a dozen girls in the village who hate him as much as you do,' Ruth said, 'mostly because he has yet to glance in their direction.'

The following morning she was called into her father's study. He didn't wait. The moment that she closed the door he got up from his seat behind the desk and said, 'I'm not pleased with you, Grace, don't think so. I don't ever want you to speak to your mother again as you did yesterday.'

'I didn't mean to. I'm sorry.'

'I have had a letter from your aunt. I haven't shown it to your mother and I think that your aunt was reluctant to write what she has written. She tells me that the reason you would not marry Henry Ellingthorpe was because you had formed an attachment to a young man here. Is that true?'

Grace silently cursed her aunt.

'I had a . . . a silly idea about him. I don't have any longer, and it didn't make the difference. I didn't want to marry Henry even if it hadn't been for that.'

'How could you even take an interest in a lad like Dennes Eliot? I wasn't aware that you had spent any time with this young man. Correct me if I'm wrong.'

Grace was horrified at the idea that she might implicate Dennes in something he had no idea about, and so she remembered what Ruth had said and didn't spare herself.

'He has never so much as looked at me.'

Her father stared at her.

'Then how on earth—'

'I don't know! I don't know why I feel like this, I would change it if I could.'

That evening when dinner was well over and Nicholas Barmouth and Anthony Hemingway were sitting alone in the study at the Hemingway house with their brandy and their cigars – it was the time of day they liked best, talking over their world, pleased with their efforts – Anthony ventured to tell Nicholas why Grace had come home. After Nicholas had listened in silence, Anthony said finally, 'We'll get rid of him.'

'The lad's done nothing.'

'I know that, but just think if he did know how she felt. Even if it is just one of these daft passing fancies that young girls have, then he might look at my money and the fact that she's an only child and get ideas.'

Nicholas laughed.

'He's just a foundryman, a good moulder, bright. He lodges with Mrs Seymour. He's just a good-looking lad, Anthony, that's all.'

'He's dirt. Don't you remember—'

'Everybody remembers, but he works hard and he never causes any trouble, and I don't see why he should be dismissed because your daughter doesn't know what's best for her.'

Fourteen

The pubs had long since turned out and the streets were deserted. Then Dennes heard someone coming, the clip-clop of a woman's feet behind him, and he turned. It was Lily.

'Dennes?' she said.

'Yes.'

'Oh. I wasn't sure there for a minute. I thought you might be somebody else.'

'Who else?'

'I don't know. Walking home in the dark isn't very pleasant.'

'You should get somebody to walk you.'

'Men who walk you home expect things.'

'I'll walk you the rest of the way. I don't expect owt.'

They walked up the High Street and turned the corner into Thornley Road in silence, and then she said, 'What are you doing on the streets at this time of night?'

'I haven't got anywhere to go.'

'Did Mrs Seymour put you out?'

'She doesn't like me drinking.'

'Oh, I see. So you have no place to go.'

'It's a fine night.'

They turned right into Baring Street and halfway down she stopped

101

outside her house. Dennes said goodnight to her and walked away but she called him back.

'You can come in but I don't want any funny business, mind you.'

'Everybody would talk.'

'That doesn't matter to me. As soon as I have enough money I'm away to my mother's.'

'Where does she live?'

'East Kilbride.'

'What about Mick?'

'I haven't heard from him in a year, not a word.' She unlocked the door and he followed her inside. She lit the lamp, and her yellow hair was bright in its glow. Dennes followed her up the stairs and into a very clean bedroom where the bed was made up.

'There you are.'

'Thanks, Lily.'

Soon it was all over the village that Dennes had gone to live with the beautiful girl who helped out at the Black Horse. At work Dennes whistled and sang, and was so cheerful that he reminded Nat of the early days, when his mother had taken his brother and left him. In the evenings sometimes Nat was lonely without Dennes and went looking for him. At the Black Horse he was there talking to Lily. Nat went there as often as he could because he missed Dennes so much, but it was difficult talking to Dennes because he was often drunk and singing and making the kind of conversation which the sober find offensive. He had fights too. More than once Nat took him home bleeding and half-conscious. Occasionally he was so drunk that he couldn't walk, and Nat would put an arm around him and Dennes would sing them back to Baring Street, his voice echoing off the buildings at the far side of the road.

One Sunday morning when Dennes ventured downstairs very late, almost dinner time, Lily was sitting over the fire. The kitchen was shining clean, the house smelled of Sunday dinner, and she was neat, her dress dark blue and fresh on and her hair shining and pinned back.

'You're too late for breakfast,' she said.

'I know.'

'Dennes . . . I want you to stop coming home drunk and bleeding every night.'

'It isn't every night.'

'Too many nights for comfort. I don't know how you can work.'

'You'd be surprised.'

'Men never surprise me. Why did you leave Mrs Seymour's?'

'I told you. I took Nat drinking and she didn't like it.'

Lily looked sceptically at him.

'He comes to the Black Horse all the time. You did something?'

'No.'

'So you didn't do anything and she made you leave and now you can't bear your own company. I've never seen anybody as drunk as you were last night, except for my husband once or twice, and he's a lot older than you and had good reason to hate himself. He was weak and useless and he would come back here and knock me around. Now I don't for a minute think that you've done something like that—'

'That's good, because I haven't—'

'So why do you do that to yourself?'

'Because.'

'I see.' Lily busied herself with the pans on the fire which were boiling merrily.

'I'll leave.'

'Leaving isn't going to make the difference. You'll do the same thing wherever you go, it seems to me.'

'I'll go somewhere else.'

'Where people don't care?'

'I don't want anybody to care,' Dennes said roughly, and he collected his jacket and walked out.

He was going to go to the pub but he couldn't face it, and to his anger he was hungry and his thoughts kept going back to the smell of the dinner – Lily made such good dinners – and the neat, clean house and the image of Lily's bare neck as she bent forward to look into the pans. He called her names, he called himself names. He walked miles across the fell and flung himself down into the heather by the stream.

103

It was the middle of the evening by the time he walked into the house in Baring Street. Lily was sitting at the kitchen table drinking tea and eating ginger cake as though nothing had happened.

'All right,' he conceded, 'I'll try not to do it any more.'

'I kept your dinner for you. I'll warm it up.'

Dennes sat down and ate his dinner and Lily cleared up. He went into the front room and there in the early evening warmth, listening to her clattering around in the kitchen, Dennes fell asleep.

Being sober all the time meant that there wasn't a lot of point in going to the pub. Dennes hadn't thought how much time drinking and getting drunk and getting sober took. There were great gaps in his life now. Also Lily was at the pub in the evenings so it was too much of a temptation not to go but if he went the men thought he was soft if he couldn't put away at least four or five pints. Almost every night he went to the Black Horse to walk her home. It wasn't far but as the nights drew in during the autumn he thought of how bonny Lily was and how the men looked at her, and he made sure that he was there so that she didn't have to walk through the streets by herself when she finished.

Being sober all the time gave him lots of energy and he went walking and worked hard and made more money and appreciated Lily's cooking the better for the lack of drink. Dennes got to the stage where he would call in late, have one or two drinks and walk home with Lily afterwards. That winter Lily took to putting the front room fire on on Sunday mornings so that by Sunday afternoon it was cosy to sit there and read or talk and watch the light fade in the early afternoons. Lily didn't work on Sunday nights so they had the whole evening together.

It snowed one Sunday early in December and they sat in the dark by the firelight watching it. Lily's settee was so comfortable that Dennes often fell asleep there; it was big enough even for him. Now he was sprawled there and Lily was sitting in the corner of the settee against the cushions and he could see by the firelight her face lit up with excitement at the snow.

'I used to love Christmas when I was a little girl.'

'Did you get a lot of snow in Scotland?'

'Sometimes. I love it when it snows at Christmas. My sister, Mary and me, we used to go outside and dance when it snowed. Everything's so nice when you're little, isn't it?'

'And then what happened?'

'My dad was killed and my mother married again.'

'Isn't he nice?'

Lily shrugged. 'He's nice enough but he's not my dad.'

'But you want to go back?'

'Aye, I want to go home.'

'Why haven't you?'

'I kept thinking Mick would come back.'

'Do you want him back?'

She smiled at him.

'You always think things'll be different, people will change even though you know it isn't true and . . . I haven't much money. I don't want to go home penniless.'

'I've got some—'

'No. I want my own money.'

'You could think of it as a loan.'

'All the way from here to Glasgow?' Lily laughed softly. 'I don't think so, my hinny,' and she reached over and touched his cheek with her fingers.

'You took me in, Lily. I owe you.'

'You pay your way and well.'

Lily lit the lamp and closed the curtains against the square white flakes falling now in twirling motions with a slight wind behind them. She stood there like she was afraid to move.

'I thought it would be wonderful, you know, being married. I thought somehow that there would be magic.'

'And wasn't there?'

She shook her head.

'I kept thinking that there almost was, like there's magic out there tonight in the snow, like there had been in childhood. Maybe that's what being grown-up is, the magic goes. It went from everything when I married Mick. He made me feel as though nothing I did was any good

105

or any use. He made me feel stupid and clumsy. At first I thought that I wanted him to come back but I know now that it was only because I was afraid of being alone. But, you know, there are a lot worse things than being alone.'

'But you took me in?'

'That was different, we aren't married. It didn't matter whether you liked the dinners or the way I keep house or – or anything about me. If you didn't like it I could tell you to go. And you aren't like Mick, you're always so pleased with everything like it was the very first time that you'd ever eaten a meal or had ironed clothes or seen a blackberry pie.' She laughed. 'You'd make anybody want to make you happy, it takes so little doing.'

'Yes, well, my mother was a mucky bitch, I can't get over the smell of polish,' Dennes said, smiling at her.

She went back and sat down with him on the settee and then she leaned across and kissed him on the mouth. Dennes hadn't thought that she might. He sat there and looked at her. Lily drew back, blushing.

'I shouldn't have done that, I'm sorry. I hear the talk among the village lasses. You never kiss anybody, you never ask anybody to go for a walk. You're not awful like the others. I kept waiting for you to try it. You know. They always do but you don't. You keep your hands to yourself.'

'I have to have somewhere to live,' Dennes said, 'I don't want to have to leave the village. It's the only home I remember.'

He wished that she had left the curtains open and the light off but the lamp cast shadows everywhere and was soft, and the curtains weren't quite the right size so there was a gap in the middle, and in the shadows the snow fell in a light dance. The magic was there both inside and out as though waiting for an invitation. She was so neglected, she was so ready to believe, in spite of a man who had not fulfilled a single one of her dreams in any small part. How could he have done that, Dennes wondered. She was beautiful, she was young, she was ready to believe in fairy tales. Why should not just one of them come true?

He did think about taking her to bed and showing her all the tricks there were, all the knowledge that had brought her kind to think that the smell of ironed shirts was halfway to paradise, but he didn't. He just persuaded her to turn off the lamp and part the curtains some way, though she said that the draught was terrible. He built up the fire to take care of that and they sat close and watched the snow as it built its way so methodically up the window ledge outside and carefully carpeted the front street.

In the morning the world was perfect like an iced cake, untrodden and unused. Lily looked rather like that too, her shining eyes on him so sure. It made him want to run away, to tell her how things were, but he didn't. He didn't want to remind her of Mick. It was almost as though she had never been touched because in all sorts of ways it became clear that she hadn't, that there had been no act of love, that Mick had taken her as though he was stepping on flowers in a garden, that he had wanted nothing but his own doubtlessly swift satisfaction. She didn't understand that there was more, she had perhaps once believed it but she didn't now. She had married Mick out of fear because she was by herself, and possibly because she saw men's hot eyes on her. She had mistaken marriage for safety and it had been a miserable discovery. But now she was beginning to understand and to believe, Dennes could see, and there was a part of him which was not pleased with himself because he didn't love her. The argument was that he had enough feeling for her to bring the illusion back, but she was just not Gwen to him, like every woman he met.

One Sunday afternoon in the winter, when he had gone out for a walk and Lily hadn't wanted to go and was lying down, he came back in time for tea and there was no tea on the table. The fire was on but there was no sound or sight of her. When he shouted up the stairs there were sounds above and a thickset man walked slowly down the stairs. Behind Dennes, from the front room, two more men came in.

The thickset man Dennes recognised, the others he didn't know. Mick Hodgson looked hard at him.

'You're just a lad,' he said, as though disappointed. 'I remember you now. I remember your mother.' He grinned at the other men. 'We all remember her, not her face of course, her skirt was always over it.'

They laughed loudly. Dennes glanced at the stairs.

'What have you done to Lily?'

'That's exactly what I was going to say to you, lad.'

'She thought you weren't coming back.'

'So you had your way with her? There's no use looking at the door, you're going to get the kind of hiding that your father should've given you years ago. Then maybe you wouldn't go interfering with grown men's fancy stuff. But then you never had no father, did you, or did you? I could be him, or Alf here. He used to like your mother, did Alf. Saturday night wasn't Saturday night until Alf had it away with your Mam. We could any of us be your father, couldn't we?'

'Lily!'

Mick smiled.

'She's not there. I sent her next door to Mrs McAndrews. She didn't want to see you get a hiding.'

Dennes moved suddenly into the only space in the room where there was nobody behind him, turned around fast and from his pocket took the kind of knife which made Mick Hodgson's eyes change. He always carried it now because of William Daniels. The blade sprang. Mick's gaze wavered.

'Come and get me then,' Dennes urged softly.

In the firelight the knife blade glinted, and when Mick made a sudden move Dennes lunged at him. He cried out with pain, the blood forming a thin line on his arm and spreading. The others looked at each other while Mick nursed his arm and backed off, and when Dennes moved towards them they cleared one to either side. He went slowly, watching carefully, turning to back through the door and outside to the yard. There he shouted again, 'Lily! Lily!'

Mrs McAndrews was in her yard.

'She's gone and it's no better than you deserve.'

'Where's she gone?'

'Home. She should've left years ago,' and Mrs McAndrews picked up the mat she had been shaking and went back into the house. Dennes put away the knife and ran off down the road as fast as he could.

* * *

Nat walked home slowly from his evening in the Black Horse. It was a fine, clear night, not late, men were still in the pubs, the street was deserted. Most of the way home, not far from the entrance to the steelworks, somebody was lying in the road. Dennes was too easily identifiable for Nat to make a mistake. In the moonlight Nat could see his thick straight fair hair. Nat got down, frightened, but when he turned Dennes over the whisky fumes sickened him.

'Now what have you done?' he said. 'Dennes? Dennes?'

After five minutes Dennes was only just conscious. Nat had never seen anybody so drunk, hardly able to walk. He tried to waken him, to make him walk, but it was a struggle and it seemed such a long way home, the short distance down the bank to the Golden Lion. He took Dennes round to the back even though it was further, he didn't want the men to see, and as he staggered into the kitchen Dolly clapped her hand over her mouth and flew to tell her mother even though Nat asked her not to. Gwen took one look at Dennes and then anxiously at her son.

'Can you get him upstairs?'

'You'll have to get Taylor to help me. He's dead drunk.'

When Dennes came to, he thought for some moments that he was back in the lilac house and that made him shudder. He had a savage headache and a tremendous thirst. He was meant to be at work. He washed and dressed and went downstairs to the kitchen, and there was Gwen seeing to the kitchen fire just as she had on so many days. He would have stood there just watching her but that she heard him and turned. She straightened.

'You certainly know how to make the village talk, don't you?' she said. 'First you go and live with a barmaid, and then when her husband turns up you take a knife to him.'

'I wasn't living with her, just lodging, you know I wouldn't do that. And as for him, there were three of them. I didn't hurt him, it was just his hand.'

She stood there indecisively for a few moments, and then went over and hugged him. Dennes pulled her into his arms and buried his face in her neck.

'I missed you so much.' He had promised himself he wouldn't say that. 'Nat had no right to bring me back here.'

Gwen stroked his hair.

'Of course he had,' she said. 'Where else would you go?'

Fifteen

The day that Gwen accepted Nicholas Barmouth's proposal she cornered Dennes in the kitchen.

'I want to talk to you.'

'No.'

'Dennes . . .' She got hold of him, made him face her, even shook him slightly. 'Listen to me. Listen.'

'I'm leaving.'

'No, you're not.'

'I'm not staying here while you marry that man.'

'Oh yes, you are. If you stay here Nicholas will help you.'

'Why should he do that?'

'Because I will ask him. You can leave the village and have nothing, or you can come with us and have the possibility of a future. Stay here. You can come and live at Esh House and be part of the family and Nicholas will help you. He likes you.'

'No.'

'Wouldn't you rather be near, wouldn't you rather have good food and warmth and live in a nice house and have the chance of a decent job than to have to leave here alone with nothing?'

He was silent.

'You've been with me for a long time now, and I care for you. I care about your future. There's no reason why you shouldn't have those things, you have brains and ability, you just need opportunity and education and somebody to help you. Nicholas can do that.'

Dennes stared at her. 'That's why you're marrying him, isn't it? So that we can have a decent future.'

'What did you think?'

'I thought you loved him.'

She hesitated.

'He can give us so much. I can't turn that down. Please, let me do this. I want to lift us out of here, and I can do it if you help me. But I want all of us there. I want to see you in a nice suit among civilised people. You deserve that.'

'I don't want it!'

'Don't behave like a fool when you're not one. This is the only chance we're ever likely to get. I'm not going to spend the rest of my life washing up glasses and waiting on other people. I'm going to be a lady.'

'I don't think ladies go around marrying men for money.'

Gwen laughed.

'They do it all the time,' she said. She paused, and then she looked clearly at him and said, 'I know you're too young to understand this, but you're intelligent enough, and in time you will. You mustn't let passion rule your life. There are other things far more important.'

The Hemingways were convinced that Nicholas had lost his mind, Grace told Alexandra. Alexandra didn't reply. She was lying on the sofa in front of the sitting-room fire. Grace was sitting beside her.

'Don't you think he's out of his head?'

'Does this mean Dennes?' Alexandra opened her eyes.

'Does what mean Dennes?'

'Well, if Mrs Seymour is marrying Mr Barmouth, is Dennes going to be there?'

'I shouldn't think so, not after the episode with Lily Hodgson. It hardly counts as respectable.'

112

'Dennes was never respectable in the first place,' Alexandra pointed out.

'True. I don't know. He's lived with the Seymours a long time now.'

Grace's parents were adamant that they weren't going to the wedding (Mr Covington said nothing other than was his best suit clean) but they all went anyway and Dennes was there, dressed in a dark suit, head bent over his hymn book. He didn't look up even when Mr Barmouth and Mrs Seymour made their vows. Grace knew because she glanced across the aisle at him several times. Afterwards, during the small reception at Esh House, he didn't eat and he didn't speak to anyone, and Grace was particularly disappointed at that because the only thing she had wanted from the day was a smile from him and perhaps a word, though she had been forbidden to go anywhere near him by her father.

He went outside. Grace couldn't think why, it was a bitterly cold March day. There was snow in the fields and on the hillsides with a wind which sent everybody huddling around fires, and the garden at Esh House, which in the summer was a picture of roses and rockeries was all dead-looking and dark. She followed him anyway. There was no particular reason not to, her parents could hardly miss her and he wasn't going to speak to her inside.

When she got out there she wished that she hadn't bothered. The house stood on a hill and there was not even a line of trees to stop the sleeting wind. One or two trees were in bud but the earliest spring flowers, the yellow, orange and purple crocuses, were flattened, the daffodils' shoots were broken off in places, and here and there the fencing was in pieces. Dennes was nowhere near the house, as though he wanted to get as far away as he could without actually being offensive. He was standing by the far low wall which led into the fields as though he might at any minute climb over the wall into freedom. As she drew nearer he turned around. The wind was lifting his fair hair, he was better dressed than ever before, but Grace didn't delude herself that he was glad to see her.

'What do you want?' he said flatly.

No young man had ever spoken to Grace in such a way. She thought of the young men she had been introduced to in London who had address and education and wit. They had fine clothes and southern accents, they read and danced and made the kind of conversation which an ignorant clumsy boy like this could never understand. Why had she carried with her this picture of him? It was gone. He was common and worse than that he was ill-mannered.

'That's not a very nice way to greet anybody,' she said.

Then he made things worse by lifting his eyes to her face, smiling ruefully and saying, 'I'm sorry. I just didn't know you were there. I didn't hear you.'

Grace glanced down at her shoes, which were not meant for gardens.

'It's very muddy out here.'

'It snowed this morning,' he said.

Grace wasn't sure whether it was sarcasm so she chose to ignore that.

Talking wasn't easy because of the freezing wind. Grace wished that she had stayed inside.

'You're less than polite,' she said.

'I have to be polite to you, do I?'

'It's usual among civilised people.'

'Is this in London? I heard all about it. Some rich, titled man wanted to marry you but you didn't want him. You wanted all this.' Grace looked out past his hand at the fields and further over at the hills and the fell, and then she looked at him.

'This is exactly what I wanted,' she said. 'You have no idea how boring it was. I hated it, I just wanted to come home.'

'I should think you would at your age.'

'My parents weren't very pleased with me.'

'No, well, you don't get many rich titles around here. The place isn't exactly wringing with them. What was he like?'

'He was very nice, tall, fair, slender, clever, charming . . .'

'Fancy having all that and money and position, and for some bit lass to tell you that she doesn't want you. He must've wondered where he'd gone wrong,' and Dennes laughed. 'He didn't taste awful, did he?'

114

Grace giggled. 'No.'

'You did get as far as that then?'

'That was how I knew.'

'Yes, you would.'

'Grace!' Her father's voice came across the garden like staccato. She jumped and said, 'Ohmigod,' under her breath, and then hurried back across the garden stumbling in the wet soil. Her shoes, she feared, would never be the same again.

Dennes wandered back inside. Nat went to him as he made his escape into an empty sitting-room.

'What were you doing out there with Grace?'

'Putting my hands up her skirt,' Dennes said, since there was nobody within earshot.

'That's not funny.'

'She followed me. It was nothing to do with me.'

'Her father wasn't very pleased.'

'Well, he wouldn't be, would he, having tried to marry her off to some posh southern lad and then finding her talking to foundrymen. Fancy expecting her to marry at seventeen.'

'My mother married at sixteen.'

'Your mother must have wanted to.'

'More than she does now, I think.'

Dennes looked sharply at him. 'What does that mean?'

'I mean if he'd been nowt but an ordinary foundryman she wouldn't have.'

Dennes said nothing, and when he finally looked up Nat was scrutinising him. 'You're very quiet for somebody who has new clothes and a bedroom all to himself. There's nothing wrong with Mr Barmouth, is there?'

'Not that I know of.'

'But you don't like him? Is that because you don't think you're going to get on with him, or is it just because you'd feel the same way about anybody who was marrying my mother?'

Dennes said nothing.

115

'Well?' Nat insisted.

He still didn't answer.

'What are you going to do, take him to the seaside and push him off a cliff edge so that she'll have his money and be widowed again?'

When Dennes still didn't say anything, Nat got hold of him by his jacket front and shoved him up against the wall. Dennes didn't look at him.

'I suppose since your own mother was a prostitute you think every woman's like that.'

Dennes was silent.

'It's true, isn't it? You wanted to bed my mother?'

He hit Dennes. Dennes didn't retaliate until the third time, and then he knocked Nat back against an ornate wooden table. Nat hurt himself so much when he fell that he couldn't get up. Dennes stood over him for a second, and then said slowly, 'I never touched her.'

'You dirty bastard,' Nat said, wincing with pain.

Dennes walked out of the room and left him there.

Dennes had never slept in a room by himself and even then there was no peace. The pretty little parlour maid came in and made up the fire and turned scornful eyes on him.

'Will you be wanting anything else . . . sir?'

Dennes just shook his head.

'Don't hesitate to ring, will you?' she said, slamming the door shut after her.

The Hemingways and the Covingtons had gone home together.

'I still think he's mad,' Anthony Hemingway confided to Alexandra's father in front of the fire when they got back, 'taking on a widow and four children.'

'I don't think I would call Dennes Eliot a child,' Mr Covington said in measured tones.

'I don't think I'd call him one either,' Alexandra said as she and Grace went on up the stairs. 'What were you doing following him into the garden? Your father nearly had kittens.'

116

'I never get to speak to him.'

'I have the feeling you will now. Not that it's going to make any difference.'

'What do you mean by that?'

'He's hardly even aware of your existence, Grace.'

They had reached Grace's bedroom now, and once the door was shut she let out a wail. 'Don't say that.'

'It's true. Anybody can see it just by looking at him. He looks . . . preoccupied.'

Grace looked carefully at her.

'Preoccupied?'

'Yes, as though he's thinking about something else all the time.'

'Somebody else?'

'Perhaps.'

'But he can't. He can't, Alex, he can't.'

'I couldn't get a word out of Nat Seymour,' Alexandra said thoughtfully. 'They don't seem very happy about their mother marrying a well-set-up man, do they? You'd think they would.'

'My mother doesn't like her.'

'Your mother doesn't like anybody,' Alexandra said.

Mary let the fire go out in Dennes' room two evenings running. The first time he put it down to her forgetting or having too much else to do, but the second time the room was too cold to sit in, and since he had taken to sitting there and reading he wasn't happy about it. He rang for her for quite a long time before she appeared, and asked her civilly to attend to the fire, and when it was done and burning brightly he waited until she got all the way back downstairs again, and then called her up again and asked her to bring some tea. Mary did not even pretend to be deceived.

'You'd better tell me exactly how you want the tea now, and whether you want biscuits, or are you going to wait and make me bring them separately?'

'It's entirely up to you, Mary.'

Mary raised her eyes to the ceiling.

117

'I'll make sure the fire doesn't go out again,' she said.

'That'll be nice,' Dennes said.

For several nights afterwards Dennes' bedroom was the warmest in the house.

Nat didn't even try to convince himself that his mother was happy when she came home from a week in the Lake District. She looked distinctly homesick and the reason for it wasn't even present.

'Where's Dennes?' she said, eyes everywhere.

'Gone out.'

'He knew we were coming back this afternoon.'

'I expect he'll be back in time for dinner,' Nicholas said pleasantly.

The atmosphere in the house changed when the master came home. Everything had to be right, and that included mealtimes and people being prompt. Dennes was rather late for dinner and they had sat down. Gwen's eyes shone when she saw him but Nicholas merely said, 'You're late. Don't let it happen again.'

Nat would have apologised and he thought that in earlier times Dennes would have too; but he didn't, he just sat down and ate. Later on when Nat was sitting by the sitting-room fire alone, Gwen came in and put her hand on top of his head and smiled at him and said, 'Did you miss me?'

Nat almost forgave her for everything, especially when she kissed him.

'Nicholas wants to take you into the office at the steelworks. I wondered whether you would like that, not to do boring clerking or anything like that but to help him properly eventually. What do you think about it, Nat?'

'I don't know anything about that side of it.'

'I know you don't but Nicholas is going to talk to you. You could train, work hard and study and do well. He's willing for you to try if you want to and he's got other plans. Now I know you won't necessarily be very enthusiastic about all of these, but you can try.'

When Nat found that these included a tutor for himself and Taylor and a boarding school for Dolly, he was inclined to object. Nicholas was infuriatingly reasonable.

'I know what you're thinking, Nat, but the school for Dolly is only Monday to Friday in Durham and it'll just be for a couple of years until we get a little bit of polish on her. She'll enjoy it when she gets used to being with girls her own age and living in the city. As for your education, I don't think I need to say any more, do I?'

Dennes was not included in any of the schemes. Nat tried not to care. They had not spoken since the fight. He thought that Dennes had no right to expect anything more than a home here. Nat wished him far away.

Nat and Taylor were taken into the office and Nicholas began to teach them foundry management. He also hired a young man called Ernest Pelton to teach them mathematics and science and engineering.

Dennes went on working at the foundry just as ever and was prompt to dinner but other than that he was never around that winter and spring. He went out, but where, Nat didn't know. The rest of the time he stayed in his room.

Passing there one Saturday afternoon and finding the door open, Nat ventured inside. On an old table by the window were piles of books, the same kind he was using for his lessons with Ernest, and there were papers in neat handwriting with pencilled comments in the margins in Ernest's scrawl.

Nat started and turned around when he heard something. Dennes was standing behind him. It was not a big room, not like Nat's bedroom, and it was dark being at the back of the house overlooking the yard and buildings, but it would have been impossible to read Dennes' expression anyhow, he was so guarded these days.

'When do you see Ernest?' Nat asked him.

'I go to his lodgings in the evenings.'

'You pay him?'

'Unlike you I don't have a stepfather.'

'I didn't think you were interested in education.' Dennes didn't say anything. Nat glanced again at the books. He didn't know what to say now. It had been such a long time since they had had a conversation. He had thought that he hated Dennes. Now he found himself wanting to talk, wishing he could think of some reason to stay, but he couldn't,

119

and he knew even without looking that Dennes' green eyes were cold on him. He wished things otherwise. He glanced at Dennes and wished he hadn't, because he had been right, they were as cold and hard as emeralds whereas once they had been warm with laughter and friendship. He turned around and walked out and listened as Dennes shut the door.

Nicholas had a wide acquaintance and introduced his new family to them. Nat was quite sure that a number of these people, including the Hemingways, would have been more than happy to ignore Gwen and her family but they didn't dare because Nicholas was such an influential man in the district. It didn't make for particularly comfortable social occasions and Nicholas insisted on them going and meeting people.

One Saturday night that summer there was a dance at a big house near Castleside, not far from Consett where the big iron and steelworks was. It was a huge place with a ballroom. There were at least two dozen pretty girls in new dresses standing around on the edge of the room waiting to be asked to dance. Dennes wasn't going. Nat only went because he had to. Grace had already been chosen for the first dance by the time he got there, and there was a crowd of young men standing about waiting for the next dance. And then Nat saw a familiar face. Alexandra Covington, standing as far away from the dancing as she could, almost invisible among the plants, wearing a very unbecoming green dress which was anything but new. She looked totally bored and, worse than that somehow, as though she would have given a lot to be anywhere else.

Nat knew by sight now several of these girls, he had been introduced to them at one time or another, some of them were beautiful and many of them were very nice, but he made his way carefully around the edge of the ballroom, not meeting any eyes, until he reached her, and there he very politely said good evening to her and would she care to dance. She stared at him for several seconds and said no, she wouldn't, and walked out of the room.

Nat was shocked. He knew very well that once you had asked a woman to dance she was your captive until the music stopped. They

120

weren't allowed to say no. And then a thought occurred to him. He was well beneath her and she knew it. He was suddenly angry and he went after her, out of the house, down a big semi-circular stone terrace, to the lawns where she was standing looking out over formal gardens.

'Why?' he said.

'I don't have to explain myself to you,' she said, and would have walked away but Nat wasn't having that. He got hold of her surprisingly slim wrist.

'You do,' he said. 'Ladies don't refuse.'

'Whoever told you that?'

'That's why, isn't it?'

'That's why, isn't what?'

'It's because of who I am – or rather, am not.'

She stared at him for a second, then suddenly her cross face changed and she gave a warm smile, and it was lovely. Her eyes glowed and her teeth were so pretty.

'Oh Nat,' she said, 'you didn't think so?'

'What else am I to think?'

She sighed and Nat let go of her wrist, and she said after a little hesitation, 'Nobody's ever asked me to dance before.'

'What, never?'

'You came past all those other girls to ask me to dance?'

'Well – yes.'

'I'm sorry. I just don't understand why you would do such a thing. You know a lot of them and some of them are very pretty and very accomplished—'

'You're very pretty—'

'No, I'm not, and if I stood on you, you wouldn't be able to walk for a week. Go in and ask somebody else.'

'Certainly not.'

'You don't like being turned down, do you? Especially by the fat poor girl.'

'You're not fat and you have no idea what being poor is like.'

'I couldn't possibly dance with you. When I was learning to dance I was always the biggest. I have to lead.'

121

'Shut up,' Nat said, and dragged her back to the ballroom.

They danced twice before going in to supper. She ate with relish. Nat had never seen a girl enjoy her food; usually they picked and were stupid about it. After supper they danced once again, though she had to be persuaded. Then she said it would be scandalous, but Nat had no intention of leaving her. He suggested that she might like a glass of lemonade on the terrace and she decided that there was nothing she would like more. She went outside, something she wasn't meant to do, but her father wouldn't notice or even imagine that she would have the opportunity to do such a thing. Nat brought her the lemonade and after a sip or two she put it down and they walked away from the house.

There was nobody about. It was a perfect June evening. Alexandra was ready to believe in anything now. The sun had gone down splendidly, dusk had fallen, the garden was still, the flowers gave off a faint warm scent.

To her astonishment, when they were well away from the house he drew her in among the green covered branches of an oak tree and kissed her. It was not at all the kind of thing that Alexandra had imagined a first kiss might be. She had thought that some shy, tentative young man would take her gently into his arms in a garden and brush his lips on hers and that the birds would sing. The only similarity was the garden. He put the heel of his hand into the small of her back and brought her to him in a way that could never have been called tentative. Alexandra didn't know Nat very well but she learned quite a lot about him in those few moments. The kiss was full and hard and invited liberty. Alexandra had never been held before, even by her parents, and not even the slightest brush of lips had ever come her way. Nobody had touched her in her life, and although her instincts told her that this was something different, it nonetheless fulfilled a great many needs which until that moment she had barely acknowledged. He was a lot bigger than she was, and for once in her life she didn't have to command the situation. All she had to do was give in, and that was the easiest thing in the world. She let him sweetly savage her mouth and it wasn't until she heard someone's voice at the other side of the garden that she drew back, was instantly ashamed and blushing for having encouraged him to do such a thing and said, 'Really, Nat,' and he coloured and lowered his eyes and retreated.

Sixteen

Gwen became pregnant that autumn. She said nothing but Nat privately thought that his mother was not happy about the pregnancy. Nicholas was obviously delighted and went around telling anyone who would listen about the coming child. He seemed convinced that he would have a son and heir and he made sure that Gwen was carefully looked after. The doctor called regularly and she had to put her feet up every afternoon. The days were short but warm and in the afternoons she would sit in the garden. After work Dennes would go out there and sit at her feet with his head resting against the chair and they would talk. Nat kept out of the way but he noticed Nicholas frowning in their direction if he came home early. Gwen had a habit of putting her hand on top of Dennes' golden hair and he would put back his head and laugh up at her.

Dolly was away at school, the boys worked. Gwen grew tired of doing nothing and tried to get back to normal but Nicholas was too concerned about the baby and wouldn't let her do anything. She complained to Nat that she was tired of knitting and sewing and sitting down all the time.

'I'll get fat.'

'You're getting fat anyway, why worry?'

She pulled a face at him. Weekends were easier. Dolly was at home and Mrs Hemingway came over with Grace to visit. Sometimes other people dropped in or were invited to dinner, and when Alexandra arrived with Grace, Nat left his studies and went into the drawing-room and had tea. It seemed to him that Alexandra had become beautiful of late. She had grown tall and had slimmed down somewhat though thankfully she would never be thin. She was a big, beautiful, almost mature woman now, with a full dark red mouth, long curling lashes around chocolate brown eyes, waving hair which to Nat's disappointment was always neat under a hat these days and the kind of figure which made him long to put his hands on her. Grace was if anything too slender as though she might faint, and quiet too. Grace had nothing to say but if she had there would have been no room for her conversation, because her mother talked in her presence as though she was not there. He could get Alexandra away to talk to her but Grace's mother kept her close, smiled on her and it was all how pretty Grace was and all about the new clothes she was having made for her. Gwen tried questioning Grace directly but her mother invariably answered for her and Nat became adept at luring Alexandra away to the other side of the room so that they could talk without the benefit of Mrs Hemingway's endless monologue.

He had tried saying, 'Perhaps Grace would like to see the new picture we bought,' or when it was fine, 'Perhaps Grace would like to see the garden,' but her mother never agreed to it. She would say, 'Oh but we're just leaving,' even if they weren't, or that she particularly wanted Grace to stay because . . . whatever.

Christmas came and for the first time in her life Gwen took to her bed. She felt dizzy and tired, she lost small amounts of blood. Finally two days after Christmas, when she had insisted on getting up, she collapsed. To Nat's dismay Nicholas wasn't there. He had gone off for a day's shooting. Nat carried her upstairs to bed and the doctor was sent for immediately, but she began to bleed copiously and by the time Nicholas had been sent for and come home it was obvious that she was losing the baby. Before teatime it was all over.

The doctor, satisfied that his patient was past the worst, gave her something to make her sleep and left, saying that she should be allowed to rest and he would come back first thing in the morning.

Nicholas went to Gwen's room and there were raised voices. Then he stormed off to his study and slammed the door in Nat's face. Gwen was white and quiet and insisted that Nat should go to bed, she would call if she wanted anything. Nat slept fitfully for about an hour, thought he heard her crying, paused by the door but there was silence and went downstairs.

Nicholas didn't stop him from going into the study this time. He was sitting by the fire with a glass of brandy and it was obviously not the first.

'All I ever wanted was a son.'

Nat told himself it was just because the man was drunk. He could have married a much younger woman if he had badly wanted children.

'It was obvious she could have sons.'

'There's time yet,' Nat said.

Nicholas looked bleakly at him. 'The doctor says not. He says she's not well enough to have more children. As if they know. Your mother's not old.'

'I thought I heard her crying,' Nat said.

'She failed me, Nat.'

'No, she didn't. Don't say that to her, will you?'

'I already did. I already shouted at her and blamed her. I didn't mean to.'

'She'll know that.'

'I've wanted a son for so long, all my life it's all I wanted. I didn't have a father, you know. My mother . . .' He looked up. 'She was like Dennes' mother, she would go with anybody. I thought when I married that life would be good, I had achieved so much. All I wanted was to have a normal family but it never happened. I just wanted a wife and a child or two. I see my workmen, that's what they have and most of them don't even look after them properly, and look at me. I haven't even got a son. One of my furnacemen, he has five sons, five big strapping lads and he doesn't bother with them. He neglects his family, his children were never at school, they have nothing but they're big and capable. They went out and found work, they look after their mother –

like you and Dennes looked after Gwen, didn't you?'

'We tried. Won't you go to her? She needs you to tell her that it's all right.'

'How can I? It would be a lie.'

'So tell her a lie.'

Nicholas smiled at him.

'You'll be good with women, Nat, telling them lies.'

'If it eases their pain.'

'Go to bed. I want to be left alone.'

Nat trudged upstairs again and judged that he had been wrong, there was nobody crying. He did try her door quietly, but it was locked.

She was sleeping now. She had stopped her grieving for the time being and as the soft sobbing ceased she huddled in closer against Dennes' shoulder. He had got up quietly and locked the doors but she hadn't moved and he went back and lay down with her and took her into his arms and she had awakened only a little. She was exhausted. He had gone to her. For once she hadn't even urged him away. The tears and the words tumbled together.

'Nicholas says it was my fault.'

Always, always, she thought everything was her fault. Always she had to be told it wasn't and even then she didn't believe it. She was a woman, she had been born guilty. He didn't believe that Nicholas had said that to her, it was in her mind, like it was her fault that William Daniels had raped her, it was her fault that a boy half her age had fallen in love with her and even though she had done everything she could not to make these things happen they were her fault.

She had given in this once and let him hold her. Whatever Nicholas had said it had finished her off, babbling that the child had been taken away from her because she had not wanted it and how sorry she was that she felt like that because all Nicholas wanted was a son. She couldn't bear the responsibility of losing his son, and all those times when she had wanted to be alone and Nicholas had been there because he wanted a son and now and now . . .

She slept. Dennes didn't sleep, he kept torturing himself with how different things could have been, with the if-onlys, even though he knew it was all a waste of time. The if-onlys never came true, the wishings, it was all longing and no substance. Dennes dreamed of escape. He dreamed of things that could never be, like having her young with him so that they could get married and have children and a future and being open together and proud. He dreamed of running away to some imaginary place where things like age difference didn't matter, he dreamed of acceptance from her family and friends, he dreamed that he was not dirtied and spoiled. He dreamed impossible things. He thought that somehow perhaps people got to start again all clean and wiped and reborn, that he could die and come back and come through so far to be worth loving.

She moved a little in her sleep and awoke suddenly, her blue eyes dull.

'Are you hurting?' Dennes asked anxiously.

'No. You won't leave me, will you?'

'I won't ever leave you.'

'I pretended.'

'What?'

'That it was for you, that I wanted you to come with me for you. That's not true. I couldn't bear to be without you.'

'I know.'

'You knew even then.' She traced her fingers down his face. 'You did lock the door, didn't you?'

'Yes.'

'It'll be all right in the morning.'

'Yes.'

'I'm not bleeding any more.'

'No.' He stroked her hair. It should have been plaited and out of the way, it should have been tidy but it wasn't, it was the way that he loved it, free, so dark against her white nightdress.

She went back to sleep, peacefully this time, folded in against him for comfort, his arms making her safe, her head against his shoulder. Dennes lay awake listening to every sound.

Light was coming into the room now, that small twinkling start to

129

the day that creeps through the most generous of curtains, where God pretends to you that the world is a wonderful place to be because you're still there, you're still alive, you've triumphed in some tiny misguided way over the night. You made it as far as the dawn and your reward is to watch the sunlight trying to dazzle you with its brilliance, only you know that there's horror in it of every conceivable kind and that the sunshine is just a fairytale. There is no magic in the dawn, sunlight creeping around the curtains like dead fingers. It made Dennes want to run somewhere far away and hide in a dark place where nothing pretended to be other than it was. The child had not survived and so much had depended on it. She didn't awaken even when he eased her out of his arms, unlocked the door and slid from the room. The servants would be about soon, everyone full of concern to see how she was, whether she had slept. Dennes put on his shoes and went out to meet the day on its own terms. The grass was silver with frost, the trees were all iced with diamonds. The sky was cloudless. Somewhere above him a bird sang. The servants were already about, had been up well before the light came. Behind him he heard Mary's for once sympathetic tone.

'Cook's made a cup of tea. I could bring you one.'

Dennes wasn't even properly dressed and she didn't call him 'sir' and she didn't use sarcasm or that clever tone that meant he had earned her displeasure because he was muck. He turned and smiled at her and said, 'Thanks, Mary, that would be nice,' and she smiled in return and dimpled and then ran back lightly into the house, into the shadows.

Seventeen

It seemed to Dennes that winter that Mary was not well. She tired easily coming up the stairs and was pale. Nobody else seemed to notice and she didn't complain of being ill but one evening in February when she had carried a heavy bucket of coal upstairs and he had got up hastily to help her, she gave him the bucket and then she fainted. Dennes picked her up and carried her over to the bed and then he poured out half a glass of water and sat her up and put the glass to her lips as she came round.

'They shouldn't make you carry that upstairs.'

'It's my job.'

'Some job,' Dennes said. 'Poorly, are you?'

'I'm fine.' She scrambled off the bed.

'Been in a hedgeback with some lad?' Dennes guessed.

Mary looked as though she was about to deny it and then changed her mind.

'If you tell they'll throw me out.'

'They're going to throw you out anyway as soon as they find out, without wages an' all.'

Mary sighed.

'Eh, he was bonny, the bastard.'

'Left you?'

'It was only the once, fair night. I had a drink of beer with him and then . . . up on the fell in the heather.'

'Nice,' Dennes said.

'It wasn't half. Nearly four months. It doesn't show, does it?'

'Not there.'

'You won't tell on me.'

'I'll tell them to stop sending you up with those buckets,' Dennes said.

'You can't or they'll know there's something the matter.'

Dennes kept a close eye on Mary for another month and then she was discovered.

'It wasn't you, was it?' Nat accused him as they met on the upstairs landing.

'Why the hell should it be me?'

'You've been around her quite a lot lately, ever so friendly.'

Dennes went downstairs. Mary had just had an interview with Mr Barmouth and was coming out of the study. There was nobody else around. She was crying bitterly.

'You leaving?'

'First thing in the morning.'

She went off crying along the hall. Dennes knocked on the study door and when he was told to come in did so. Mr Barmouth was sitting at the desk. He looked up.

'What do you want?' he said.

'It's about Mary,' Dennes said.

'What about her?'

'You're not really going to turn her out without a penny, are you?'

Mr Barmouth looked at him.

'Why not?' he said.

'Well, what is she going to do? Her father died and the only money her mother makes is dressmaking and you know what that's like.'

'You want me to give that little trollop money?'

'You do have a lot,' Dennes said.

'Look, lad, she went with some . . . gypsy in a ditch.'

'It was just a mistake,' Dennes said.

132

Mr Barmouth looked hard at him.

'Was it now? Or is it that you have a more personal interest?'

'You know what'll happen to her if you don't help her. She'll end up making her living on her back because that's all that's left.'

'She should have thought of that.'

'It's not much of a prospect for one mistake. Couldn't you help her?'

'Why should I?'

'No reason.'

'But you have a reason?'

'Me?'

'Yes. You would do that.'

'I didn't.'

'Sure about that, are you?'

'I said I didn't.'

'Then why are you so concerned about her?'

'Because I know what it's like.'

'You know what what's like?'

'My mother was like that.'

Mr Barmouth laughed.

'Your mother was like what?'

'Her parents put her out—'

'Is that what she told you?'

'What?'

'That she had parents who were horrified at what she'd done?'

'They— they lived in a big house and my father was a soldier and she played the piano.'

Mr Barmouth began to laugh again. His laughter made Dennes feel sick.

'That's what she told you, is it?'

'Well, yes.'

'Your mother had no parents, none that she knew—'

'How do you know?'

'Everybody knew. She was born around here, in an orphanage. There was no piano, there was no soldier, your mother was a slut right from the beginning. She would go with anybody from being a child. I

133

like the bit about the big house though. She had imagination. She always had imagination. That's why she made such a good whore.'

Dennes wanted to hit him. He had never wanted to hit anyone as much. He had tried so hard to hold on to the idea that there had been something for his mother and before her, that somewhere there had been a vestige of respectability, that somewhere in her life there had been even moments of happiness, that some time somebody other than him had looked after her, cared for her, tried to make her life a little easier.

He knew very well by now that Nicholas Barmouth was within distance of hating him and he considered sometimes whether it would not have been much better to have defied Gwen and left the village altogether when she married Mr Barmouth, because he knew now and he thought that Mr Barmouth knew that she had too much feeling for Dennes. Perhaps it had always been so, he couldn't be sure. All he knew was that when she walked into a room it was him she looked for first. Her eyes lit up when she saw him. She loved him not as she had claimed, not as she loved Nat but as a woman loves a man and he thought that Mr Barmouth must have been blind not to see it right from the first. Now he was punishing them both as much as he could for something which could not be helped. And in his heart Dennes couldn't blame him. To bed a woman who belonged morally to another man was beyond thought and she did belong to him now, even though Mr Barmouth had wedded, bedded and impregnated her. Nothing made the difference. Only her sense of right and wrong had kept her from indulging that love and now they were all three of them ruining their lives over it. He felt almost sorry for Nicholas Barmouth.

He had been foolish to come here and think that he could make the difference for Mary. He was only glad that he could not make things any worse.

He walked out. That disconcerted Nicholas, he could see. He went up the two flights of stairs and knocked on the door of Mary's tiny attic bedroom. She opened it. Her face was tear-stained and a shabby bag on the bed was almost full of her belongings.

'You tried to talk to him?' she said as she shut the door behind Dennes.

'It didn't do any good.'

'It was nice of you. You didn't have to do that. He doesn't like you to begin with. What do you stay for?'

'I feel responsible.'

She smiled.

'Do you always feel responsible for everybody? He'd just think you'd done it to me.'

'Yes, he did.'

'You're lucky you didn't get a good hiding,' Mary said and fastened the bag up. 'Arguing with Mr Barmouth, it's never a safe thing to do, you know it isn't.'

'I just didn't want you on the streets with a bairn.'

'Why, what's it to you?'

'The same thing happened to my mother.'

Mary shivered. Dennes took a small money bag out of his pocket.

'Here,' he said.

She backed off.

'Don't you pretend to me that Mr Barmouth gave you money for me. He wouldn't do it and I'm not taking money from you.'

'Take it.'

'I won't.' She backed off further. 'You sweated in the foundry for that.'

'I don't need it.'

'You will. Sooner or later you'll leave here and then you will.'

Dennes pressed the money into her hand. She started to cry again and push it back at him.

'You've got nobody,' he said.

'Yes, I have. I have, my Mam.'

'Your mother can't keep you. She can hardly keep herself by all accounts.'

'We'll manage. It's my own fault I'm in this state.'

'It isn't the baby's fault though, is it? If somebody had bothered to help my mother things would have been different.' He forced the

135

money into her hand, closed her fingers over it and she kissed him wetly on the cheek. Dennes got himself quickly out of the room before she could cry over him any more.

By the summer Gwen was pregnant again. Nat knew long before she told him and so, he suspected, did Dennes who went about with a carefully blank look and a cheerful attitude which Nat knew camouflaged the rage that he felt because she was not well.

They had both been very careful of her that spring because she was always quiet and tired. She cried a lot, Nat thought, though never in front of him. Nat tried hard to be jealous of Dennes. When Nicholas was not at home Dennes was always fetching and carrying, reading to her when she was tired, making her smile with his stories of people she used to know who didn't bother with her now that she was so grand.

One September evening when Dennes had left the company and gone upstairs to his room, Nat followed him there. Nicholas had long since made it clear that Dennes was not welcome at any time other than meals and if Gwen would not have created a huge fuss Nat felt sure Nicholas would have made Dennes eat with the servants. Nat spent most evenings enduring boredom in Nicholas's presence and at least, he thought, Dennes didn't have to put up with that.

He knocked lightly and Dennes answered so he went in. Dennes was lying on the bed, reading, but he put down the book and sat up.

'Something the matter?' he said shortly.

Suddenly Nat couldn't say anything, he was so upset, not just because Gwen was pregnant, because they were here at all, because he and Dennes were no longer friends, because things never worked out. He went over to the window and stood there while his throat closed.

'It's a bloody awful view,' he said tightly.

Dennes got off the bed and came over.

'I'm frightened,' Nat said. It wasn't what he had been going to say but out the words came. Dennes put an arm around his shoulders just as though they were still friends and Nat shrugged him off and moved nearer the window. 'I don't know what you stay here for,' he said roughly.

'I'd miss the warm family atmosphere.'

Nat couldn't help but smile at that.

'I wish we were back at the Golden Lion,' he said.

'I never go there. I can't bear it. I can't think how it's still standing without us. It's like an insult somehow, like all we have left is the past.'

'That's not true,' Nat said quickly. 'Every damn afternoon you have at home you spend with my mother.'

Dennes said nothing to that.

'You do know she's pregnant, don't you?' Nat insisted. 'If anything happened to her . . . Why did he marry her, why? If all he wanted was a family he could have taken a young girl. God help them, any of them would have had him with his money.'

'He loved her,' Dennes said softly and not looking at him.

'How can you say that, Dennes?' Nat turned and glared at him. 'Does he treat her like he loves her?'

'Not now, no, but he did before, when he thought that she cared about him.'

'If she didn't care about him what did she marry him for?'

'Because it was the sensible thing to do for the future.'

'That's the worst reason I ever heard for getting married.'

'She was thinking about us, to make things better for us.'

'This is better? I don't know why you stand it.'

'Let's go to the Black Horse and have a pint,' Dennes said. 'They've got a new girl in there, you'll like her, Nat, she's as bonny as a picture.'

Nat considered for a moment.

'All right,' he said finally. 'Let's go.'

Gwen was ill, worse than she had been the last time. Nicholas refused to acknowledge it when Nat requested a doctor. She was sick constantly, she didn't sleep. She had to be coaxed to eat anything and she had a cold and then a cough which she could not get rid of. Nat got the doctor when Nicholas was not there but she did not improve. She lost weight steadily until the only thing large about her was the baby and her eyes. The sickness didn't stop. By the time the baby was almost due she was too tired to get out of bed and every day she said less.

Nat and Dennes no longer talked about anything that mattered. As often as he could Nat came home early from the office. In the evenings Taylor was there and Nicholas. Nat asked Nicholas if Dolly could come home from school but he wouldn't listen.

'Your mother isn't ill, Nat, she's having a baby. It's perfectly natural,' he said.

'If anything happens to her I'll bloody kill him,' Nat said to Dennes. 'I hate him so much I can't breathe freely when he's in the room. How can he do this to her?'

'He wants to believe it. She is having his child.'

'She's not going to live through it and you know it,' Nat said, to his own horror starting to cry because he had believed until the words were spoken that his mother could not die.

They were standing in the garden at the side of the house. Nat couldn't bear to be in the warmth indoors as though everything was normal. The wind was cold and bitter there and dried his tears too fast.

'Don't you go and cry in front of her,' Dennes threatened.

'Oh shut up, Eliot, you hard bastard.'

'God, Nat, it's freezing out here.'

'I don't care!' Nat drew his sleeve over his eyes.

'Haven't you got a hanky?'

'Who are you, somebody's bloody mother?'

'Here.' Dennes handed him a big linen square. 'And don't blow your nose on it,' he said.

A fortnight before the baby was due Nat came home in the middle of the afternoon to find the doctor's horse and trap outside and when he rushed in Nicholas was walking slowly down the stairs. He looked up vacantly when he saw Nat and stopped for a moment.

'I was going to send for you.'

'My mother?'

'And my son. I lost my son.'

The doctor came out of Gwen's bedroom and along the hall. He walked down the stairs as far as Nat and said, 'I'm sorry.'

Nat ran. He ran up the stairs, Nicholas staring after him, and burst into the room. There was so much blood Nat couldn't believe it. There were people in the room, nurses, saying things to him. How they had tried to save the child as though somehow the child was all that mattered. The person on the bed was not his mother, had never been anybody's mother, so very dead.

They ushered him out of the room quickly so that he was scarcely in it and then Nicholas was there, talking to him. Nat didn't remember what he said.

'Where's Dennes?'

'He tried to insist on seeing her. I couldn't have that. She was in a great deal of pain. It was just so sudden. I didn't realise that she was so bad, that she was dying or I would have let him see her.'

'Where is he?'

'I don't know where he is.'

It was early evening when Dennes came back. Nat had been watching for hours. He came in the back gate from the fields and up the back stairs to his room. Nat followed him there and somehow he had known what he would find, Dennes calmly packing.

'Are you going far?' Nat said.

'Just to the nearest pub.'

He was badly bruised about the face and, from the way that he moved so carefully, in other places.

'Did Nicholas hit you?'

'No. Two men were up from the works laying the new paths. Big Irish lads. He got them to bray me when I tried to see Gwen.'

'The pub won't help.'

Dennes smiled.

'I'm going to the Golden Lion,' he said. 'When I've had a few pints I see the past ever so clearly.'

'God Almighty, Dennes.'

Dennes looked at him.

'You have to stay here.'

'After what he did to my mother?'

139

'You have to. There's Dolly to consider and Taylor. And the funeral. And the future. You do have a future here and it's the only place. You can't drag them away now or everything your mother did was a waste of time. Dolly's nearly a young woman and Taylor's good in the office, you said he was. It'll be Barmouth, Hemingway and Seymour some day. Just wait.'

'And what are you going to do?' Nat said sarcastically.

Dennes picked up his bag.

'I'm going to get drunk,' he said.

Eighteen

When Dennes came to, it was because somebody turned him over with something hard that hurt. He opened his eyes and was looking at the wrong end of a double-barrelled shotgun and then he remembered the drinking and the storm and the need for shelter. He remembered the broken-down house. He remembered thankfully passing out. He didn't remember the slight, grey-haired woman or the gun.

Some time had passed, maybe a night, maybe more. He had a savage thirst but he didn't dare move.

'Get up,' she ordered.

He had to get up slowly because his limbs were stiff from sleeping on a cold floor.

'What are you doing on my land? I don't like tramps.'

'I'm not a tramp. I live in the village.'

'If you live in the village what are you doing here?'

'I was drunk.'

'What's your name?'

'Dennes Eliot.'

'Eliot?' She looked hard at him and scowled. 'Oh yes, I see it now. You look just like your mother.'

'How do you know? I could look just like my father, couldn't I?'

'I thought you didn't have a father.'

141

'It was a joke,' Dennes said patiently.

'You have nowhere to go, you're drunk, dirty and obviously penniless, looking down the barrels of a gun and you think it's funny?'

'No, I don't think it's funny.'

'I don't think it's funny either. You get off my land.'

Dennes went. Nearby there was a stream but when he knelt down to it she shouted after him.

'Don't drink that water, it's not clean!'

The woman, Dennes tried to recall her name and couldn't, was soon gone from sight. He walked over the fields to the old quarry and stood there on the edge looking down at where he and Nat had dumped William Daniels' body. He kept looking down into the water. The thirst was becoming a torment, the edge looked so inviting. No more thirst, no more daybreaks, no more long nights. Then a voice said softly behind him, 'Can you swim?'

It was her again.

'I'm not sure,' Dennes said.

'You'll regret it a minute or less after you've done it,' she said, 'you don't drown straight away, even if you can't swim. It's very deep and you'll keep coming back up until your lungs burst and every time you do you'll wish you hadn't been so stupid.'

'I wasn't going to.'

'Weren't you?'

'I'm not on your land any more,' Dennes pointed out helpfully, but he moved slightly back from the very edge. As he did so the scene in front of his eyes seemed suddenly to intensify, and then it was as though it reached out and banged him on the face, and then it was all over.

He thought at first that he was dead, he must be dead because the last thing that he remembered was falling over the quarry edge, and then he opened his eyes and he was in a neat blue-and-white bedroom and he was in bed. The bed was not far from the window and winter sunlight was coming in. From outside he could hear hens clucking around. The cover over him was warm. He was thirsty but not like he

142

had been. He sat up. By the bed was a big jug of water and a glass. Dennes poured out a glassful and swallowed it without breathing and then he lay down again and stayed still and went on listening to the hens. They sounded so happy, so busy, as though they were women gossiping while shopping. After a while he fell asleep again and when he awoke the grey-haired woman was standing by the bed.

'You better?'

'Yes.'

'Sure?'

'Yes, thanks.'

'You need a bath.'

It was in some ways like his arrival at the Seymours had been, and it hurt so much to remember it, only this time the clothes were bigger and there was a razor which she said had been her husband's but would do, and some time later Dennes went into the front room where she was sitting.

'I don't usually sit around like this,' she said, 'but it's Sunday.' She got up and came back soon afterwards with a pot of tea and milk and sugar and cups and saucers, and a big pile of sandwiches. Dennes accepted and bit into one. It was chicken. It tasted wonderful.

'I had to wring its neck,' she said, 'it wasn't laying.'

Dennes waited for her to take a sandwich before he had another one.

'I've had something to eat,' she said, 'these are for you.'

Dennes demolished the sandwiches at the kind of speed which he knew would create indigestion later, and when they had gone, as well as two cups of tea and a large slice of apple pie which she said she just happened to have left, with thick cream, he thanked her and sat back.

'So, are you going to tell me why you wanted to throw yourself off the quarry edge?'

'I didn't want to.'

'Didn't you? You were very close to the edge for somebody who didn't want to. One slip and that would have been it. It's very deep. People go over there and are never found.'

'I know.'

'So you were thinking about it?'

'It was just a possibility. I'd been drunk.'

'I don't approve of drink,' she said.

'If you like.'

'I don't like. I think it's a disgusting way to behave. Do you know how I got you back to the house? I found two men to carry you and they told me all about you, how Nicholas Barmouth threw you out of his house after his wife died, how you lived with a married woman and knifed her husband when he came back, about the drinking and fighting and the way that you squandered your money. I suppose you're going to say that this is all wrong so that I'll take you into my house and feed you chicken sandwiches every day.'

And then he remembered her name.

'Not every day, Mrs Kelso,' he said.

She went off to milk the cows. Dennes watched from the doorway of the byre.

'Think you can do it?' she said. 'It's not as easy as it looks.'

'Neither are most things.'

'Come here then. Sit on the stool. You always milk from the right.'

'Why?'

'Don't ask daft questions, and go gently, mind you. Life's easy until a cow stands on you. Just think that you're stripping the milk from her.'

'What's she called?'

'She's a cow. She doesn't have a name.'

'I thought all cows had names. I thought they were all called Daisy and Buttercup. Hey, I'm doing it,' and he was. The milk spurted into the bucket.

'Don't get enthusiastic. There's another to do,' she said and went away.

Dennes eventually milked both cows. It took him a very long time. His hands and back ached. He went into the kitchen with Mrs Kelso afterwards and she made him a cup of tea.

For some time a good smell had been coming from the house, and now on the kitchen table was a brown pot filled with meat, vegetables

144

and gravy. There were potatoes and there was fresh bread and a big oblong of butter on a white plate, and in a jug on the table was some pink liquid which Dennes strongly suspected was alcoholic.

'I thought you didn't like drink,' he said, after sipping cautiously.

'This isn't drink,' she said, 'it's sloe wine. I make it.'

The meat was beef and among it there were shiny pieces of golden turnip and orange carrots. The beef had to be spooned from the pot and there were bright red tomatoes with it and the gravy was better than Dennes had ever tasted.

'What's in it?' he said and he almost expected her answer.

'It's sloe wine,' she said.

After he had eaten Dennes was very tired. She washed up. He didn't offer to help and she didn't ask him and when it was finished she turned to him and said, 'You can stay if you'll work but I won't pay you anything. You can sleep in the barn and mind you, I'm not a young woman, but the doors will be locked and I keep a shotgun by the bed.'

She gave him a pillow and a blanket and Dennes went off to the barn. In the dark sky an odd star twinkled, he could see it through the door up in the hayloft. He didn't want to face the night, he was tired of nights, the way that each day had one like a great big hole for you to fall through. He lay for a while ready to take on the long dark hours but Mrs Kelso had tired him out with fresh air and work, filled him full of good food and wine. Within ten minutes he was asleep and he slept more soundly than he had done in a very long time.

Shona Kelso was up before him, it was late but she said nothing. Dennes offered to milk the cows again and she was obviously glad. She made the breakfast and Dennes fed the hens. He stayed out there watching them eat their corn, and he went over to one dark red hen and while she pecked about he stroked her. When she had done eating at least for a little while he picked her up and she put her head under his arm.

'That's Trudy,' Mrs Kelso said as she came into the yard, smiling.

'I see. Your cows don't have names but all your hens do.'

'As a matter of fact the cows do as well,' she said, 'it just seemed so silly.'

'And what are the cows called?'

'Emerald and Bryan.'

'Bryan?'

'It's my favourite name,' she said.

There were fresh boiled eggs for breakfast with brown bread and the sweetest butter that Dennes had ever tasted.

There was a lot to do but all of it was interesting, and Mrs Kelso had made what was almost a religion out of producing and eating good food. Her cellar was full of homemade wine: birch sap, honeysuckle and apple. It was the apple which was Dennes' downfall that evening. It didn't look much but the smell of it was almost as good as the taste, and it tasted better than anything he had ever drunk in his whole life. Much of the wine wasn't bottled, it came in gallon jars and it was from these that they poured out tumblerfuls. Dennes slept even better that night than he had the night before. Mrs Kelso forgot to lock the doors but he didn't tell her. He gazed happily up at the stars from his bed in the hayloft and then fell into a sound and happy sleep.

There were few visitors to the farm. The milk was collected, people called to buy butter and eggs. It was not like a real farm; she had Jacob sheep – the black-and-white ones – two cows, a couple of pigs, the hens, half a dozen ducks who had to themselves a very big pond at the back of the house and a lot of lush land which was meadow, neatly walled because she kept it so, and the house and garden where she spent most of her time. She had glasshouses, something Dennes had only seen at Esh House, and here she told him she grew tomatoes and grapes and cucumbers. The house itself was a big old farmhouse in stone and Dennes thought that he had never liked a house more. It had a big kitchen with an open range and off it small rooms, the dairy and the pantry and down some steps the cellar. Then there was a dining-room and a parlour, both spacious, and upstairs were three big bedrooms and a small back room. There were views of the valley from every window.

She soon became less suspicious of him but Dennes went on

sleeping in the barn. She fed him the best meals that he had ever tasted, pork in apple wine, beef in elderberry, partridges roasted with their livers chopped with ham, pheasants drenched in butter. Dennes tried not to be happy but it was impossible.

Sometimes he went drinking with Nat and although she didn't approve she gave him money so that he could have drunk a lot more than he did. Dennes was ashamed for how he felt about her, he didn't like to go off and leave her there because she seemed to have no friends and he would make excuses to Nat and come back early. She stopped making him sleep outside, he had to himself a big bedroom, a clean heavenly big bed with light pleasing furniture such as he had never seen before. Shona had a lot of books and during the dark nights Dennes was glad of them because he and Shona sat over the kitchen fire – they hardly ever used the parlour – and after she had produced the most exquisite meals that he had ever eaten they drank apple wine and they read. Sometimes it was recipe books which they read out to each other and sometimes it was funny stories. They read aloud to each other and the wood fire crackled and burned so friendly. It flickered in the shadows of the room. The cats would come in and sit on their laps. Shona had a dog called Bert, who had been supposed to be a sheepdog to some neighbouring farmer but had never quite got the hang of rounding up sheep, and Shona had taken him. He slept at the foot of her bed but sometimes he would push open the door and Dennes would wake in the night to find the dog on the bed with him, breathing warm doggy breath all over him and taking up a lot of room.

Nineteen

Dennes had been right, Nat thought, the day of the funeral. Dolly was almost a young lady. She would soon be fifteen. She wore her expensive clothes modestly but stylishly. She was softly spoken, she even cried softly for her mother. He had told her nothing that would make her dislike Nicholas. That wouldn't help. The man had fed and clothed her, sent her to school, done nothing wrong in her eyes. The more Nat saw of her that week the more he became convinced that Dennes was right.

Taylor was the same. He cried over his mother and at the funeral he kept an arm around his sister and Nat knew that they couldn't leave Esh House. All he could have taken them to was a tiny cottage in a back street and the kind of life which they had almost forgotten. They were grieving but there was no hate in it. He had that all to himself. The losing of Dennes was like another bereavement. Nat had never felt so alone.

Going back to work was easier. Nothing was different there. He even pretended that he would be going home at half-past five to his mother and Dennes, and when they were not there he couldn't stand it and retreated to the Golden Lion. It was a mistake. It seemed to him that the room there echoed of Nicholas smiling at his mother as she went around talking to the customers. He passed the lilac house and that was no better; William Daniels seemed to hover in the cold little yard.

He couldn't find Dennes. His enquiries brought nothing but the information that Dennes had been there at the Lion, had even left his bag, the woman said, so he was coming back. He was not at the Black Horse. Even the sight of the pretty barmaid didn't make Nat smile.

The only place where Nat could find any comfort – and he gratefully avoided the churchyard – was the awful little house in the back street where he had come with his mother and father when he was not much more than a child, and that too was hard because they were both dead now and he had the responsibility of his brother and sister without Dennes' help. Nat had never felt so old. He understood then what Dennes had meant about the past being the only place to go. He wished that just for a few minutes he could hold on to the happiness that he had known then. Yet at the time it hadn't seemed like happiness. They had been poor and over-worked, ill-fed and ill-clothed and it was just so awful to think that he had now the things which he had so much wanted then, a beautiful home, a good job, security, nice clothes, good food, even servants and a horse. He had everything and had lost what really mattered. He wished that he could go back and have his mother and his father again, and this time appreciate them. He remembered how ungrateful he had been as a child, that he had thought his father such a small person, so unimportant and stupid, and he saw now that it was not so. And he wondered why it seemed to be part of God's plan that your parents had to be either old or dead by the time you knew how much they had cared for you, how much they had done. It seemed so cruel, as though God was laughing at all attempts to be a decent person. He knew now, when he had met other men, that his father had been good and had loved him. His father had had dreams, it was true, and those dreams had been his undoing, but Nat thought it was better to have dreams than not to have them. When you didn't the night was too long, it bettered you with doubts and regrets and guilt and left you in the grey dawn, tired and hot and defeated.

He couldn't find Dennes anywhere. He went into a pub he hadn't been in and downed five pints before he went home. Dennes was right, it did help. He had missed dinner. Nobody said anything to him. Later Dolly brought him some sandwiches to his room and hugged him.

'Are you drunk, our Nat?'

'Not really.'

'Next time,' she said, 'you should take Taylor with you.'

'I will,' Nat promised.

She kissed him and went off to her bedroom and Nat swore to himself that he would look after her and do the right thing as his mother had wanted.

Dennes didn't think about Gwen, he couldn't bear the image of her in his mind. He pretended that she had never existed, it was the only way in which he could deal with the problem. He never went back to Esh House and mostly he avoided Nat, even after seeking him out and telling him where he was staying, other than the odd time that they went drinking, and then Nat talked about the steelworks and what he was doing and Dennes told him about Shona and the farm. They never mentioned Gwen or talked about the past.

That winter Dennes rarely left the farm and he was glad. It was as though nothing else existed, he could hide away with Shona in the darkness, in the comfort of the farm and it was the greatest comfort that Dennes had ever known. He felt safe as he never had when a child, with big fires, good food and wine, the books, playing card games with her, reading, laughing, knowing that nothing could hurt him here. He did almost all the outside work during the bad weather and Shona rewarded him with the kind of food that most men only dreamed about.

And then he had the nightmare. He dreamed it was the day that Gwen had died and he was trying to get to her. She was calling out his name and he was running and running along the hall towards her bedroom door and the more he ran the further away he was until she was screaming and there was blood and she was lost from sight.

He awoke in the dark, cold night, lit a candle and made his way downstairs, the sheepdog following. The kitchen was the warmest room, so he went in there. The fire was nothing but grey ashes. Dennes sat down at the table and put his hands over his face.

He heard Shona on the stairs, her feet making the stair rods clink, but he didn't move. She came into the kitchen. She didn't say anything; she lit the lamp and began with the fire, and when she had finally coaxed it into life and tiny flames began to flicker and spurt she sat down at the table and said, 'Not crying, are you?'

'I'm a man.'

'Is that a definition of one?'

Dennes smiled through his fingers. 'No. I've just never cried, that's all.'

'When the fire gets away I'll make you some tea.'

'It was just a dream.'

'Very unsatisfactory – dreams. The good ones always stop before you get to the best bit but bad dreams, they go all the way.'

'This one did.'

'Yes.'

'I've never been very good, you know, Shona.'

'Neither is anybody, don't you find? It's strange that we should expect to be when everything in life is either a dreadful disappointment or a swiftly passing pleasure.'

'It hurts so much.'

'But not enough to make you cry?'

'I can't cry, I don't know how.'

'Do you want an old woman to cuddle you?'

'No, but I want you to.'

She laughed and took him into her arms.

'Eh, lad,' she said, 'it's a bonny tongue you've got to match your face. Thank God I'm not young.'

'I love you, Shona.'

'You're daft, you are.'

'Have you loved people who've died?'

'My husband, my son, my parents. Almost everybody. That's why I live here. I can't bear other people who don't understand. My son was nearly five years old. He would have been about your age now. It was the hardest thing that happened to me.'

'And your husband?'

'It took all the joy and all the light from my life when he died. Other men were so small afterwards. I couldn't bear company, the stupidity of it. I contented myself with this place and the animals.'

'Was it easier?'

'No, it was the only way I knew how.'

'But you got used to it?'

'I used to go and stand on the quarry edge and tell God that it was his fault and that I was going to kill myself, and then I decided that I would punish him even worse. I would live as long as he had decided I would and I would curse his name *every day*.'

'And do you?'

'Not now. It's as if he opens your eyes to the tiniest things so that each day is a miracle, the weather changing and the animals and the food is twice as good—'

'And the wine is three times as good.'

Shona laughed.

'Oh aye,' she said, 'the wine,' and she kissed the top of his head and let him go.

She made him some tea. He went back to bed to drink it and when the slow winter light came at last he fell into a velvet sleep and in it there were no dreams and beyond it there were no fears.

Twenty

The spring was easier, Nat found. In some ways living as they began to live then was better than things had been when his mother had been alive and Dennes had been there. It took Nat a long time to admit it to himself but it was true. There was a peace at the house which had not existed before and he wondered whether Dennes had known this and had left on purpose because he knew that his presence made things worse.

Dolly did not go back to school, and when the first grieving was over Nicholas began to lavish things on her. At first Nat wished that he wouldn't. He wanted his hatred of Nicholas to remain pure but it was difficult to be unmoved by what Nicholas did for Dolly. She was not beautiful like Grace Hemingway but she was a very pretty girl, now in expensive clothes, cared for, educated, playing the piano for Nicholas's guests. Nat knew that Gwen would have been glad to see her there.

Nicholas was kind to Nat and Taylor and he began to teach them how to run the steelworks and it would not have been honest for Nat to say that he disliked the work. Nothing pleased him more than to spend the day in the foundry at Nicholas's side, learning as much as he could as fast as he could absorb it. Taylor was happy in the office but Nat liked to be down in the works as well, watching the different processes, the pouring of the steel, the skills of the moulders and the fettlers, the way that men worked so well together, the castings cooling only yards away from booted feet.

Nat began to admire Nicholas Barmouth. He had knowledge, he could do everything his workmen could do and he had business ability as well. He ran his works the way Nat would have done, he knew each man by name, he knew their problems and how hard their jobs were. He was a fair employer as far as Nat could tell, his men were decently paid and housed. And most of all Nat enjoyed the way that Nicholas treated him when they were there, with respect. This man, seen here, was the kind of man that Nat would have wanted for a father. They talked constantly about work and Nat loved every second.

On Sundays he and Taylor and Nicholas would sit either by the fire or, if the weather was fine, in the garden after their dinner with a cup of tea apiece and discuss the works. The flowers began to come out, the lawns were growing, the trees were in bud. Everything was getting better. Dolly treated Nicholas like a father. She adored him. She kissed his cheek when they met, he smiled on her.

As the weather warmed and the summer arrived Nicholas decided that they ought to have some kind of quiet social life, and to Nat's delight he began to ask more people over, as well as the Hemingways who came to dinner occasionally.

Grace had by this time refused three eligible men. Nat saw why men fell in love with her. She was so beautiful by now that everyone stopped talking the minute that she walked into the room. The men couldn't but look at Grace and she was so natural, so ordinary.

One Saturday evening that summer she came straight over to Nat, smiling. She was wearing a blue dress which made her eyes look even deeper. Her skin was perfect, pearly, her yellow hair gleamed and shone. Nat sat next to her at dinner. She didn't say much, but the young man on her other side talked so much that she didn't need to.

Alexandra sat opposite and after dinner, in the garden, it was she who came to Nat and said, 'How's Dennes?'

'He's staying at Mrs Kelso's.'

'At the farm? Yes, I heard. She's a strange woman.'

'I haven't been there,' Nat said, 'sometimes we go for a drink.'

'Grace's father and Nicholas tried to do business with her a few years back – there's sharp sand below some of her property. They would have paid her good money too but she didn't want to know and the Church Commissioners wouldn't help.'

'Maybe she didn't like the intrusion.'

'Maybe not.'

'Aren't things good with you then?'

Alexandra looked gratefully at him.

'The mines are worked up. It's only a matter of weeks before we close. My father has had to dismiss what servants we had.'

'What are you going to do?'

'I don't know. We should go to the farm and see Dennes. Does Mrs Kelso get upset at visitors?'

'I can ask him.'

The result of this was that Mrs Kelso invited them to tea and Alexandra wished she hadn't told Grace because she insisted on going.

'You haven't been asked,' Alexandra pointed out.

'Please, Alex, let me come. She won't mind.'

'It isn't the done thing.'

'Oh, please. I haven't seen Dennes since Mr Barmouth married Nat's mother. You wouldn't begrudge me an hour or two in his company.'

Shona Kelso showed nothing more than pleased surprise to find Grace at her tea table.

'What did you bring her for?' Dennes asked Nat privately.

'She wanted to come.'

'Whatever for? She's like something out of a toy shop, for God's sake.'

After tea Dennes offered to show them the pigs. Only Grace was keen and went. Alexandra grinned at Nat.

'That must be a first for her,' she said.

Grace went to see the pigs and the hens and the ducks. She had hens at home but they had never before been interesting. They went into the field by the pond and there to Grace's mortification she slipped and fell

157

in a fresh cowpat. Worse still, Dennes couldn't stop laughing and although Grace knew that she should have been pleased to see him laugh, it made her angry.

'You haven't changed, have you?' she said, getting to her feet, wrinkling her nose at the smell. 'You're just a horrid, common boy!'

'Oh, come on, Grace.' He backed off as Grace advanced on him clenching both fists but he was laughing so much that he couldn't stop her. 'If you hit me I'll chuck you in the pond,' he threatened. 'Mind you, you'd smell better.'

Grace was almost in tears. She ran back to the house and when Dennes followed some time later Shona had loaned her another dress. It was brown.

'You should've worn that colour to begin with,' Dennes recommended, 'and then only the smell would have distinguished you.'

This was too much. Alone with the man of her dreams in Mrs Kelso's kitchen she touched him for the first time. She tried to smack him round the ear but he was too fast and grabbed her nearly off her feet.

'Hey, hey. Whoa.'

'You laughed,' Grace said wetly.

'It mattered, eh? I didn't know. Is it your best frock?'

'It wasn't the— it wasn't the dress.'

'What was it then?'

Grace didn't answer. She shook her head and sat down on a chair and Dennes got down beside her and pushed back a wet curl from her eyes.

'Come on, you can tell me,' he said softly.

'I made a fool of myself.'

'You have to have an audience to do that. There was nobody around.'

'You were there.'

'Me?' Dennes laughed again. 'That doesn't count. Come on. Come and sit in the garden with me.'

Shona's garden was tiny. Fortunately it was also empty. They sat down on the lawn. Dennes lay down and closed his eyes and then he turned over on to his stomach and settled himself on his elbows and watched her as she pulled the heads off daisies.

'What do you do?' he asked her.

'Do?'

'Yes. At home.'

'Nothing much. I keep my dress clean.' She smiled at him. 'My mother has spent my whole life telling me not to do things. The only time it was the other way round was when I wouldn't marry Henry Ellingthorpe.'

'Haven't they forgotten about that?'

'They're never going to forget about it. My mother thinks I'm going to be an old maid now. She's terrified about it.'

'Can't you marry somebody else?'

'Around here? There isn't anybody, just Peter Clifford and the vicar's son. Besides, I don't want to marry them. Peter reads poetry and Aidan is studying theology. I ask you.'

'But you didn't like the rich lads in London who did nothing. Maybe you should do something else, some lasses do.'

'Like what?'

'I don't know. Office work. Nursing.'

'My parents would die first.'

' 'Tisn't much of a prospect either way,' Dennes said.

He lay down on his back again and closed his eyes because the sun was so hot. Grace tickled his nose with a daisy and he opened his eyes, laughed and grabbed her. Grace shrieked. He rolled her over and tickled her and she got the giggles and laughed until she ached. She had never behaved like this before and it was wonderful. Her mother would have been horrified.

'Give in!'

'No!' She pushed at him and then got up and ran, out of the garden, around to the side of the house, past the duckpond and into the wood, shouting and laughing when Dennes caught her, very out of breath. There between the shadows and the sunlight in the wood he brought his mouth down on hers. Grace had dreamt of him doing such a thing for so long that when it actually happened she was frightened that he

159

would realise she wanted him. The kiss was full and sweet, better even than she had dreamed and he took her into his arms. Grace stopped him but very reluctantly and was rewarded by a curious gaze.

'You aren't like I thought you were at all,' he said.

'I hope this is complimentary, Dennes.'

'I thought you were a vain, conceited, rich, little b—'

She put her fingers on his lips.

'Please,' she said and he started to laugh.

'You're all right,' he said.

Grace thought of all the fulsome compliments that she had received on her beauty and smiled.

'So are you,' she said, 'mostly.'

Alexandra called from the house.

'Grace! Grace, where are you? We have to go.'

Dennes released her and they walked slowly out of the wood and back to the farmhouse.

She fairly floated home and there Mr Barmouth was sitting with her parents. Grace tried to get away. She wanted to retreat to her bedroom and think about Dennes but she couldn't. Mr Barmouth told her how well she was looking, asked her all about her afternoon so Grace was obliged to be inventive. It was hours before she made her escape and she was bored. And then she lay half the night thinking about Dennes, so happy, so pleased, wondering what would happen now.

Her mood lasted. The weather changed but Grace didn't care. She ran across to Alexandra's house the following afternoon in the pouring rain and drank tea with her in the old summer house as they had since children when they wanted to share secrets and the rain stotted off the roof.

'He kissed me.'

Alexandra stared.

'Where? When? What was it like?'

'In the wood after tea and it was . . . it was the best thing that ever happened,' and Grace related the details while the rain poured down.

All that week she waited for him to contact her. Every day she fully expected a note or that she would see him or that he would send a message with Nat. It was a very long week, possibly the longest of her life. For some reason her parents invited Mr Barmouth to dinner three times. They also asked him to go with them to a church flower festival. By the eighth day Grace was crying, by the end of two weeks she was wishing all kinds of evil fates on Dennes. She and Alexandra sat in the summer house again. The weather had improved but Grace's mother thought she would spoil her complexion by sitting in the sun.

'Why did he kiss me if he didn't mean it?'

'Impulse.'

'How could he do that, Alex?'

'They do.'

'It's happened to you?'

'Once.'

'You didn't tell me. Who was it, Peter?'

'Nat.'

'Maybe it's something only common boys do.'

Grace gave up going into town in hope of seeing Dennes. She tried not to think about him. All the following week Mr Barmouth was at the house every day and Dorothy had insisted that Grace be dressed up, and that meant a fuss about her hair and her dresses and not being able to see Alexandra or go walking on the fell to dip her feet in the icy waters of the stream there, or to sit with a book in Alexandra's summer house pretending to read and thinking wistfully of that one kiss and wondering how long the memory of it would have to last, because it was obvious to her now that there was not going to be another.

Alexandra's father had bought her a small white dog, a West Highland terrier which she called Ruffles. When the days were fine that summer they took him for walks. Sometimes Peter Clifford came by. He was studying to be a doctor and was home for the summer. But Grace wasn't able to go to Alexandra's because Mr Barmouth was always at the house. It was frustrating not to be able to do what she wanted to do before the summer weather was finally over. It wouldn't last, it never did.

Sometimes during the days which followed Mr Barmouth asked her to walk around the garden with him, and when she was invited to his house with her parents he filled her arms with flowers before she went home. She was only grateful that Dolly was mostly at home or Nat was there to dilute his stepfather's boring conversation. She was dying to ask Nat if he had seen Dennes but pride forbade that. She wanted to cling to him when Mr Barmouth was around. She hovered so near that she was worried Nat would get the wrong impression. She begged him to teach her chess.

'I thought you hated boardgames,' Nat said.

'I do,' Grace said miserably one Sunday afternoon when it was pouring with rain and she was desperate to be with people her own age.

'Come on then.'

They went through into the study and Nat closed the door. Grace's shoulders went down with relief.

'So,' he said, 'what is it?'

'You know what my mother's like. I think they want to put me in a glass case.'

'I know.'

'They treat me like an oil painting, only there to be looked at. Your stepfather is as bad. He keeps telling me how beautiful I am and giving me roses. I hate roses. I hate the smell of them, it's so sickly.'

'Grace! Grace!' came her mother's voice from the hall.

The study overlooked the side of the house. Grace looked desperately at Nat and he quickly unlatched and pushed up the window, climbed out and held out both hands.

'Come on, hurry up.'

Grace took handfuls of her skirt and managed with his help, and after he slid shut the window they ran up the yard. It was raining heavily. They went in at the stairs which led up to the loft from the carriage house. There was plenty of loose hay to sit in and the window looked out over the valley. Grace subsided thankfully into a pile of hay and sighed at the silence.

'I haven't seen Alex in an age,' she said. 'I'm not allowed to go past the doors.'

'Why?' Nat said, sitting opposite.

'I don't know. Nat, can I ask you something?'

'What?'

'Why do men kiss girls they don't love?'

'Do they?'

'Haven't you?'

'I suppose, yes. Because it's nice?'

'It is nice,' Grace said, smiling in remembrance. 'You know I don't think I can stay at home like this much longer. My mother never lets me out of her sight. Do you think there's anything I could do?'

'You mean go away?'

'Yes. Be a housekeeper or something.'

'It would have to be a long way,' Nat said, 'or they would bring you back.'

'I haven't enough money to go far.'

'I don't think anybody would take you on as a housekeeper, Grace, you're too well-bred and beautiful. You stand out. Besides, you've never worked, you don't know anything about it and you would have no references—' He stopped. The door at the bottom of the stairs was creaking open.

Dolly's voice said softly, 'Are you up there, our Nat? Grace's mother is looking all over the place for her.'

The following afternoon Grace was asked into the sitting-room where her mother and father were both looking pleased.

'We've got some good news for you,' her mother said. 'Something we're very pleased about.' She squeezed Grace's hand as Grace sat down.

'What is it?'

'Nicholas has asked me for your hand in marriage,' her father said, 'and I have consented. We have hoped for so long that this might happen.'

'I was worried,' her mother confessed, 'especially after Henry Elling-thorpe, and now everything has worked out for the best. You won't have to leave here, I know how much you care about the place, goodness knows why. You won't have to move away. We'll see you every day—'

163

'And of course there's the business,' her father said. 'When you have a son he will inherit everything.'

'It's perfect,' her mother said.

'Mr Barmouth?' Grace said.

'I know he's a lot older than you are, but Grace, these things can be such a blessing,' her mother said. 'He understands what marriage is like and he'll be able to look after you and give you everything you need—'

The floor of the room had begun to do strange things, reminding Grace of how little she had eaten lately. Nothing kept still. She told herself not to faint, that only stupid women did such things but it was no good and oh, the blessed relief of nothingness.

'I thought that new corset was too tight,' her mother was saying as Grace came round.

She was on the sofa. Ruth was holding smelling salts under her nose. Grace pushed Ruth's hand away and coughed. Her father had gone. Mrs Jackson appeared with tea on a tray. Her mother tried to insist that she should eat something.

Grace attempted to explain that she couldn't marry Mr Barmouth but her mother only told her to hush until she felt better, and when she did feel better all she wanted to do was cry, so Ruth put her to bed and there she stayed, in the half-light, in the silence, trying not to think. Later her mother came to her.

'We'll have a big party for your engagement. Everybody will be invited and oh, Grace, I've got such plans. Wait until you hear what I think we might choose for your wedding dress but there, I think there's been enough excitement for one day. You rest, my dear,' and she leaned over and kissed Grace on the forehead, something she rarely did.

'I can't marry him, Mother.'

'I know that you don't love him, Grace, but I think that by now you must have learned from your first mistake. This will be a very good marriage for you, believe me. Nicholas adores you and there's nothing better than a devoted husband. I know. Everything will work out for the best. Do try to get some sleep, dear.'

Her head went round and round. The light faded and came again, the birds greeted the dawn. She dressed and went downstairs to catch her father before he went off to work and he smiled at her protestations, and when she accused him of not listening he said that he was perfectly willing to listen when she was feeling more like herself and patted her hand and went away to the office.

The autumn evenings were cutting in. Alexandra was glad of them. Now that she had no help there was so much to do. All that summer she had looked after the gardens herself, growing vegetables, digging flowerbeds, cutting lawns and hedges and in the early autumn the fruit had to be harvested. It was more important than ever this year.

The vegetables and the apples and pears were stored carefully, the plums were bottled and jammed and so were the strawberries and raspberries. When it was all over she was so relieved. To close the doors early and know that coal for the fire was one problem they did not and probably never would have was so comforting.

The pits were closed down: her father was like somebody else. He shut himself away, his life's work was over, the men had gone. He had no conversation. He sat over the fire. Alexandra was dreading the winter with him, he no longer wanted to socialise and the house was so big for the two of them. Worst of all her mother's portrait hung over the fireplace and seemed to look accusingly at her. Her mother had been like Grace, small and blonde and blue-eyed and very pretty. Alexandra, to her dismay, was just like her father.

One evening in early November when she was washing up in the kitchen there was a sharp knock at the back door. She had locked the doors early, it was dark and cold. Now she went over and said, 'Who is it?'

'It's me.'

She opened the door to Grace and by the kitchen light saw the wet tear-stained face turned up to her.

'Grace. Whatever's happened?'

165

Grace stumbled inside, went to the fire, held up cold hands.

'Is it your father? Your mother? Something awful? Tell me.'

Grace turned slowly from the range. 'Mr Barmouth wants to marry me.'

Alexandra would have laughed but for the fact that Grace was crying.

'Not seriously?'

'He came and asked my father.'

'Well, what an optimist,' Alexandra said lightly. 'How very conceited. How foolish. He's practically an old man. The lecherous person. I hope you sent him packing. It's not worth crying over, Grace.'

'My father has told me that I must.'

Alexandra stared.

'Whatever for?' she said.

'He doesn't want me to be an old maid and Mr Barmouth is so nice and so respectable and it would be so comfortable to have me near—'

'That would make you Nat's mother,' Alexandra said helpfully. 'You're not laughing. Your father doesn't mean it, Grace, he can't. And as for Mr Barmouth, he wants his head looking at.'

'He does mean it, they both do. I think really, it's all to do with business. Mr Barmouth is a lot younger than my father and naturally they don't want the business splitting and that would be nice and neat. Nobody else involved when I married.'

'He can't mean to.'

'My father's tired of me not being married. My mother is afraid that no one will ever ask again.'

'When they think it through they'll change their minds. They'll have to,' Alexandra said.

Grace said nothing.

'You haven't agreed to marry him?'

'They didn't ask me. They somehow assumed that I would. There's to be a big party at Mr Barmouth's house to announce the engagement, a surprise party.'

'Some surprise,' Alexandra said.

* * *

166

Alexandra went to see Nat. She hadn't intended going to see him but it seemed the only thing to do. When she went there it was impossible to be alone with him. The atmosphere in the house was so light and Alexandra envied that. Her house seemed to echo with emptiness and her father's sense of defeat and her loneliness. Grace was her only real friend and if she married Mr Barmouth that wouldn't last because he was so much older, and so were his friends. She would have to spend her time with them.

Nat offered to walk her home. She had known that he would. It was dark and bitterly cold and when they got to her house she asked him in.

'I think I ought to get back.'

'I have to talk to you. Come into the kitchen, it's warm in there.'

'I thought you seemed awfully edgy. What's wrong?' Nat followed her inside. 'Where's your father?'

'In bed, I expect. All he does these days is sit over the fire and then sleep.'

'Isn't there anything you can do?'

'What, do you mean financially? Take in washing? Start a school?' She took his coat and sat him down and poked the fire until the blaze was high. 'This isn't about money or about me.'

She sat down in the other comfortable chair across the fire from him and said bravely, 'You know the big party that Mr Barmouth is planning?' Nat didn't say anything but he nodded. 'It's to announce his engagement to Grace.'

The hard-gained peace of the past few months seemed to explode in Nat's head like a fire-cracker, to be consumed and lost in that instant, and after that he thought it was some kind of terrible joke.

'Nicholas marry Grace? He's . . .'

'Twenty-five years older than her. Yes, I know, but her parents have insisted.'

'They can't do that.'

'They have. She's stood up to them as best she could. They haven't offered her a choice.'

167

'She said she would?'

'I don't think she was asked.'

'But that's awful. He can't do that. He just can't. She's so young and . . .'

He got up and walked around the kitchen. He didn't say anything for a while and neither did Alexandra, and then he looked at her.

'There isn't a thing we can do.'

'Nat, there's got to be. She's talking about running away.'

'She can't. She doesn't know what anything's like.'

'Will you think about it?'

The next evening Nat went to the farm. Dennes was in the byre milking Bryan. Nat went in there and stood for a few moments, unsure what to say.

'Nicholas has asked Grace to marry him.'

Dennes looked up, stopped, stared.

'What?' And then he laughed. 'The dirty old bugger,' he said.

'She's going to.'

'She wouldn't do that, not in a million years.'

'Her parents have decided that she is.'

'You mean it, don't you?' Dennes finished milking the cow and they carried the milk up to the dairy. There was nobody around. Shona had gone into Bishop Auckland and was not back yet. They went into the house and had a glass of apple wine.

'It doesn't make any sense. Are you sure about this?'

'Positive. They think it's right for her, that's what Alex told me.'

'But she's so defenceless. She'll never stop them.'

'I know that. She's talking about leaving.'

'What, running away? She wouldn't get ten miles. They'd just bring her back.'

'We're having a big party at the house to announce the engagement.'

'Jesus.'

'I thought you might have an idea.'

'Like what?'

168

'I don't know. I can't think of anything short of dropping him into the furnace at work.'

'That's not a bad idea except that it would muck the steel up.'

'There is another way.'

'What's that?'

'You could marry her.'

'I could?' Dennes stared at him.

'Yes.'

Dennes said nothing more.

'You've thought about it, haven't you?' Nat guessed.

'Yes, but only in my worst moments.'

'How come?'

'Last time you were here . . . I made myself stop thinking about it, Nat. She's pure as the driven bloody snow and I'm . . . well . . .'

'You know what he's marrying her for, don't you? For the same reason as he married my mother. He'll bed her until she gives him a son.'

Dennes said nothing to that.

'Don't you fancy her, Dennes?'

'Yes, of course I do. Everybody who's ever met her fancies her. I just don't care about her like that, that's all. I like her well enough, I like her better than I thought I ever would, but to wed and bed a lass like that without loving her, it would be an awful thing to do.'

'Better that she marries him? Imagine what that would be like.'

'I don't want to.'

'If she runs away it could be even worse—'

'Will you shut up? I'm trying to think. It might not work, she might refuse.'

'Give over.'

'And old man Hemingway would never take me into the works.'

'She's his only child, what's he going to do? You do want revenge for what Nicholas did, don't you?'

'Not like that. Not through some bit lass who has no choice.'

'How did you think to get it?'

'I don't know, but not like that.'

169

'We've got nothing and I'm not going to let him do this on top of everything else. You know how he is, you know how he'll treat her, just like he did with my mother.'

'Your mother didn't love him. If she had done, it would have been all right and you know it,' Dennes said.

'Grace doesn't love him either and it's worse than that. My mother was nearly his age. She knew what marriage was like. Just think if Grace doesn't produce a child, or like her mother she only has one female child. Think what that would be like. Years of hell. There's something else as well.'

Dennes eyed him. 'You spent a long time working all this out, didn't you?'

'She wants you.'

'That's not true.'

'The other Sunday when we walked back from the farm she . . . she shone and she's been miserable ever since, not just because of Nicholas—'

'It was just a kiss. I don't think she'd been kissed much before, that's all.'

'Well, I don't think it is. I think she cares for you.'

'That's not a reason to marry her, Nat, that's a reason *not* to. I don't want to marry anybody. I'm going to stay on the farm with Shona and play cards and drink apple wine and get old. And never think about anything ever again. I couldn't leave Shona.'

'So you're going to let her marry him?'

'If you're so keen, you marry her.'

'And lose the other half of the foundry?'

Dennes looked straight at him.

'I like the way you say that. Why don't you just be honest for once and say you love the other lass?'

Nat smiled ruefully. 'What if Grace cares for you like you cared for my mother?'

'That would be the worst reason. Mind you, I'd do almost anything to stop him from getting what he wants.'

'Well then.'

'I couldn't do it. I don't want her. I don't want any woman. I never did want anybody but Gwen.'

Twenty-One

Grace couldn't sleep or eat. She had cried so much that she couldn't cry any more. She could no longer bear to be in the same room as Nicholas Barmouth. Worst of all, now that she had stopped protesting, her parents took for granted that she was reconciled to her forthcoming marriage. They did not see or want to see her unhappiness. He was there all the time and her parents welcomed him. Grace found herself being civil to him, making conversation, taking walks around the garden.

The engagement party drew nearer. At Esh House Mrs Appleby did what she called 'turning out the house' in preparation for the engagement party. Each glass of the chandeliers was washed, new curtains were bought and new rugs. Every time Grace and her parents came over to Sunday dinner the house looked brighter and cleaner and her parents and Nicholas looked so happy. Grace saw Nat's worried gaze on her. She knew that there was nothing he could do so she pretended. She smiled at him, forced herself to look happy, stayed close to Nicholas. The effort exhausted her but she couldn't sleep and even the idea of eating sickened her.

She had not imagined that time could go so quickly when you hated each minute. Her mother had new clothes made for her. She was constantly at the dressmaker's, standing still for hours while pins were put in and rearranged around her and alterations were made. Her mother talked excitedly about weddings. Nicholas bought her small expensive gifts, a wooden jewellery box lined with velvet with her name carved on the top, gold earrings set with coral.

Two days before the party he came to the house, and when they were alone in the garden he took her into his arms and kissed her.

With his hands and mouth and the nearness of his body, he replaced the kiss and the embrace which Dennes had given her. She panicked inside. It was as though even the memory disappeared. She tried to get away and he held her. He told her that he loved her, and his enthusiasm overcame the restraint he had so far shown her. It was not a disgusting kiss. On the contrary, it had experience, it had expertise, it spoke to Grace of things she knew nothing about. He smelled of cigars and expensive cloth; it was the smell of her father's study. She pulled back as hard as she could and he let go of her.

'I'm sorry. I shouldn't have. Not yet,' he said.

Grace muttered things, she didn't know what, and he took her back inside. She felt bruised and yet almost invisible, as though the person she had been was gone. Nobody cared what she felt or thought, nobody listened. They did not see her as she was, she was just something to hang fine clothes on, something to be admired, something to be bedded to breed.

When he had gone, when it was late and her parents were in bed, Grace packed. She took what little money she had, her jewellery and the clothes that she liked best, and when it was morning she walked to the station and got on to the first train that arrived.

It was early evening before Nat found out that Grace had run away, and that was only because Dolly had listened to Anthony Hemingway at the library door. He went to the farm to tell Dennes who was outside locking up the ducks and hens. The white ducks had to be persuaded inside, but they couldn't be left in case the fox got them. Sometimes it was a long process. Luckily Dennes was just shutting the door on them, and he stood in the cold dark evening and listened as Nat explained hastily. Dennes didn't say anything for a few moments and then, 'She'll

174

never survive. She doesn't know anything. Why the hell didn't they leave her alone? I don't understand. They bring the lass up to be useless and then force her into an impossible situation. What did Hemingway expect her to do, put up with it?'

'She could be anywhere,' Nat said.

'Somebody must know something. We've got to find her, Nat. She sticks out like a sore thumb, something'll happen to her. Doesn't Alexandra know where she is?'

'I don't know. I haven't seen her.'

They walked back to the village and to Alexandra's house. She answered the door herself and took them into the kitchen, but it was obvious that she did not know Grace was missing.

'Has she got friends to go to, relatives?' Dennes asked.

'Nobody, except an aunt in London, and I don't suppose she has the means to get to London. Her parents never give her any money. Where could she have gone?'

'Newcastle?' Nat ventured.

'We'd never find her there,' Dennes said.

'Durham maybe,' Alexandra said.

'I'll go there,' Nat offered.

'She could have gone to Darlington. She's been there before.'

'I'll try that,' Dennes said.

'Haven't Nicholas and her father got people looking for her?' Alexandra asked.

'I expect they have. Let's hope we find her first.'

Darlington was a familiar place, that was why Grace decided to go there. It was more friendly than Newcastle, just a mill town, a market town. She was stared at right from the beginning. Women of her looks and expensive clothes did not get on to trains alone, carrying bags. She ignored the stares.

It was a cold autumn day. She walked down from Bank Top station into the town itself. It had wide streets and big buildings. She wandered about High Row, the main shopping area, with her bags; there were few women about which made her even more conspicuous. It was mid-

175

afternoon by then and she imagined the women at home getting ready for tea. Her home seemed far away now.

She didn't like to ask the way to a hotel. Her bags were weighing heavily on her hands and arms. She turned off into side streets looking for a place to stay, somewhere that would take a young woman on her own, and as she did so somebody knocked into her, sending her bags flying. By the time Grace had recovered the boy had picked up her belongings and run away very quickly down the street and around the corner. Grace set off to run, protesting, but there was nobody about, her skirts hampered her, her hat came off and he was so much faster. By the time she got to the end of the road he had disappeared.

Grace wanted to sit down and cry. She didn't know what to do. She couldn't go to the police, they would send her home. She wandered the streets until the short autumn day drew to an end and the lamps made the pavements look eerie to her. Then she found a park and went in and spent the night there, cold and hungry, huddled well away from any prying eyes, policemen or anybody that might do her harm. It was the most fearful night of her life. She thought back to the fire in her bedroom, to her comfortable home, she thought of her mother's table and things back there didn't seem so bad until she brought to mind the image of Nicholas smiling at her.

The next morning, more hungry than ever and very frightened, she saw a notice outside a hotel offering work, and when she went in they set her on in the kitchen washing dishes. It was hard work and there was no respite.

She worked all day without anything to eat and by evening was so desperate for food that she felt faint. She began to eat other people's leavings. It made her feel sick but at least she didn't feel faint any more, and after a while the sickness left her.

The washing soda made her hands sore. Grace had not thought that the world contained so many dishes. It was well after midnight when she finished, only to be told that she would be paid at the end of the week.

'But I have no money,' she declared, and the fat little man who was the hotel proprietor looked her up and down.

'Nowhere to stay?'

'No.'

Grace remembered the night before, but when he showed her up two flights of stairs into a small room containing little but a double bed she wished that she had said nothing.

'There are other ways to make money,' he said. 'A bonny lass like you. I have customers who would pay well for a few favours.'

'I'm tired,' Grace said.

He went out and shut the door and locked it behind him.

Grace could feel the tears behind her eyes. She was more frightened now than she had ever been in her life. She felt hungry and dirty and wretched. She lay awake fully-dressed for a long time watching the door, certain that at any moment a man would appear. She fell asleep at last, exhausted.

The second day there was even worse. She was awoken early to begin work and spent all day and all evening in the kitchen being given nothing to eat. She ate everything which she found on the plates.

When it was very late she was taken up to the room again and locked in. It was, Grace thought, like a prison. They had kept watch on her all that day. She sat down on the end of the bed, she even lay down and dozed a little and then suddenly she was awake, starting at the sound of footsteps on the stairs, two sets, heavy, like men's.

Her gaze was fixed on the door. She got slowly to her feet and backed away. The door unlocked, there was talk and the hotel owner came in, smiling.

'There she is,' he said, as though Grace were a prize pig. 'You won't find a bonnier lass in all the north.'

Grace flattened herself against the far wall as the second man walked in. He was much bigger. He was young and tall and fair. Grace stood for a moment, unable to believe her luck.

'Dennes!' she said and began to smile, and although she had never done such a thing in her life she ran the short distance across the room to him and got hold of his arm, just in case he was a vision and was going to disappear.

'You can't do that,' the hotel manager said as Dennes guided her out of the room.

'Do you want the law on you?'

'You can't just take her out of here. I'll call my lads up from the bar.'

Dennes took his guiding hand off Grace's waist, and when she turned around to see he put the man up against the wall and stuck a nasty-looking knife under his chin. He walked the man downstairs like that and then let go just before Grace reached the outside door. He followed her outside.

She couldn't say anything, the fear was all mixed up with the relief and made her legs tremble. It was late and dark and very cold. Grace couldn't stop being frightened. She just wished herself at home in her own bedroom, and the more she thought about it, the worse her situation seemed to have been. She thought what might have happened and stopped there in the street. Dennes put an arm around her.

'It's all right,' he said.

'I'm so tired.'

'There's a hotel just up here. I stayed there last night.'

'I can't stay in a hotel with you.'

'Don't be daft,' Dennes said. 'Mind you, it'll have to be the one room. I haven't got much more money than our train fare home. I'll sleep on the floor.'

It was strange to Grace to be there alone with him. The little hotel was so friendly after the place she had just been. Nobody seemed to think it odd that after a night alone Dennes should bring her here with him. The woman behind the reception desk even smiled at her.

The bedroom fire was soon lit, and although it was anything but luxurious it was clean and neat. She stood there holding out her hands to the blaze. Best of all was the tray which had on it a great pile of beef sandwiches and two big pint pots of beer. Grace sat down on the one rickety chair by the fire and ate and drank, and she thought she had never tasted anything as good. She ate slowly and watched the flames, and Dennes took off his jacket and lounged on the bed. She had never been in a bedroom with a man before, and she thought that he could have been a stranger, that he could have paid money for her, that she would not have been able to stop him, that life could have become a long series of nightmares. She looked quickly at him and he smiled and the doubts vanished and the images went.

'Did my father send you?'

'He wouldn't send me, would he?'

'Nicholas then?'

'No. Mind you, they must be near to finding you. It isn't exactly difficult. They remembered you at the stations. Even some of the shopkeepers.'

'What did you say to the awful man in the hotel?'

'I asked him if he had a pretty lass around, that I was willing to pay.'

'How did you know?'

'I didn't, it was just a guess. I'd spent a lot of time over the past two days in shops and in pubs and on streets. It was such an awful place it just seemed the type. I was thinking about giving up and going home.'

'I'm glad you didn't.'

'I was thinking you must be somewhere else. I've got Nat in Durham doing the same and your father and Nicholas have men out looking for you. You're tired—'

'You don't think they'll find us tonight, do you?'

'How could they know? There are a lot of hotels here, Grace, don't worry.' He got off the bed and picked up his jacket. 'I'll give you a few minutes to get ready for bed—'

She stood up in alarm.

'Don't worry, I won't go far.'

'You can't sleep on the floor, Dennes, there's no carpet and the draught under the door is freezing.'

'I've slept on plenty of floors.'

'There isn't even an armchair.' The rickety dining chair she had sat on was surely only meant for people to put their clothes on. 'Just sleeping on the same bed can't hurt surely,' Grace said, 'and I'm frightened.'

'Take your time,' Dennes said and went out.

179

Grace was half-inclined to lock the door after him but she didn't. She took off her clothes and had a wash and put her underclothing and her petticoat back on again and then she went to bed. She turned out the lamp, lit one candle and lay watching the shadows which the fire made on the wall. She felt almost safe now.

When he came back he took off his jacket and his boots and lay down on top of the bed. Grace gave him a pillow and a blanket.

'Are you all right?' he asked softly.

'Yes. Thank you, Dennes.'

'No trouble.'

'Dennes . . .'

'What?'

'I can't go back.'

'We'll talk about it in the morning.'

'I didn't run away just to go back. They aren't going to make me marry him.'

'Nobody's going to make you do anything.'

Grace was turned towards him but Dennes wasn't looking at her. He was lying on his back staring up at the ceiling. He looked even better by candlelight. Grace had dreamed about having him to herself like this, but never in such circumstances. When she didn't say anything more Dennes looked at her.

'Don't worry,' he said.

'I am worried. If I go home, my father will force me to marry Nicholas. He will.'

'I won't let him. I promise. Now go to sleep. You have bags under your eyes like sacks of coal.'

'Did I thank you?'

'Yes.'

'I'm so grateful,' she said, and closed her eyes and went to sleep, warm, full and secure.

In the morning they ate a huge breakfast before they left the hotel. Grace felt much better after her night's sleep and the food. They went to the park, the same one where she had slept. She could not believe that she had done such a thing and to come here now with Dennes was so different, so much easier that it raised her spirits.

'Why did you come and find me?' she said as they sat down on a bench.

'I knew you'd have a hard time on your own and I wanted to talk to you.'

'What about?'

'About what you're going to do.'

'It doesn't involve you.'

'It could. Have you considered? Now that you've run away, Nicholas Barmouth probably won't want you. Will your father have you back?'

'I'm not going back.'

'You could stay here, find work and lodgings. I could help you with that.'

'I don't want to do that either.'

'What did you think you were going to do?'

'I didn't think at all. I just had to get away from him. He kissed me. He smokes cigars and he smells of them and— he smells old.' Grace wasn't looking at Dennes. She didn't like to talk to him about things like this. 'It was just so disgusting.'

'There is another way out.'

'What's that?'

'You could marry me.'

Grace looked at him then, but he had developed an interest in some people walking by at a distance.

'So that's why you came here,' Grace said. 'Why on earth would you do that?'

'Two reasons. Firstly, I hate Nicholas. It would give me a lot of pleasure to take you from him, and secondly because in the long run I would stand to gain a great deal.'

'You mean the foundry.'

'Yes.'

'That's very hardheaded of you, Dennes.'

'Yes.'

Grace got up. 'If you want the foundry and you hate Nicholas that

181

much why not say that in the first place? And if I want to stay here and find work and lodgings?'

'We could probably find something.'

'I'd be alone.'

'I'd bring Alex to come and see you.'

Grace sat down again and reached out slender fingers and touched his fair hair.

'When I was sixteen I would have given anything in the world to marry you. When Henry Ellingthorpe proposed to me all I could see was you. He was a terrible disappointment. He had blue eyes.' She drew back. 'You couldn't marry me. Shona wouldn't have me at the farm.'

'I'd leave the farm.'

'Do you mean we'd have one of those little houses off the main street?'

'Probably.'

'You'd make me go to bed with you.'

'You could have a room to yourself.'

'It would be an awful risk,' Grace said.

'If you want you can stay here. There was a sign in a dress shop window. We could get you a job and a room somewhere.'

Grace thought back over her life: her mother constantly telling her how lovely she was, the dressmakers, the clothes, thinking about her appearance all the time, being careful of her hands, being made to go around puddles, never getting dirty as a child, having her hair put into rags each night because it was naturally straight, trying to sleep on the rags and weeping, not being able to play with the local school children, not going to school, not doing anything useful, her mother telling her never to run. Her childhood seemed to her now to be filled with white and the constant danger of dirtying it.

'You really want the foundry?'

'Only half of it. I want Nat to have the other half.'

'You want to take everything from Nicholas?'

'Everything.'

Grace thought of Nicholas and her father not listening to her, not caring what she thought or felt.

'It might not work.'

'Possibly not.'

'Then you'd have to keep me for the rest of our lives. What if you wanted somebody else?'

'I won't.'

'How do you know?'

Dennes looked down.

'I don't feel like that,' he said.

'I'd have to cook and clean and look after you.'

'Couldn't you do that?'

'I think Alexandra would show me. I've never done anything like that, my mother wouldn't let me in the kitchen. I could have my own kitchen. I don't know anything about kitchens. I don't even know how to light a fire.'

'It can't be that difficult. Lasses not nearly as bright as you do all that.'

'Yes, but their mothers showed them how. You think I'm bright?'

'Of course you are.'

'Nobody ever told me that before,' Grace said, and laughed.

Twenty-Two

'I can't believe that you asked her to marry you.'

'I can't believe it either,' Dennes admitted.

They were staying out of Shona's way because Dennes hadn't told her yet. They were outside. They always, Nat thought, had their important conversations outside, mostly in the winter when you could hardly catch your breath for frost.

'I just couldn't let her marry him, that's all,' Dennes said.

'There must have been some other road—'

'There was. I could have encouraged her to get work and find a room—'

'She wouldn't have lasted a week.'

'I offered to help with that.'

Nat felt guilty now as though there ought to have been a better way out, as though he had sacrificed Grace for revenge and ambition and he knew that Dennes didn't want to leave here, to be without Shona's company, the animals, the comfort, the idea that it might last. He felt sick.

'I wish I hadn't talked you into it now.'

'There was nothing else to do, or if there was I can't think of it. She was in an awful state. You should have seen the place and that greasy little bastard, ready to sell her to somebody, anybody. She was so frightened. She'd had everything stolen, she hadn't eaten or slept and she was terrified to come back here and face her father and Barmouth.'

'So when's the wedding?'

'As soon as I can arrange it.'

'There'll be hell to pay,' Nat said. 'She's all either of them's got. They're going to be very angry and Nicholas will have a fit. He does love her.'

'Good,' Dennes said.

'What if he comes after you like he did before?'

'I'll risk it. I don't think he will.'

'Why not?'

'Pride maybe.'

'And old man Hemingway?'

Dennes grinned.

'They shouldn't have made her do it, should they?' he said. 'Can you imagine what kind of a foundryman's wife she'll make? I bet she can't boil a kettle.'

'You'll have to leave here and find a job.'

'I know. We'll manage, we'll get a house . . .' Dennes' voice trailed off.

'It won't be that bad.'

'She's not my style, and as far as I can see I'm not hers.'

'Well, she's the same age as you, she's twenty years too bloody young to be your style,' Nat said. He looked carefully at Dennes. 'Do you ever think that we would have been better off at the pub, you and my mother together?'

'She wouldn't. This is a very small town and I think she thought we wouldn't survive here like that and maybe she was right. And she wanted things for you and Dolly and Taylor. She wanted what you've got. We just have to remember not to let go of that.'

Nat went home.

Dennes went inside. Shona was banking down the fire.

'Has Nat gone without saying goodnight?'

'He realised it was late.'

'There's something happening, isn't there?'

'I've asked Grace Hemingway to marry me.'

'Really? I didn't know that you were that way inclined.'

'I'm not, but her parents want her to marry Mr Barmouth.'

'How very crude,' Shona said, wrinkling her mouth. 'Did you want to bring her here?'

'Of course I didn't, Shona, I'll get a job and a house.'

'I'd be sorry to lose you. The thing is, why should you marry her?'

'I owe Nicholas Barmouth.'

'Revenge is a very bad reason for marriage, Dennes, or do I mistake you and you're in love?'

'No, I'm not in love.'

'She's very beautiful.'

'That sort of thing doesn't matter to me. He'll make her miserable, Shona, I'm not going to let him do that. He did it to Gwen and it was awful to watch. All he wants Grace for is because she can give him a son. I don't think that's much of a reason for marrying anybody.'

'Isn't that the reason most men marry?'

'Is it?'

'You're decided on it, are you?'

Dennes had brought Grace back to Alexandra's house and there she stayed. Alexandra's father rarely moved from the sitting-room fire except to go to bed. She even took his meals to him in there. He had no interest in anything and though he must have known that Grace was there he asked nothing.

Grace didn't venture beyond the house during the time it took Dennes to find a job at a nearby steelworks, and a house, and to arrange a special licence so that they could be married. Grace had sent her parents a note saying that she was well and didn't want to be found and they gave up the search after almost a week. Nobody but Nat and Dennes knew she was there.

As Grace and Alexandra sat over the kitchen fire one night not long before the wedding, Alexandra said, 'You don't have to marry Dennes. You could stay here.'

'Do you think they would let me do that once they found out? Besides, I want to marry Dennes.'

'Are you sure?'

'He's the only person I've ever wanted to marry. Now I can. Will you teach me to keep house?'

Alexandra nodded but said nothing.

'It couldn't be worse than being married to Nicholas Barmouth,' Grace said.

'Nothing could be worse than that,' Alexandra agreed.

Twenty-Three

Nat would have given a great deal not to have become involved in what followed. Seeing Grace and Dennes was not easy because Nicholas had been so happy. Nat would have thought, watching Grace and Nicholas together, that it was obvious she cared nothing for him, but perhaps he was blinded by his own love. Nat was far from guilt-free about this.

Dennes got a job in a foundry nearby. The house that went with it was not ideal but at least they had somewhere to live. It was a two-up and two-down. It was an overstatement really to call it a house. It was a back-to-back and it was the house at the back of the street as opposed to the house on the front of the street. You went through a tiny, dark, dirty, wet tunnel to get to it. You stepped up into it from a yard which it shared with a similarly unfortunate abode. The yard sloped in the middle with a sink, and had at the far end of it a coalhouse and an outside lavatory. At one side was the huge end wall of the Variety Theatre and the yard went out and down a step into yet another back street not far from the railway. It was called Back Railway Street, which seemed fair enough to Nat, but it was known locally as Irish Back Street because of the number of Irish people still around. They had integrated themselves somewhat into the town, and clusters of them living side-by-side were not as common as it had once been.

Inside the house were just two rooms downstairs and a pantry. It had the steepest stairs of any house Nat had ever seen, and two small rooms upstairs.

Nat thought that if he had been Dennes he could never have taken a lady like Grace into such a house, but then it was not really a matter of choice.

From her attics and unused rooms Alexandra had found them a variety of furniture, some of it quite good, and linen and crockery and cutlery and a lovely Turkish rug. Shona had helped to provide what she could, and Nat bought them things, a clock and some candlesticks, and Dolly bought a rug which was really too nice to go in front of the kitchen range but was cheap by comparison to the very faded and old (though thick) Turkish rug which they put down in the front room. Goodness knows what the neighbours would think if they saw it, he thought.

Nat had told Dolly and Taylor what was happening almost from the beginning. He knew that they had been shocked by the idea of Nicholas marrying Grace, and that Dolly understood immediately that Grace did not want to marry him. Nicholas was no longer some father-like figure to Dolly. She saw him as a person now and that was not easy for her. As for Taylor, when Dolly had been shocked at the knowledge that Nicholas was intending to marry Grace and said, 'But he's an old man,' he had replied, 'Mam married him.'

'Yes, but Mam was old too. Grace isn't.'

More than once they all gathered at the little house in Back Railway Street and there in the yard Dolly whispered to Nat, 'Won't Grace hate it here?'

'I suppose she just won't hate it as much as being married to Nicholas.'

They were married on the first Saturday possible. Dennes had left the farm with many looks back. Only Nat and Alexandra went to the church; it was not the local church, Grace was too well-known there. Dennes had approached the new Primitive Methodist minister, who knew no one and seemed quite happy to perform the ceremony.

190

Miraculously nobody seemed to know, but this was probably due in part to the fact that Grace's first name was Beatrice. She had never before been glad of the fact, having hated the name. Now it proved a hiding place for her identity.

The chapel was so big and so empty. When it was all over they came out and stood around awkwardly. They had agreed that there would be no fuss or somebody would notice. They would notice soon enough. Nat walked Alexandra home and they parted company at her gate. She kissed him lightly on the cheek before going in.

Dennes and Grace went back to the little house in Irish Back Street and lit the fire and put the kettle on and didn't know what to do next. Dennes felt quite sick. He had never felt quite so sick. He didn't want any tea, he didn't want anything to eat. He wanted to run away back to the farm, back to Shona and the animals. Suddenly his idea to take revenge on Nicholas Barmouth seemed stupid and childish and unimportant, and this girl looked more out of place here than anybody anywhere else in the world could have done, he felt convinced. Besides that he had not even kissed her properly since their marriage, and he just wanted never to have to. She was so young, so trusting and innocent, she made him feel dirty even just to stand near her when she was so pure. He could not believe that he had suggested she should marry him, and yet when he looked at her he knew that there had been no alternative for her. However bad this was, it could not be half as bad as the day she married a middle-aged man whom she cared nothing for.

She kept looking at him and then away as though she could not believe it either, and when Dennes glanced around the room he wished more than anything that he could have taken her somewhere decent to live. He wanted to apologise for the house, he wanted to apologise for the wedding, he wanted to apologise for himself, but he couldn't.

They sat in the front room on a sofa which, like all the rest of their furniture, was much too good for the house. It was the most comfortable piece of furniture Grace had ever sat on, and big enough for both of them. She was a little bit apprehensive but Dennes was so easy to be with. He talked to her about inconsequential things. Grace didn't dare ask him if he missed the farm. She knew how much he had liked being there.

'We could ask Shona for Sunday dinner. Alexandra showed me how to make Yorkshire puddings.'

Dennes smiled at her.

'That would be nice,' he said. 'I found her a lad to do the milking and things. She can't do it all by herself any more, especially not this weather.'

Grace didn't care about the weather, in fact she was rather glad it was such a cold night. The fire burned merrily. Dennes would make good money. They would be all right, and if it was nothing like her life had been so far, there was a certain excitement in that.

Later on the bed came down in the front room which she had all to herself. She felt guilty about that because Dennes had suggested she should sleep there, as the fire made the room so pleasant. She tried to talk him into staying there with her but he said only, 'That wasn't the agreement. Let's just leave it as it is for now. You won't be frightened?'

Grace smiled in remembrance of this when she went to bed. How could she be frightened with him in the house? He could do anything.

She lay for a while watching the fire. In the street somewhere beyond someone was singing drunkenly, happily, almost melodically, Grace thought. In time she would make Dennes fall in love with her and then he would stay with her in the big bed by the fire and take her into his arms.

Nat wished that he could have been anywhere else in the world when Nicholas Barmouth found out that his bride-to-be had married a foundryman and gone to live in Irish Back Street. Nat and Dennes had talked about what might happen, that it would not take long before the discovery was made and in fact it was only the next day, Sunday afternoon. Anthony Hemingway came to the house and his voice was raised so that you could hear it well beyond the study.

'They'll probably have you killed,' Nat had told Dennes.

'They'll get somebody else to do it, like Nicholas did last time. He always gets other people to do his dirty work. Of course if he does he'll have Grace to contend with.'

This had not occurred to Nat. All depended now on whether Anthony Hemingway could distinguish between anger and hatred. If he couldn't, Dennes was in trouble. And Nicholas Barmouth would know for certain that Grace had never had any kind of regard for him.

That afternoon, possibly for the first time ever, Anthony Hemingway's carriage arrived in Irish Back Street, and from it two big men got out and hammered on the door. When Dennes answered it, the first said, 'Mr Hemingway wants you to come to the house.' He glanced at Grace as she stepped forward. 'Not you,' he said.

It was the first time that Grace had met lack of respect in the village and she stepped back. Dennes muttered reassuring words and went with them, half-expecting to be driven out of the village and dropped into the quarry, but nothing happened. At the Hemingway house they left him outside Anthony's library. Dennes didn't bother knocking on the door, it seemed superfluous. He walked in, but slowly, shutting the door behind him. Anthony was standing behind his desk, not far from the fire. It was a big, elegant room and there were so many books. Dennes loved it.

'Do enjoy looking around,' Anthony said, 'it's the last time you'll ever be in this house. Make the best of it.'

'I didn't ask to come here. You sent for me.'

'You took my daughter.'

'You make her sound like a parcel. You made it impossible for her to stay.'

'I didn't think she would ever do such a thing. I'm not sure why you married Grace. I don't think that I want to hear any lies from you and I don't think you're capable of anything else. Perhaps you were taken in by her beauty, much better men than you have been, and perhaps she married the worst young man she could find to hurt her mother and me because we tried to persuade her into a good marriage and if you choose you can tell her that yes, we are hurt because

193

she married a no-good bastard like you—'

'I don't use language like that in front of my wife,' Dennes said.

Anthony ignored the interruption. 'I think the real reason that you married her is because she was vulnerable and because she's the only child of people who have all the things you've never had, brains, respectability, money, so I'll tell you this. You'll never be in this house again, never accepted and you'll never see a penny of my money because I'm going to disown Grace legally. You've dragged her down as far as you possibly could. I wish you joy of her, keep her, she's yours.'

'Is that all?' Dennes said. 'You could have written me a letter.'

'I didn't know you could read.'

'I think I'll go now, Mr Hemingway, unless you're going to order the carriage to take me back.'

'Just think how lucky you are that I didn't have you beaten senseless.'

'Oh, I do,' Dennes said.

He walked slowly back. It was dark now and the pavements were frosty. He was quite hungry. He thought that she was probably sitting there in the dark, fire out, not a thought for a meal, frightened, crying, but when he opened the door of the house the lamps were lit, the fire was bright, there was an appetising smell of onions and meat and she was fussing over a pan of potatoes on the fire. She turned around and she was wearing an apron. It made Dennes smile.

'Well?' she said.

'Your father wishes us joy.'

'Does he really? He didn't cut your heart out then?'

'He couldn't, there's nothing there. My stomach's fine though. That smells wonderful.'

'I hope it will be,' Grace said critically. 'I have the feeling these potatoes are going to turn to mush before they're ready. They aren't good, you know.'

'I'll get some from Shona.'

'Did you see my mother?'

'No. Your father told me never to darken his doors again and that he wasn't giving us any money. Oh, and he's going to disown you.'

Grace sniffed, wiped a tear, put down the potatoes.

'He probably doesn't mean it,' Dennes said.

'He never says anything he doesn't mean.'

'How very boring,' Dennes said, and was rewarded by what was almost a smile.

'I wish things hadn't been like this. I wish I could have taken you home and my parents could have come to the wedding.'

'It never works like that.'

'I used to believe it did, didn't you?'

'No, never,' Dennes said.

She looked at him suddenly. 'What was that about your heart?'

'The way to it is through my stomach. Is the tea ready?'

Nat felt sorry for Nicholas. He didn't want to feel sorry for him but it happened and there was no way to deny the feeling. Nicholas shut himself into the study rather as he had done when Gwen died, and not just once. He stayed in there for longer and longer periods every night, and on the Saturday when the engagement party should have been taking place, Nat ventured in there very late to find Nicholas slumped in a chair by the dying fire with an empty whisky bottle beside him. Nat felt inclined to join in. Things got worse. The following morning he was called into the study and with narrowed eyes Nicholas said, 'You knew what was going on, didn't you?'

Nat hadn't expected this.

'Didn't you?' Nicholas said again, and before Nat could think of anything to say he came over and hit him hard with the back of his hand full over the face. No man had ever done such a thing to Nat before. The fights he had had were fair, with boys of his own age when he was younger, and since then nothing. He was off-balance somehow to begin with and went back into the bookcase just behind him. It hurt so much that he couldn't think.

'Answer me!'

'Yes, I knew.'

195

'How could you do such a thing after all I've done for you?'

'I didn't do anything.'

'No, you didn't. You didn't tell me, you didn't stop her, you . . .' He hit Nat again, only this time with the front of his hand, and just as he did so Dolly walked into the room.

She cried, 'Nat!' and ran over and got in the way, and Nat grabbed her by the waist and drew her out of Nicholas's reach, behind him.

'I suppose she knew as well, and your brother? All of you, laughing at me.'

'We weren't laughing,' Nat said from a safe distance.

'I took you in, worker's brats, all of you! You're ungrateful, ungrateful and disloyal.'

'Grace didn't want to marry you,' Dolly said.

'Be quiet, Dolly,' Nat urged her.

'You should have known she didn't. How could you think that she loved you? Her parents made it so that she had to do something.'

'Not him,' Nicholas said. 'Anybody but him. A girl like that, so lovely. He matters to you, doesn't he?'

'She loves him.'

Nicholas's eyes narrowed.

'That's not possible. I don't believe it.'

Nat didn't say anything.

'Are you trying to tell me that Dennes Eliot professes love for her?' Nat didn't answer. 'He did it from revenge then. You're not in a good position to play games, Nat. Answer me.'

Behind Nat Dolly was starting to cry. He turned around and took her into his arms, and then walked her to the door, opened it and pushed her out into the hall. Then he stood against it so that she couldn't get back in again.

'You're no better than him,' Nicholas said. 'I thought that you were, for a while, and all this time I trusted you and treated you like my son. You didn't really think that you were cleverer than me, that you could deceive me like that? You didn't really think so, did you, Nat? Well, you're going to have plenty of time to think about what you've done, because I'm going to throw you out and I'll see to it that nobody takes you in or helps you because if they do they'll suffer the same fate. Let's see how you like the street.'

The little house in Irish Street had already become a haven. Outside of it things went on in disharmony, people shouted, children cried, there were Saturday night brawls, but inside the four rooms Grace created magic. Dennes was interested enough in his work and his new workmates to be satisfied there and he made good money. They lived quite simply. She cleaned and shopped and cooked and saw Alexandra and looked after Dennes and it was the best way that she had ever lived. Dennes didn't interfere about how the house was run and however bad her attempts at cooking were he didn't complain. In fact he was the least difficult person Grace thought she had ever met. She realised now what her father was like, how fussy, how everything had to be exactly to his taste and exactly to his liking and how much of her mother's life went on around this, making sure that none of his acid remarks were voiced.

Grace was quite well aware by now that her very new husband was capable of the kind of remarks which would have dissolved stone but he didn't make them. He was careful with her and encouraging about what she did. Under this new and free way of living, Grace blossomed. He didn't tell her what to do or how to do it. He didn't tell her who to see or where to go. Alexandra came often to the little house and Grace soon became very proud of her shining house, her golden-topped pies and her delicious dinners. And Dennes was so complimentary. She didn't have to worry about what she wore or how she looked, she didn't get bored because there was plenty to do and she could do what she wanted when she wanted and go out as she chose, and she wasn't frightened any more. Dennes was a much bigger man than her father and they were living in a small house, but he didn't take up any room somehow. She felt as though the place was all hers. When he came home from work he was a delightful intrusion. He wasn't moody. He had taken to kissing her when he went out and when he came home, not necessarily on the mouth but just wherever he could reach as he went by, her hand or her cheek or once just under her ear. It made

Grace laugh and because they otherwise never touched she was aware
of him every second, how he moved, how he looked, what he said.

One evening that second week when Dennes was having a bath by
the kitchen fire, he shouted her name. Grace was in the front room
keeping out of the way. She had put all the hot water she had into the
big bath and hoped it would do until there was some more.

'Grace!'

'What?' She came to the doorway. 'There isn't any more hot water
yet.'

'I know that. Just come here a minute.'

A man without his clothes was a new area to Grace. He was quite
casual about such things, but Grace had been brought up in a house
where people only saw one another fully clothed. In a small house
these things were different.

'What?' she said, going over and not looking at him.

He reached out wet hands and pulled her down into the bath tub.
Grace screamed. The water went everywhere. He pulled her down on
top of him. Soaked, Grace thumped him.

'You fool!' she said.

'Is the water warm enough, Gracie?'

'Don't call me "Gracie". You're an idiot.'

'Give us a kiss then.'

'Dennes—'

'Go on.'

Grace looked into his green eyes and then his arms tightened around
her and he kissed her mouth like he had done that day at the farm. The
difference was that she had stopped him then. Now she didn't. He
drew her down very close and taught her how to kiss him. She didn't
stop his fingers from peeling apart her wet clothing so that he could
reach her shoulders and her throat and breasts. The kissing was a
serious business and so was the feel of his hands. In her imagination
there was a noise outside, quick footsteps through the passageway.
Somebody stepped up into the yard and banged hard on the door.
Dennes stopped kissing her, took his hands off her. The banging went
on and on.

Grace felt thoroughly foolish now as she got out of the bathtub and pulled her wet clothes around her and dripped her way to the door. When she opened it, Taylor was standing there. He didn't notice her disarray. He was actually crying and his words were incoherent.

By the time he was inside and the door was shut, Dennes was out of the bathtub and drying himself briskly.

'What?' he said as Taylor knocked the tears away.

'Our Nat.'

'What?' Dennes began throwing on his clothes.

'He said not to come for you. They knocked him about.'

'Who did?'

Grace was staring.

'Nicholas's lads. He threw us out – at least our Dolly and Nat. I wasn't there.'

'Where's Dolly?'

'On the front street. She isn't hurt but she was frightened to come through the passage.'

'Go and get her,' Dennes told Grace.

Dolly was huddled against the big doors of the Variety and she had been crying too. Grace put an arm around her and walked her through the passage and into the house.

'They've hurt our Nat bad,' she said, 'and he said not to come to you. He said if we did they would come.'

Dennes was dressed now. He put on his boots and his jacket and his cap.

'Come on,' he said to Taylor, and when they went out he slammed the door after him.

Grace put the kettle on, changed into dry clothes, mopped up the floor. Dolly helped her to empty the bath tub and when the area around the fire was free they sat down by the blaze and waited for the kettle to boil.

It was a cold night with a frost. Dennes felt it more keenly because he had just left a warm bath, a warm room and a warmer wife. They walked briskly down the street and took the quickest way through the back streets down to the bottom of Ironworks Road. Dennes would have run but he didn't want to draw attention to himself. He didn't stop that brisk pace until he came within sight of the gates of Esh House. They were closed and Nat was lying on the outside of them. Dennes got down beside him.

'Nat? Nat? I'm going to leave Taylor here with you and go for the doctor—'

Nat didn't move but after a minute or two he opened his eyes. 'I told him not to go to you.'

'Don't be soft.'

'I don't want a doctor. I can get up if you give me a hand. I'm all right.'

'Where does it hurt?'

'I'm all right.'

'You sure?'

'Just give me a hand.'

Taylor and Dennes got him on to his feet and very slowly, almost carrying him, began the long walk home.

They put down the bed in the front room, made up the fire and Grace bathed the cuts and bruises. Dolly was persuaded to go to bed. Taylor went up with her because she was still frightened. Grace tidied up in the kitchen. Dennes stood by the front room window with his back to the wall, and when it was quiet and Nat was as comfortable as he could be, Nat said to him, 'I don't want you going there.'

'There's not a lot you can do about that.'

'It was my fault.'

'You're just like your mother, everything's your bloody fault!' Dennes said.

'If you go there they'll kill you. That's why I didn't want to come here.'

'You stupid sod, Nat, where were you going to go?'

'I don't want him coming after you.'

'I don't know why he didn't. Why take it out on you?'

'I told you. It was as much my fault—'

'I'm going to put him on the bloody street before I'm finished with him and as for Hemingway—'

'He didn't do anything.'

'He did enough. He tried to marry his daughter to his partner so that they would have a child for his stinking bloody foundry like she was a piece of meat—'

'Love her, do you?'

'I don't love anybody!' Dennes said savagely and in the silence which followed he looked up. Grace was standing in the doorway.

'I think Nat should rest now,' she said.

Dennes turned to the window.

'Go to bed,' he said.

When Dennes left Nat he didn't go straight to bed, he was too angry to sleep. He walked down the yard and out into the back lane and he stood taking great breaths of frosty air. He thought back to his wife's sweet mouth and soft body. He thought back to having twice since then given her orders, and he knew that she had overheard what he had said to Nat. She would not come to him like that again.

He went back inside and locked the door, and looked in on Nat before he went to bed.

'You all right?'

'Yes.'

'You want anything, you shout. I'll hear. Don't worry about it, Nat, we're not going to let them win.'

Dennes was sleeping with Taylor who turned over restlessly at the noise as Dennes walked into the bedroom.

'He'll be all right, but it'll take a while.'

'Why did they bray our Nat up like that? He didn't do anything. I wish I'd been there.'

'I'm glad you weren't,' Dennes said. 'I would never have got both of you back here in that state.'

'Why, though? You were the one who did it.'

'He just happened to be there, I think.'

'Nat liked him, you know. Admired him. Wanted somebody like that. He liked working with him. It was you.'

'You want to blame me?'

'Yes.'

'Well, that's a first in your family. You're right, it was my fault right from the beginning.'

'I don't like you, Dennes.'

'Taylor, I could have been sleeping with my wife,' Dennes said, and he turned over and closed his eyes.

Twenty-Four

It took a long time for Nat to get better. Dennes got Taylor a job at the steelworks. Taylor didn't complain but Dennes knew that he hated it. Having had a taste of the office and a few years of good living, Taylor disliked the small house, the hard work and the new poverty. Dolly was no longer a young lady. She helped Grace to do the housework. She didn't complain either. Dennes wouldn't have stood for either of them saying a word and he thought they knew it.

Over the cold weather Nat slept downstairs, but when he was well enough he insisted on sleeping in the bigger bedroom with Taylor so that Grace and Dennes could have the privacy of a double bed in the sitting-room and Dolly could have the smaller bedroom upstairs.

Dennes said nothing about this arrangement, but he did not pretend to himself either. He had tried to be kind to Grace, but the house was so crowded that they were never alone together and she no longer smiled on him or encouraged him to kiss her when he went out or came home. He knew that he was not easy to live with any more. The anger that he had felt over Nat had had nowhere to go and was waiting for an outlet. The others treated him carefully. Nobody argued or contradicted him. Sometimes a silence fell when he walked into the house. Only when Nat was there did Dennes feel comfortable, and Nat became frustrated at having to stay still and off work until he was better.

The first night that Dennes and Grace went to bed together she turned away from him to undress. Dennes didn't want to make things any worse. He sat on the far side of the bed and did the same. It was such a relief to get out of his clothes, even though the air in the room was bitter. He got into bed. Grace was sitting in the lamplight brushing out her hair. She wore a white cotton nightgown, richer than anything a foundryman's wife would ever have been able to afford. It had embroidery at the neck with a tiny ruff with ribbon at the neck, and a big collar edged with embroidery, and ribbons and lace at the wrists. Dennes thought it was one of the prettiest things he had ever seen. She finished brushing out her hair and began plaiting it.

'Can't you leave it?'

'It would be all cots in the morning. I can plait it in the dark if the light's bothering you.'

'No. I like to watch.'

That made her turn slightly further away so that he couldn't see. Dennes turned over away from her and stayed like that even when she put out the lamp and got into bed. She did so carefully so that she wouldn't touch him, holding her breath as though he was a dangerous animal going to pounce. She lay there rigid, he could feel her, her breath ragged. In the end Dennes turned over and she jumped and drew back.

'What's the matter with you?' he said softly. 'What do you think I am?'

'I think you're cold and bad-tempered and nothing like the person you pretended to be.'

'I'm just angry. Nat got hurt and that was my fault. I should have known.'

'How could you have?'

'I knew what Barmouth was like.'

'Let it rest.'

'I can't. They had no right to hurt him like that. I did it. It was my fault right from the start. Nat didn't do anything.'

204

She was still as far away from him as she could get without actually falling out of bed. Dennes took his pillow and pulled off the top cover.

'What are you doing?'

'I'm going to go and sleep in the kitchen.'

'Dennes, it's cold. Dennes—'

He shut the door on her voice. She was right, it was cold and he was not used to it any more. It brought back the past, the fears, the dirty smells of the house, trying to keep Joseph warm, trembling, waiting for her to call him. Everything mixed up in his head, the cold floor under the mat, feeling guilty all these weeks over Nat. He dreamed how things used to be, his mother drunk and laughing, the awful feeling of never having enough to eat, being knocked across the room by some man who was staying, Joseph crying and the kitchen floor by the dead fire on a winter's night. His mother was calling him from her bedroom.

'Dennes. Dennes.'

He awoke. Grace was standing there with a candle, touching his shoulder and saying his name.

'Come back to bed.'

He went. The bed was so soft and warm that it made him shiver at first. Grace kept well away from him. Dennes curled up and went to sleep.

The following night Nat was restless. He wandered downstairs in the middle of the night when the fire was banked down and the house was cold. He was half-dressed, shirt and trousers, and was beginning to wish that he had stayed in bed when he heard the front room door and Grace walked in. She put down her candle and smiled at him.

'I thought I heard you. Let me build up the fire and I'll make you some tea. You're not in pain, are you?'

Nat shook his head and then he sat down and watched her bring the fire back to life, swing the kettle over it.

'Dennes blames himself, you know,' she said.

'Nicholas was drunk, he's been drunk ever since. He wouldn't have done that otherwise.'

'They beat you very badly.'

'People love to see other people brought down.'

'You care.'

'What about?'

'About Mr Barmouth, about losing the foundry. About other things perhaps.'

'About other things particularly.'

'So why did you do it?'

'I couldn't let you marry Nicholas. I saw what he did to my mother. I didn't think he would go this far. I misjudged him. I thought he cared sufficiently about us not to do this. Gambled and lost. I should have known, of course. He did the same kind of thing to Dennes when my mother died, though not nearly so brutally. He didn't hate Dennes as much as he hates me.'

Grace put her fingers up to his cheek and reached up and kissed him.

'Do you have to go into the kitchen in the middle of the night and make up to Nat?' Dennes grumbled when she got back into bed.

'What are we going to do?'

'I don't know yet. I'll get Nat a job.'

'And then what?'

'I don't know. We might have to stay here for always like this. Wouldn't that be lovely?' Dennes said.

Shona came to Sunday dinner very often. She brought wine and eggs for them, sometimes a chicken, butter or milk. That Sunday, it was April by now, she asked them when they were seated at the kitchen table what they were going to do to make money now that Nat was better.

'I thought I'd get him a job at the steelworks,' Dennes said. 'Why, have you got another idea?'

'I think there might be sharp sand up on the fell above the farm. People have wanted to go there before and look for it. I wondered if you might be interested. If somebody could find it and get permission from the church they could drill.'

'A quarry, you mean, on your land?'

'Wouldn't it spoil the look of things?' Grace said.

'A fell's a fell,' Shona said. 'Mind you, I don't know anything about it.'

After dinner Dennes and Nat walked up there. It didn't look like a place where anybody could make a living, Nat thought when they reached the fell top above Shona's farm. It gave a new meaning to the word 'bleak'. The wind blew low across the heather so that the whole thing was a rippling mass, and there was nothing to see for miles but sheep and the odd stone shelter.

Nat looked hard, as though some miracle might appear. A miracle was what they needed now, he thought. He had sacrificed the home that his mother had provided for himself and Dolly and Taylor for revenge and ambition. Dennes had sacrificed Shona and dearly-bought peace of mind and the farm, and now they had nothing. But the biggest sacrifice of all had been Alexandra Covington. It had sometimes seemed to Nat that if things had gone on as they were, if Nicholas had believed in him, trusted him, treated him like the son he so desperately needed to be and taken him into the foundry with a future, he could have gone to Alexandra Covington and asked her to marry him. He knew that she liked him, he knew that she wanted him, he didn't know any more than that; he had never been sure of her because she had been for so long so far above him, and now she was back there and he was back here and she was out of reach just the same as ever. It was true that she occasionally came to the house, but he couldn't talk to her any more because he had given her up. And it was not as though Grace was happy. Dennes was incapable of making anybody happy now, his guilt weighed so heavily on him that Nat thought he had rarely seen anyone so cold and angry. They couldn't even talk about it, because it was not just the way that Nicholas had treated Nat, it was all the rest. It was the way that Dennes had loved Gwen and ruined her marriage, how Nicholas had therefore tried to win another woman whom he loved, and there Dennes had again been in the way. There was no way out of this, just Nicholas enraged, calling on the Irish boys with their sticks and boots and hatred of anyone who had any more than they had. They had enjoyed it. Their laughter had rung in his ears for weeks. They had loved his pain and his cries.

Dennes was standing there looking blankly across the fell.

'Do you see anything?' Nat said.

'I see a lot of hard work.'

'That's what I thought.'

'It would take money. We'd have to keep on working at the foundry as well.'

Shona had said that she would loan them some money to get started.

'It could work,' Nat said. 'There's a big demand for this kind of stuff.'

'Depends how much there is. There'd be all sorts of problems. We'd need horses and . . . how far is it to the railway line from here? What are you smiling at?'

Nat was, though he hadn't noticed.

'You want to do it, don't you?'

'It's the quality of the sand that matters, you know.'

'I do know.'

'Do you?'

Dennes started to laugh. He cuffed Nat round the ear and Nat thumped him in the chest, but when they went home to Irish Back Street Nat was happier than he had been in a long time. Only Taylor had nothing to say, and when Nat was able to get him by himself in the front room and ask him what he thought of the scheme, Taylor said, 'I don't know what we're doing here. I don't understand why we had to get mixed up in this in the first place.'

'Did you want Grace's father and Nicholas to make her marry him?'

'It's nothing to do with us, Nat. It's not our problem. We've lost everything, and for what? We're worse off now than we've ever been. It's Dennes' fault, he admits it. We had a nice home, good work that we liked, the chance to manage a steel foundry, and now what have we got? Nothing, and Dennes telling us what to do. The next time he tells me what to do I'm going to shut his mouth for him,' and Taylor walked out of the house. Nat went back into the kitchen, but he did not imagine that the conversation had been lost on Dennes who didn't even look up.

They went ahead with the idea of the quarry. Beginning was quite complicated. There had been geological surveys done of the area; most of the sand was buried close to the surface and would not be difficult to find. Permission to drill and test-bore to find the depth and quality of the sand had to be given by the mineral agents of the Church Commissioners, to go on to the land and take samples from it. This took time, to find out whether the sand was there in sufficient quantity, and when it was they had to lease the quarry on a royalty basis for so much a year and so much a ton.

In the meanwhile they also worked at the steelworks to gather as much money as possible. They lived as cheaply as they could. Grace found this difficult, Nat knew, but Dolly was used to it and taught her how to feed a lot of people on little money. It wasn't exactly exciting but it did help. Grace got rather thin and white under the strain.

When Nat and Dennes stopped working at the steelworks, Taylor kept on so that they would have one wage coming in, and that was when the hard work started. They had to put a road in. Every day they worked in the bottom of the quarry to make money, and at night they dug the road. Because it was a peat bed the road kept disappearing. It was like working backwards, sometimes twenty hours a day just to keep things going. Often they didn't go home at all, but slept a few hours in the small tin-sheeted buildings they had erected for shelter, and to protect the sand, and for the mill. The sand had to be dry, the wetter the sand was the harder it was to mill. Dry sand flew through the mill.

Quarrying was the hardest thing Nat had ever done. The physical effort of actually getting out the rock in the first place was enormous, removing the various strata above it and then carrying the sand to the mill a few tons at a time with a horse, breaking the rock from oversized pieces and then shovelling it by hand into the mill.

All that autumn and throughout the winter they worked seven days a week as many hours as they could bear. When it was wet the sand clogged up the holes and could not go through the mill. Hard frosts made the stone harder as well. The winter was so bad that getting up and down from the quarry was almost impossible and the work was excruciating in the cold weather, drilling and blasting and hand-shovelling while the weather did its worst around you. There was nothing to stop the biting winds, the snow, the sleeting rain and the sheer cold up there on the fell top. When they did come home to warm baths and soft beds and hot meals, Nat could have cried with gratitude.

Taylor was still working at the steelworks but there was little money. Neither Grace nor Dolly mentioned it, but when Nat questioned him Taylor got up and walked out of the house into the winter night. Nat caught up with him in the back lane.

'What have you been doing with your pay?' he said.

'It's my pay, isn't it?'

'It isn't yours. Not a penny of it. Taylor, we're starting to make some and there will be enough, but just at the moment there isn't. We owe Shona a lot for what she lent us. We have to pay her back before we can make a profit. Now give me your pay.'

Taylor dug into his pocket and produced some coins.

'Is that all?'

'That's all, yes.'

'What did you do with the rest?'

'I went for a drink.'

'A drink? You don't go drinking again, do you hear me?'

'You're not my bloody father, Nat!'

Nat took him by the jacket lapels and banged him up against the wall hard.

'Next time you don't bring your full pay home I'll bray you,' he said. He hauled Taylor up, and Taylor wrenched free and ran down the road. Nat went back inside. Dolly's eyes faltered.

'You didn't tell me he got drunk.'

'You want me to tell tales on my brother now, do you?' she said and ran upstairs.

Nat turned to Grace. 'He got drunk.'

'He's having a hard time, Nat.'

'We're all having a hard time.'

'Yes, well he didn't ask for it,' she said.

'And I suppose you think we did?'

'Don't start on her,' Dennes said.

'You could try treating him like an equal,' Grace said.

'What does that mean?'

'You don't, you two. You treat him like an inferior person. Like you treat Dolly and me.'

'We do not!' Nat said.

'Yes, you do.'

Nat wasn't used to arguing with women. His sister wouldn't have dreamt of it.

'How many times has he been drunk lately?'

'You aren't here.'

'How many times?'

'Nat, ease off,' Dennes said.

'I'm going to bed,' Grace said and walked out.

'That's the entire family, Nat. I could do with getting drunk myself. Are you sure it wasn't envy? I'd give a whole lot for a pint.'

Grace came back into the room and put a handful of money on the kitchen table.

'What's that?' Dennes said.

'It's my grandmother's pearls.'

'They were all you had.'

'Here, go to the pub and have a drink.'

'I'd choke,' Nat said.

'Dennes, here.' She put some of the money into his hand. 'Take him to the pub before he gets any worse.'

Dennes took the money and ushered Nat out of the door, but that night when they were in bed and she was almost asleep, Dennes said softly, 'When I have some money I'll buy you some pearls.'

'I don't like pearls.'

'Something you like then.'

'What I like is not to be treated like a fool and for Nat not to take things out on his brother and sister,' Grace said.

It was at about this time that Peter Clifford, the doctor's son, came home from Oxford. He was now a doctor himself and had joined a

211

practice just this side of Durham. He was a very pleasant young man, and he and Alexandra met up several times at the few social evenings which she attended that spring. She missed Grace. Going to the little house in Irish Back Street was not much pleasure. Grace was obviously unhappy, and because Dolly was there they could not talk. Grace would not or did not have time to go walking, so Alexandra had had to look elsewhere for company. She missed Nat too because he and Dennes were always at the quarry, and now that Nat and Grace were no longer her social equals her father did not like her going to see them. She had thought that he would not notice but he did, and people told him that she went there. It was all very unsatisfactory, so when she ventured to a small dance and Peter was there and asked her if she would dance with him, Alexandra was flattered and accepted.

She soon grew to like him. He was educated and intelligent, he was interesting. He was a gentleman, he knew how to look after her, he liked books, he liked her. Sometimes on Sundays he came over in the afternoons and spent an hour or two over tea, talking and laughing. He loaned her books, he talked about his work. When the spring came they saw one another regularly, and when Alexandra did venture to the little house in Irish Back Street she told Dolly and Grace all about him. Alexandra was no longer lonely, she was happy now. She dreamed that her life could work out, that Peter might ask her to marry him. She pictured herself in a pretty house in Durham with a garden and roses and a child. She thought of how she would run the house, make wonderful meals, talk to Peter about his work, organise dinner parties.

One Sunday afternoon when Peter had had to go to work, she waited until after dinner and walked along to see Grace. Grace could hardly be working on a Sunday afternoon, she might even have time to go for a walk. It was a warm day, the flowers were all out.

When she got there the house was silent but the back door was open as usual so she ventured inside. Nat was sitting at the kitchen table with papers scattered in front of him and there was nobody else about. Alexandra hadn't seen him much since he had left Esh House. He looked thin and was frowning, but when she went into the house he put down his pen and smiled and offered to make her a cup of tea.

'Where's Grace?'

'They've gone for a walk. You've missed them, to Shona's, I think. Dolly wanted to see the lambs.'

Nat hadn't much to say. Alexandra couldn't think.

'I hear you're seeing Peter Clifford,' he said finally, as she sat down by the fire in an easy chair which had once been her grandmother's.

'Yes, he's . . . he's working today. Doctors, you know.'

'Yes.'

Nat said nothing more and Alexandra was reminded uncomfortably of the night they had danced together, and how he had kissed her as though he couldn't wait another minute to do it. Peter had never kissed her. She wished that he would.

'How's Nicholas?'

'He's drinking a lot, so my father says. He's dismissed the servants, everything is just left. You must miss it all, the house and the foundry and everything.'

'Yes, I do.'

'Grace's father hasn't been very well lately. I thought I would come over and tell her. He hasn't been to work for a fortnight. Quite often Nicholas isn't there either.'

The frown returned to Nat's face.

'That must make things very difficult.'

'I'm sure it does. How's Grace?'

'Fine.'

'Is she? She works much too hard.'

'There's a lot to do and we aren't much help, trying to get the quarry going and make some money.'

Alexandra ran out of conversation before she had half-finished her cup of tea. She had never thought to have a stilted conversation with Nat. He obviously didn't want her there, though she was not sure why, and she couldn't look into his cool blue eyes without remembering how he had kissed her. She left as soon as she could and walked around by the doctor's house to see whether Peter was home, and when he was she was invited and stayed to tea. She liked his parents, they were the kind of people she would have wished for herself. His father talked to

213

her and made her laugh, his mother encouraged her to eat chocolate cake and told her how pretty she looked and Peter smiled and ate cake and drank tea and Alexandra could not help comparing Peter and Nat. Nat had made her feel uncomfortable, Peter would never have done that. He talked freely and easily to her, asked questions about what she had been doing and later when his mother and father left them alone he took her carefully into his arms and kissed her. Alexandra was so pleased, it was the kind of first kiss which every girl dreamed about, gentle and cautious. It didn't make her head spin and her lips smart, and there was no hand at her back urgently pressing her into his chest, but after Peter had walked her home, when it was late, she thought how thin and silent Nat had become. She wasn't altogether happy about having walked away from the little house in Irish Back Street, her half-empty teacup placed on the kitchen table.

It was the following week that Dorothy Hemingway came to see Grace. Nat had told Grace that her father was ill and Dennes had urged her to go home and see him, but Grace didn't feel that she could do so until she was asked. She had waited patiently for a message, so when her mother came she ran into the yard and hugged her.

'Mother! I'm so glad you came.'

She tried not to notice how her mother looked distastefully around the house.

'I'm glad to see you, Grace, how are you? You look lovely but then you always look lovely.'

Grace wished that the front room fire had been lit, but of course it was not, it being mid-week, and it was too cold to take her mother in there.

'How's Father?'

Her mother's eyes filled with tears. 'He's very hurt, Grace.'

'Yes, I know. I'm sorry.'

'How could you? How could you marry a man like that? Is he kind to you?'

Grace considered. She didn't see Dennes much any more, he was at work except on Sundays, and if it was fine, even then. They needed to work as many hours as they could. Dennes wouldn't argue with her. Sometimes he teased her and called her 'Gracie'. The only time they were really alone now was in the bedroom, and there he very carefully turned away from her and went to sleep. He never touched her. But he was not unkind. They didn't have much money yet, but he never kept a penny of it. She didn't remember the last time he had had a drink. Quite often he brought things home from the farm, milk and butter and eggs, sometimes chickens, and if he had free time he went to the farm and shot rabbits or pigeons so that they would have meat at the weekends. He was, Grace thought now, the very opposite of her father. He would never have shouted at her in front of anyone and certainly hadn't in private, he didn't try to bully her or humiliate her or make her do anything he wanted. He never complained about anything, he constantly admired the meals that she made and he was cheerful. He made her laugh. He never lost his temper except with Nat, and if they were going to shout they went outside. Sometimes from the back lane she could hear swearing but it was never in front of her, and although Taylor said Dennes was awful to work with and yelled all the time, Grace had no evidence of it.

'He's very kind,' she said.

Her mother stared. 'Indeed?'

There was something else too. Twice lately he had had bad dreams; she had awoken to find him urging her out of bed because he thought that the roof was falling in, and each time it had taken her minutes to convince him that everything was normal.

'Your father isn't well,' Dorothy said. 'Ever since you left he hasn't been the same.'

'I'm sorry,' Grace said.

'I don't mean to blame you. I know you think we were wrong. We thought we were doing the best thing. Are you happy?'

'I am now. You will stay and have a cup of tea?'

Her mother said that she shouldn't, but she did, and Grace made tea and proudly gave her mother a piece of cake which she had made herself. They talked of inconsequential things, but her mother hugged her before she went home and Grace was so happy that when the men came home that Saturday evening she ran to tell Dennes. He wasn't there.

'Where's Dennes?' she said, looking behind Nat.

Nat glanced at Taylor. 'He went for a drink.'

'What, now?'

'He said he wouldn't be long.'

She spent the evening watching for him, not realising until then that she had been looking forward to him coming home. They ate, the evening darkened and finally she went to bed. And then he came home. She heard the voices in the kitchen, Dennes and Nat. She put on a dressing-gown, a very nice Oriental silk one which had been Alexandra's mother's and much too small for Alex, and she ventured barefoot through the door. They stopped talking abruptly when she walked in. Dennes didn't look to her like somebody who'd been drinking.

'You're very late,' she said.

'Oh, don't you start. I can go out, can't I?'

'You didn't come back for tea.'

'I wanted a drink.'

'A drink?' Nat said. 'You're as bad as Taylor.'

'It's none of your bloody business.'

'You must have had a pailful,' Nat said.

'So?'

Grace looked hard at him. She had seen people drunk, falling over, laughing, swaying, speech slurred. There was no evidence of that.

'It costs,' Nat said.

'Oh, don't bloody start that again.'

Grace flinched over the swearing. She was quite well aware that they did that when there was only the two of them, she had overheard it before, but never in her presence.

'We haven't got that much of it.'

'Oh, shut your face,' Dennes said, and she began slowly to realise that, sober, he would not have spoken to Nat in such a way in front of her.

'Ignore Nat,' she said. 'Come to bed.'

'He's always going on about money.'

'I know.'

He went happily with her, went to bed and was completely silent.

He didn't get up the next day which was Sunday, and she left him there. After dinner he came into the kitchen, dressed and silent. Grace was darning socks by the kitchen fire. It was a job Dolly had taught her. She hated it.

'Is there anything to eat?' he said finally.

'No.'

'Do you want me to apologise?'

'No, I like you to come home late, drunk and foul-mouthed.'

'It was only once.'

'Is that meant to be an excuse?'

'I don't have to excuse myself to you.'

That was too far and Grace knew it. 'Did something happen?'

'Like what?'

'I don't know, that's why I'm asking.'

Dennes actually smiled. 'That would be nice and simple, wouldn't it?' he said.

'I'm just trying to help.'

'I don't need your help,' he said, and walked out.

He didn't come back. Tea-time came and went. She imagined him coming back late and drunk again, but although it was late he was sober and Grace knew now how to recognise the difference. She was in bed, turned towards the window and didn't speak to him. He came round to her side of the bed and sat down. The curtains were opened, Grace liked them that way and the night was not dark.

'Don't be cross,' he said softly, 'I won't do it again.'

'I don't care what you do,' Grace said, turning her face towards the pillows.

He got up. He undressed and slid into bed and went to sleep. Grace was inclined to hit him. The only time they ever saw each other was on Saturday nights and Sundays, and in spite of everything she looked forward to these times. She had been so happy after her mother came and now he had spoiled it.

* * *

Grace was frantic to go home and see her father.

'You can't just go,' Nat said, 'your mother will send for you if he'll see you. You know she will.'

It was the following month. Dennes had been very late back that Saturday night again, though he had not been drunk, and they were hardly speaking. She wished he was there so that she could talk to him.

'Do you think it's something serious, Nat?'

'If it had been she would have sent you word, wouldn't she?'

'She said when she was here that he wasn't well, but she didn't say much. I feel as though I've done it.'

'Did she say that?'

'She implied it.'

'You can't be blamed for that. They didn't leave you much choice.'

'Why doesn't Dennes come home?'

'I don't know. Don't you know?'

'We aren't talking, not really,' she confessed.

'Why?'

'I got angry.'

'When he got drunk? It was only once, Grace.'

'You were angry,' she said.

'I was thinking about the money, as usual.'

Dennes was very late back, the house was quiet. As far as she could tell he wasn't drunk, and when he got into bed she had a better chance to judge because he said, 'Don't pretend you're asleep.'

'I wasn't pretending. Where have you been?'

'Nowhere, just out.'

'You're awful to me,' Grace said.

'No, I'm not. You don't know what awful is. You have no idea what men can do to women,' and he moved away and turned over and went to sleep.

The following day was Sunday. After they had eaten he said to her, 'Will you come for a walk with me?'

'No.'

218

'Grace, you don't like it when I don't come back, and when I do you still don't like it.'

'I don't want to be with you.'

She was washing up and he was standing behind her, and when she turned around he had his hands at either side of her so that she couldn't get out of the way.

'You are with me, we're married.'

'You don't care about me.'

'I do care about you.'

'No.'

'Oh, come on, Gracie. We can go on to the fell, over by the stream—'

Grace stood like a stone. 'No,' she said.

He stood back.

'All right. What would you like to do?'

'Nothing.'

Dennes walked out of the kitchen without a backward glance. Grace couldn't move, she was so upset.

He came back in the middle of the evening. Grace had cried most of the afternoon, had braved tea with the others and then retreated to the front room. Nat had tried to talk to her but Grace couldn't. She was lying on the bed facing the window, and she didn't turn or speak when Dennes walked in. He didn't walk straight in, he hesitated in the doorway and then slowly closed the door. He sat down on the bed.

'I didn't mean to make you unhappy.'

'Well, you have.'

'Yes, I know. I can try harder.'

'I don't want it to be like that. I thought you would love me. Other men did.'

'No, they didn't. They just wanted to lift your skirts.'

'What a dreadful thing to say.'

'There's more to love than passion.'

Grace turned over and looked hard at him.

'How would you know? You're hurtful and condescending and arrogant.'

'I don't think I want to hear this.'

219

He got up and left the room and banged the door. He didn't come back. Grace wished that she had not said everything that she had said. She didn't see him all week, and that Saturday night she was in bed when he finally came home. At least he was sober. She didn't even acknowledge his presence when he came to bed, and it took Grace a long time to get to sleep in the pale summer night. And then it seemed that she had only just got to sleep when she awoke in that way in the night that is instant awareness, and she knew why. He was talking out loud, nothing intelligible, just denial. She thought at first that it was the same dream, the roof coming in, and that he would grab hold of her as he awoke and try to pull her out of the bed but he didn't. He sweated and shook and said 'no' several times until Grace got hold of him.

'Dennes. Dennes!'

He opened his eyes to the still summer night and Grace forgot that they had been fighting on and off for weeks. The look in his eyes made her reach out, but he turned face down into the pillows.

'Was it the roof dream?' she said.

'No.'

'What was it then?'

'Nothing.'

Grace reached out and touched his back and he said, 'Don't.'

'Dennes—'

'Just leave me alone.' He moved as far away as he could without actually falling out of bed. Grace couldn't get back to sleep, and she didn't pretend to herself that he was sleeping either. He got up early and went to work before anybody else was awake, and a little later when she was sure he had left the house Grace got up too.

During the afternoon, as she was ironing, a message came from her mother to go to the house.

'Shall I come with you?' Dolly offered.

'I think I should go by myself.'

Dolly hugged her.

'I hope he'll be all right,' she said.

It was strange going back to the house as a visitor. It was in its full

220

summer splendour. Grace ached for how long she had not been there, for how she had left. Her mother welcomed her, smiling and took her upstairs. When Grace saw her father she knew how ill he was.

'He doesn't always remember everything,' her mother said gently. 'He's not going to die, he's just not well.'

He had lost weight, he had lost his colour but he smiled briefly when he saw her and held out his hand. Grace sat down at the side of the bed.

'You haven't brought that boy with you, have you?' he said.

'No, I . . . I haven't brought that boy. He's at work.'

'Where does he work?'

'He's started quarrying sharp sand. You remember.'

'He was always a good worker,' her father said grudgingly. 'So's Nat. Nicholas should take Nat back. He's all the son there'll ever be now.'

'Will you take Dennes back?'

'He spoiled his own life and now he's spoiled yours. There's no real good in him, Grace, he'll never make anything. You look tired.'

'I didn't sleep well, it's the summer nights.'

But her father was soon tired, Grace could see. She kissed him and left him to sleep and then she went downstairs to the sitting-room and had tea with her mother. She ventured to the window. Her home had the best views of anywhere she had ever been, she thought, the hills in the distance, the rose garden which her mother loved so much, the lawns paling from the summer sun.

'Do you see Mr Barmouth?' she said.

'He's not well either. You young people, you're so resilient.'

'You're not that old, and neither is he.'

'He doesn't go to the works any more and now your father can't. It's left to the men.'

'Nat could help. Father said Nicholas might take him back on. He didn't do anything.' Grace knew very well that Nat would have given anything to go back to Barmouth's foundry. 'He spent a lot of time in the foundry, and Taylor didn't do anything either.'

'They let themselves be influenced by . . . by your husband, Grace.

221

How could you marry him, he's so low.'

Dennes came home promptly from work on Saturday and ate his tea with them, though it could hardly be seen as an improvement on the drinking and the absence since he had nothing to say and didn't touch her. That night he had the dream again. Grace didn't wake him, she watched him sweat through it until he woke himself.

When he finally woke up, he turned face down into the pillows and lay still for a while, and then he turned over and looked at her.

'You could have woken me. Or did you sleep through that?'

'Last time I woke you you told me to leave you alone.'

'I must have been a braver person then,' Dennes said with a shudder.

'What's the dream about?'

'Nothing much. I'm running along a hall somewhere.'

'And what happens?'

'Nothing, it just goes on and on. Endless. I want to stop but I can't. I never get there and I don't wake up.'

'Maybe it's Esh House.'

'Maybe.'

'Or have you lived in other houses with halls?'

Dennes didn't answer that. He got out of bed and put on his clothes and left the house. Grace had no idea where he went. She told herself she didn't care.

Twenty-Five

That autumn, Alexandra's father died. He just gave up and gradually he said less, he moved less. He sat by the fire in the study. He ate less, he drank more and he did nothing. He sat looking into the fire at the coal which he had spent his life getting out of the ground, and one evening when she went in to wish him goodnight he was dead in the chair.

Having him dead was not really so very different. For so long now he had not talked to her, and he had never taken much interest in her. The only difference was that the house seemed huge, dark and cold, and she closed the doors of most of the rooms. She brought Peter and the others home with her from the funeral. Peter was good at conversation; Alexandra was grateful to have him there. He smiled and was courteous which was just as well, because Nat and Dennes between them could barely manage a smile or a word. Alexandra didn't understand why. They sat around and drank tea, and in the middle of it Dennes got up and walked out. After a moment or two Grace followed him.

He was standing in the gloom of the hall.

'Is this your dream?' she said.

He turned around. 'No.'

'Alexandra's father has just died, Dennes. Why can't you try and behave like a person occasionally?'

'Oh, I don't know, envy possibly.'

'Envy? How could you envy her the fact that her father has just died?'

'I wish my father had just died.'

'Or your mother?'

'For choice about twenty years ago.'

'That's absolutely awful. Why blame your mother for everything? Don't you think it was men who got her like that?'

Dennes looked quizzically at her.

'I never expected you to defend her.'

'Didn't you love her at all?' He laughed. Grace didn't like it. 'Will you come back in and make conversation?'

'I don't think my conversation's quite up to the doctor's level.'

'You don't like him, do you? Is that envy too?'

'Now how could it possibly be? He has a good family, a nice home, an education—'

'And Nat doesn't like him? Is that how he feels about Peter, because believe me, Dennes, it isn't very polite—'

'You think Nat should like Peter?'

'Why shouldn't he?'

'Try thinking about it, Grace,' Dennes said, but he went back inside and had another cup of tea.

Alexandra had given everybody tea and cake and then she paused before she said, 'I suppose this isn't a very good time to say it, or maybe it is because it's a nice thing to say. Peter has asked me to marry him and I have said yes.'

Peter went to her, smiling, and put an arm around her. She smiled into his eyes and that was when Grace realised what Dennes had meant. There was nothing about Nat that gave him away, not a look, not a word, but she thought back over the months since he had come to live with them. She had thought that it was the hardship, losing his mother, losing the foundry and the way of life and Nicholas, and having to begin again in the tiny house and the work at the quarry. She thought those were the reasons for his silence, and now she saw that there was something else. Alexandra was about to marry the most

224

eligible young man in the area. He was educated and well-dressed, well-spoken, personable, respected and liked, and there was nothing Nat could do. Just watch.

She stayed behind later when the others had gone. Alexandra sang as she washed up. Grace dried the dishes for her.

'I never thought it would happen, you know,' Alexandra said, smiling. 'He's so nice and he wants me. I can't believe it.'

'Do you love him?'

'Of course I do. We can live in Durham and have a nice house with a garden and children—'

'What about this house?'

Alexandra stopped smiling.

'I know, but I don't think Peter will want to live here, it's too far, and as he gets used to the practice he'll need to go and live among his patients, I mean properly among them.'

'Alex, have you ever thought about anybody else, I mean anybody except Peter?'

'There's never been anybody except Peter, and now there never will be,' and she smiled happily and dried her hands on a towel.

Twenty-Six

Grace didn't remember the first time that she thought Dennes had somebody else. It wasn't a swift realisation, it was a gradual thing. He came home less. He was there every night eventually, but he was always preoccupied and quite often he went drinking, though he never came home drunk again. She didn't know how she knew there was another woman, because if anything he was kinder than before and he did everything he could to make things easy. That was how she finally became suspicious. It was all just too good. They began to make money, not a lot by her standards, but enough so that they stopped working quite so hard, came home every night and talked about moving into a bigger house. There was enough and to spare for food and clothes, and Dennes was so cheerful. He made her laugh. It was a pleasure to be around him, and when the days drew in, though he was not there in the early evenings and could not be at work because the light was soon gone, when he did come home, they sat over the kitchen fire and played card games and talked and read and drank Shona's apple wine. Shona came to the house for Sunday dinner every week and Grace tentatively questioned her, thinking that she might be wrong and that perhaps Dennes was spending time with her. It was true that sometimes he went there, but it did not explain away the absences. A less suspicious woman would have thought that her husband was falling in love with her, but Grace didn't believe it. When he tried to touch her, she moved back from him, and the harder he tried the further she moved back, and the more Dennes was not at home.

Even on Sundays sometimes when Shona was there Dennes stayed away all day. He said, if asked, that he had been to the quarry but Grace had a feeling this wasn't true, and every so often he had the dream again, where he was running along the hall, and he talked in his sleep often.

The weeks went by, Christmas came and there under the tree on Christmas morning was a small square box with her name on it in Dennes' wiggly handwriting. When she opened it with everyone's eyes on her, it was a pretty ring with an amber stone which she well knew he couldn't afford to buy her. She thanked him very briefly and later put the box in a drawer in the sitting-room. Alexandra came over for tea, and when they were alone Grace told her what Dennes had bought her and showed her the ring.

'He's got somebody else,' Grace said as they sat down together on the settee. 'He doesn't love me, he never did and now he's got somebody else.'

Dolly and Taylor and Nat and Dennes were playing a noisy game at the kitchen table. Grace glanced up at the door as Dolly squealed with excitement.

'I don't understand what you mean. This is a small town. People would know. And why should he? I thought you said he was kind to you.'

'He is. He's so . . . attentive, almost as though we weren't married, like I was the other woman except . . .'

'Except?'

Grace looked at her and then she said very softly, 'We're not really married. We never touch each other.'

Alexandra stared.

'In the beginning it was because he didn't want me, because he didn't really care and I wasn't going to – to do that with somebody who had only married me out of revenge—'

'It wasn't just for that, surely.'

'I don't know, and now . . . now he'd do anything seemingly to get me to – to let him have me. That's what this is.' She put the ring into its box and back into the drawer.

'If he has somebody else, why does he want you?'

'I don't know. He's so good to be with, he's in danger of being perfect, and that was never true of Dennes. Anything but. I liked him better when he was honest with me. Now he's so nice to me I could kill him.'

'Just be sure you haven't got this wrong, Grace.'

'What am I meant to do?'

'You could always ask him.'

'Oh yes, he's likely to tell me, isn't he?'

That night when they went to bed, Grace turned towards the wall and ignored him. The room was still warm because the fire had been on all day and was even now just dying down. She wished that she was somewhere else. He had never loved her, he had never wanted her, he had married her because he hated another man and that was the only reason. Dennes moved close and said her name. When he did so again Grace turned over.

'You think you can buy me, don't you?' she said.

'Buy you?'

'Dennes, I didn't marry you because I cared about you. I married you because there was no other way out, because you were a less distasteful alternative than Nicholas Barmouth, and I have no intention of making my body available for you because you think it's your duty to make short work of my virginity.'

There was silence. Grace wasn't surprised.

'I wasn't going to make short work of it,' he said lightly.

'I'm not putting up with you,' Grace said.

'We're married.'

'If you want to force me, go ahead and do it—'

'I don't want to force you. What do you think I'm like?'

'I know less and less.'

Grace tried to move and he held her there until she stopped, and then he slid down the straps from her shoulders and began to kiss her, not her mouth, the sides of her neck and her shoulders and all down the column of her throat, and it was impossible to remain objective, Grace discovered. Firstly she was angry and secondly she was now rather frightened.

She remembered having talked to Ruth generally and Alexandra in particular about this, and they had agreed from what they could glean from other people that the first time you went to bed with your husband it was painful and messy and apparently there was quite a lot of blood, that it was something men enjoyed and women put up with. Grace wasn't prepared to put up with anything, especially now. She lay quite still and closed her eyes and tried to think of something else while Dennes pulled the straps over her arms and down to her waist and started kissing her mouth. Being held against him half-naked while he assaulted her mouth with the kind of kisses which Grace had only dreamed about was too much for her temper. She tried to push him off her, she turned her face away. Dennes let go, and when he did she turned completely away, face down, her body desperate for him. He started to kiss her back and slide the nightdress down her body and she turned over again.

'You don't love me.'

'Grace . . .'

'You don't love me.' Grace choked over the words.

'Grace . . .'

'Go on then, have me. I'm well paid for, aren't I? You keep me, own me, buy me things. Go on, take me.'

The silence was awful. The tears brimmed and fell. When Grace could stand it no longer she turned over into the comfort of the pillows and wept.

That night in the very depths of the darkness, when the fire had gone out and there were no shadows in the room, Grace awoke. For a few moments she did not know what had awoken her, and then she heard him. She thought it was her name on his lips at first, but it wasn't, and then she knew why she had thought so because it was similar, and she

230

knew that she had been right. He was seeing another woman.

'She's called Gwen.' Grace had gone over to Alexandra's. It was a bitterly cold day, too cold to snow, the trees were white with frost and Alexandra's kitchen was the only really warm room in the house.

'I don't know anybody called Gwen.'

'Well, he does. He talks about her in his sleep, so softly, like a man in love,' Grace said bitterly.

'You've got to talk to him, Grace.'

'How can I?'

'There's nothing else to be done. You have to.'

The following Saturday Alexandra came to Irish Back Street in the middle of the evening, worried.

'Ruffles has gone missing. He's been gone for hours and Peter's staying over in Durham because he's working. Will one of you come and help me look?'

Taylor had gone out. Dennes had been missing all day. Nat was busy doing the paperwork for the business, but he stopped.

'I'll come and help you,' he said.

'Oh, thanks.'

'Won't it wait until the morning?' Grace said, 'He's probably just gone after rabbits.'

Alexandra stared at her. 'He's never out this long, Grace.'

'You won't be able to find him in the dark anyway.'

'I've got to try. Don't you think it's worth trying?'

'I do,' Nat said, 'come on,' and he put on his coat and went with her.

They walked quickly back to the house. It wasn't as dark a night as Alexandra had thought it might be.

'It wasn't dark when he went out. I wouldn't care but he's been out most of the day. I didn't intend letting him out again, but he slipped out.'

'Don't worry. I'll go and take a look around.'

'I'll come with you.'

231

'No, just wait there a few minutes. I won't be long.'

Alexandra waited. Saturday nights were not a good time for her to be out, even though the house was a little way from any other houses, and certainly from the public houses. She was impatient. She walked around the kitchen getting more upset as he didn't come back, but when he did and she ran to the back door she was so relieved that she said, 'You've found him!'

Nat looked at her. 'Yes.'

Alexandra stopped. 'He's hurt?'

'He's dead, Alex.'

'No!'

'He was lying in the field just over from the house. I think some poachers must have shot him, probably by mistake.'

Alexandra didn't even want to cry. She felt quite cold.

'He was always running away,' she said.

'Where do you want me to bury him?'

'Over by the pond. It was his favourite place.'

'Go in then, and I'll do it.'

'I want to be there.'

'I'll shout you—'

'Nat, nobody's ever shielded me from anything in my life other than the weather, so don't go soft on me now. I want to help.'

They buried the little dog, and when they went back inside she smiled and thanked him.

'Would you like some tea before you go home?'

'No thanks.'

'I'm sorry to drag you out late on a Saturday night. I know you work hard.'

'I was glad to do it.'

'If Peter had been here . . . I wish . . . It's very nice, you know, being engaged, having somebody there just for you. I didn't think it would happen to me. I won't ever have to go to a dance again and have nobody to dance with.'

'As long as he doesn't read you too much poetry.'

She smiled. 'I know. All I can ever remember from school is the one about the celandine. "There's a flower that shall be mine." Peter knows a lot, but he cares about people, wants to help them.'

'That's nice.'

'You don't like him?'

'Oh, yes, I do.'

'People don't say things like that about people they like. I wanted you and Dennes to like him.'

'No, I do like him. He'll make you very happy. He'll have plenty of money and you won't have to worry about anything. He'll always have plenty of customers.'

'Yes.'

'I have to go.'

Nat was almost to the door when it happened. Suddenly she wanted to cry. If only she could not cry for a couple of minutes until he left, it wouldn't matter. Unfortunately the tears didn't wait. She covered them up with both hands and Nat came back to her and she apologised.

'He was all I had left of how things used to be. My father gave him to me.'

The crying didn't stop. Alexandra was quite well aware that the tears were not just for the dog. She hadn't cried over her father; she thought she didn't have any tears for him. She hadn't grieved over him, she hadn't mourned him. She had thought that she was going to get away with not doing these things because she had been so far away from him for so long before he died, almost as if they were estranged. There was nothing to say and nothing to do with him for so long, and it was in that lack that she found the tears. All the things they had not been to each other mattered now, because she knew that she would never have a chance with him again.

Nat took her into his arms, and it was the only place that she wanted to be. He was big enough for comfort, big enough to hide against. When the tears finally stopped she was shaking and didn't want to let go; it seemed so important to put some distance between the losses in her life and the fact that she was still alive, that she had the future and that she could be happy.

'I must look awful.'

'You never look awful,' Nat said, holding her tight against him with his cheek down on the top of her head.

'I'll be all blotchy now.'

He drew back slightly and looked at her and smiled, and then he kissed her just on the cheek and stroked her hair. When he kissed her on the lips, Alexandra had the chance to relive the first kiss he had given her at the dance in the garden. She wondered why she had denied to herself how good it was, how necessary. She hadn't realised until now that she was missing his lips, how hungry she had been for that kiss.

She was well aware that he was not Peter. She knew that she ought to have stopped him, but he held her so close in the way that she needed to be held. Peter didn't understand what it was like to have your parents die, what it was like to be left, the loneliness, the way that rooms echoed but Nat understood, she knew that he did even though he didn't say anything. She was trying not to hate this house now that she was lonely here. She could not understand how she had ever liked it, this monument to her father's success, the success that had come too late, for her mother had died soon after they had moved in. She remembered the short happiness, the beautiful woman whom Alexandra did not favour in any way. She knew that she had disappointed her father, that if she had been a boy he would have liked her, big and dark like he was, practical, sensible, able to take charge. She had taken charge after her mother had died, but she had understood since that men didn't like capable women, that she ought to have been like her mother, small and fair so that she could look up to men and admire their better minds and be content.

When she was with Peter she was careful not to express her opinions, to talk to his mother, to defer to his ideas. But there was a part of her which did not want to be as men wanted, to be herself, strong in mind and body and ready to take part in life.

Nat was not like Peter. In the world Nat came from women worked hard and had to be strong. She didn't have to hold back with him because he was solid like a wall. She could kiss him freely instead of waiting. She kissed him and enjoyed wanting him closer and being bold enough to make sure that he knew. The kisses were so good. And he encouraged her to hold him close. He drew her down on to the settee and his hands found their way under her clothes. His fingers and palms were rough from work and cool on the warmth of her body. Alexandra undid the buttons on his shirt but she hesitated when she got to his belt.

'Go on,' he urged her softly.

Her fingers shook over the belt buckle, and when it was undone she stopped again.

He pulled her down under him. Alexandra wanted to panic but couldn't. She wanted to stop him and didn't. He pushed her skirts and petticoats up and took down her underwear, and his hands were so gentle and his fingers were so caressing, and Alexandra was lost. He undid his clothes and parted her thighs and got hold of her. Alexandra had never imagined that she would give her virginity to a common man in the kitchen of her home on an old settee. She had dreamed respectable dreams of warm dark bedrooms on her wedding night, of an educated man like Peter with a good background, sheets smelling of lavender and the glow of a fire.

The kitchen smelled of baking. Peter would have been polite and gentle, hesitating, perhaps even talking to her. Her dreams had never included anything beyond the kisses and smiles. It wasn't dark here, the fire burned brightly, the lamps were lit. Nat didn't hesitate. He didn't talk to her, he wasn't even particularly gentle, just sure that she wanted him, careful and certain. Alexandra had never thought that anything could be so indecent and hurt and be so wonderful all at the same time. She held him and gave herself freely and hoped that he would go on exquisitely knifing her apart until she died.

It was a long time before anything else mattered again but when it did it mattered quite appallingly, and Alexandra had to stop herself from blaming him. He was obviously quite ready to take the blame, standing there calmly watching her.

'You wanted to do that before, didn't you?' Alexandra said, understanding.

'Yes.'

'At the dance?'

'Before that.'

'A long time before that?'

'Yes.'

'Well, now you have. I think you ought to go.'

'Alex—'

'I think you should go now.'

When Nat got back Grace was sitting over the fire.

'He hasn't come home,' she said. 'Was Ruffles all right?'

Nat explained about the little dog. Grace said she was sorry.

'Do you want me to go and look for Dennes?'

'You look worn out. Go to bed.'

'I couldn't sleep. Have we got any wine?'

'Yes, in the pantry.'

They sat letting the fire go down, drinking apple wine.

'Do you know where he is?' Grace said.

'No idea.'

'He's out a lot.'

'Yes, I know.'

'You don't know where he goes?'

'Just to Shona's and the pub sometimes and the quarry, of course, he's obsessed with the quarry.'

Grace finished her glass of wine. 'He's got somebody else, Nat.'

Nat stared. 'Whatever makes you think so?'

'Don't you think so?'

'No! He wouldn't do a thing like that. What would he do that for?'

'If his wife didn't want him, hadn't ever let him touch her don't you think he might?'

'I think any man might.'

'You think he has, then?'

'I don't know.'

'Would you?'

'Probably.'

'He talks about her in his sleep.'

'Does he?'

'He calls out her name. Do you think that's true love, Nat, when a man calls out a woman's name? He dreams about her, sometimes very bad dreams.'

'He's loyal,' Nat said. 'There are a lot of things that he doesn't do well, but he does loyalty. I think if there was another woman he would tell you. He wouldn't deceive you. Anyway, I think he loves you.'

'Why?'

'Because. He watches you, looks for you, looks after you. He wouldn't do that to you.'

'He has. Shall I tell you what she's called?'

'I think you should talk to Dennes.'

'He isn't here. She's called Gwen.'

Nat said nothing. His throat went dry and the room was suddenly too warm.

'You know her, don't you?' Grace said.

'No.'

'That's not true, Nat, I can see by your face.'

'No.'

'If you know her then you know where he is. Why don't you go and find him and fetch him home?' and she got up and put down her glass and went into the front room.

It was very still after that. Rain had begun, not the gentle kind of rain, but the kind which seems determined to knock the glass out of the windows, not with a wind behind it, just great sheets of the stuff. Nat put on his coat again and left the house. It was an awful night now, so dark, so wet, the kind of night that makes you doubt there will ever be a dawn to follow it. Nat walked down the main street, past the railway gates and up the bank at the far side. It was a long way to the top and after that it levelled out. The pub at the top was shut, the streets were empty, up past the school and in at the creaky gates towards the cemetery. He had always thought in a daft joking kind of way that it would not be a bad place to end up because there was a view and it was, he thought with some prejudice, the best view in the world, with the dale spread out below in all its incredible glory. He couldn't see it of course, but his memory drew him the picture, the stone walls, the sunshine playing on the tiny square fields, the deep dale, the high hills, the fell tops, it was the most beautiful place in the whole world. His mother was buried there and Nicholas Barmouth had raised a stone to her big enough to dwarf the others, so that even now with the rain and the night it was instantly recognisable. So was the dark form leaning negligently by the wall as though he belonged.

'What the hell are you doing here?' Nat said going to him.

'Nothing.'

'Well, there's not much else to do in a graveyard, you stupid bugger. Howay.'

Dennes didn't move. It wasn't raining quite as much now, just softly, though he was soaked through so it didn't really matter.

'It's a charming spot of a wet Saturday night. Didn't you fancy the pub then?'

'I keep dreaming.'

'You can't live in a cemetery, you know. It just isn't done. I mean you can spend a lot of time here later, but right now it isn't the thing to do.'

'I dream the hall at Esh House.'

'It's not much of a dream, eh?'

'No, just the hall, running along the hall, never getting there, never getting there in time. Sometimes the roof comes in before I get there, sometimes it just goes on and on. I never get there. Never.'

'Grace is worried about you. Come on, let's go home.'

'I can't.'

'Dennes, it's freezing here, you can't stay or you'll be permanent.'

'I don't care any more.'

'Well, I care. Howay.' Nat pulled him away from the wall and walked him carefully towards the gates.

To Nat's dismay when they got back Grace came into the kitchen.

'So,' she said, 'you found him.' She looked Dennes up and down. 'Where have you been?'

'Nowhere.'

'You've been with another woman, haven't you?'

And Dennes became angry straight away, Nat could see. His green eyes darkened and narrowed.

'You what?' he said.

'You're seeing another woman.'

'What's this "another"?'

'I know that you have somebody else, it's no good to pretend to me.'

'You know a lot more than I do, then.'

'Liar! You go and see her a lot. You even dream about her. You talk about her in your sleep. You care about her.'

Nat was convinced this had gone far enough.

'Grace—'

'You say her name.'

'Do I?' Dennes said, like somebody not quite awake.

'Dennes—' Nat said.

'Over and over,' Grace said. 'I have to lie there and listen.'

Dennes didn't say anything for a minute, and Nat wasn't happy about that. The time he stopped talking was the time he was about to do something, but he didn't.

'You don't have to lie there and listen, Grace. You could go and sleep somewhere else—'

'I would if there was anywhere.'

'All right. From now on you can sleep in here. You're no bloody good to me anyway.'

'I wouldn't let you touch me now if you were going to die for lack!' Grace said. 'But you don't need me, do you? Oh no, you've got Gwen, haven't you?'

'Gwen?'

'Yes. Gwen. You do remember? You speak her name ever so softly.'

If Nat could have thought of anything to say he would have said it, the silence went on for so long and Grace knew triumph when she saw it.

'You love her, don't you?' she said. He didn't answer. 'Don't you, Dennes?'

'Yes.'

Nat could barely hear the word but he closed his eyes over it.

'You went to her tonight, and all those times when you pretend that you're somewhere else, you go to her,' Grace accused him. 'How could you?'

'I couldn't help it. I've loved her for so long.'

'But you married me.'

'I thought it might be all right. I didn't want there just to be the past. I wanted to have something else. I wanted to try and have something more. I wanted somebody . . .'

Grace stared at him. 'What are you talking about?' she said.

'She's dead, Grace,' Nat said.

Grace glanced briefly at him and then back at Dennes. 'How can you love somebody who's dead?'

'That's the easy bit. She's always there in my mind. I can have her all to myself now. Nobody can take her away from me.'

'I think you're quite mad,' Grace said.

'People go mad with grief all the time. Nobody notices or cares. Nobody ever speaks her name.' He glanced at Nat. 'Not even you. You never talk to me about her. Sometimes I say her name out loud over and over. I think if I do it often enough she won't be dead, she'll have some kind of presence in the world if I say her name. And it eases the hurt. I can picture her in my mind so much better when I say her name.'

'I thought it would make things worse if we talked about her,' Nat said.

'How could things be any worse, Nat?' Dennes said, smiling. 'He wouldn't even let me see her. I keep dreaming about the hall, running down the hall at Esh House. She's calling out my name, she's saying it over and over and he won't let me see her. He tells Harry to call the men in from the garden and they get hold of me and they— they hit me. One of them's got a stick. They're big Irish lads and they bray hell out of me and all the time I can hear her calling my name. She isn't really by then, but I think she is. I think she's still calling my name.'

Grace was staring at him.

'No,' she said. 'You couldn't have.'

240

'Grace—' Nat said.

'No. You really couldn't have. Nat's mother?'

'She wasn't just his mother, you know,' Dennes said, still smiling slightly.

'She was old.'

'No, she wasn't. She was only seventeen when she had Nat. She wasn't old at all.'

'Have you any idea how awful that is?'

'Grace—' Nat said again.

'How could you love a woman like that when you could have had me? You're disgusting! You're vile!'

'Stop it, Grace!' Nat said.

'How could you? How could you want her?' The tears began to run freely down her face. She went to Dennes and banged her fists against him. 'You're filthy and low and I despise you.'

Nat got hold of her and shook her slightly.

'Stop it!'

She pulled free and ran from the room, and after that the silence was huge. Nat's clothes had got to the stage where they had been wet on him for so long that they were drying stickily. He hauled off his jacket and threw it on to a chair.

The fire had been banked down for the night but Nat brought it back to life. He would make some tea. He glanced at Dennes who had sat down on the old easy chair nearby and was watching him.

The flame spurted and broke free. Nat checked the kettle for water and put it over the fire. Dennes took off his jacket and his shoes and they sat and watched the fire. Nat didn't want to do anything else for the rest of his life now, he was so weary. When he turned around again Dennes had laid back and gone to sleep.

Nat got up and walked softly across the room and opened the sitting room door. A candle burned. Grace had not gone to bed.

'Get out,' she said without turning to see who it was.

'It's me,' he said.

Grace looked up. 'You could have told me.'

'I didn't know until tonight, and then it wasn't my business to tell you. Try not to think too badly, Grace.'

'I'm going home in the morning.'

'Do you think that will solve anything?'

'Yes, it will get me out of this horrible little house and away from the likes of you and him.'

'It'll certainly do that,' Nat said.

Twenty-Seven

When Alexandra awoke the next morning she lay in bed for a long time thinking about Nat, trying to convince herself that he was just a no-good common workman who set out to seduce innocent girls, but he wouldn't fit into the picture properly, and all the time her mind replayed her the cool blue eyes, his mouth on her bare skin, his hands caressing. She got out of bed, called herself names, and after she had built up the fire she went and had a long hot bath. She spent the morning convincing herself that she could not possibly be pregnant and the afternoon with Peter, wondering whether she looked any different now that she wasn't a virgin.

She felt wretched, she felt guilty, she wanted to go over to Irish Back Street and slap Nat hard over his sweet mouth and hand the responsibility to him.

Peter kissed her when they were alone that evening, he kissed her properly and put his hands on to her breasts and it was the wrong time.

Alexandra went on with her life as though nothing had happened. Her period came, so she was not pregnant. She was rather disappointed. She had had this vision of herself where she marched up to Irish Back Street and flaunted her pregnant state, and then she tried to forget about Nat. She deliberately didn't go, she didn't see him. She saw Peter almost every day. They had set a date for the wedding. They were going to be married before the end of August.

It was some days before she heard that Grace had left Dennes and gone back to her parents. She went over but Grace's mother said that she was ill and could see no one.

After a week she went again and this time she was allowed to see Grace in the drawing-room. Grace was thin and pale and wore a green dress which looked as though it had been made for somebody else, it was so big on her. Alexandra didn't know what to say.

'Is your father any better?' she ventured.

'He's getting worse. The doctor says it's hardening of the arteries. He doesn't know anybody, he can't remember anything. My mother is distraught and now . . .'

'Peter and I have set a date for the wedding.' Even as she said it, Alexandra was given in her mind a totally unwelcome picture of herself down on the old settee in her kitchen with her fingers pressed across Nat Seymour's smooth back and her skirts up to her waist. She wiped her mind determinedly.

'When is it to be?' Grace asked.

'August the twenty-third. You will come.'

'As long as you don't invite Dennes or Nat, I'd love to.'

The idea of having Nat at her wedding made Alexandra feel suddenly quite ill.

'You must have been glad to come back to your parents.'

It was soothing to hear Grace talking about the disgusting little house, how awful it was, how badly Dennes had gone on, how Nat had always taken Dennes' side in everything, how hard the work had been. It comforted Alexandra, thinking of how easy her marriage would be, her husband the doctor. There would be no ups and downs of business, like when you owned mines or quarries or foundries. She would live with Peter in Durham and know the best people. She would never have to redden her hands with work. She would have new dresses and go dancing and enjoy herself.

She looked across at Grace and thought how things had changed, how she had envied Grace going to London, parties, opportunities. Grace would have no more opportunities now. She was nothing but a daughter in disgrace. She would probably never leave this house again to live anywhere else. She would stay here and be told what to do, her opinion would never be asked, there would be no social life for her, she would have no children and no friends. The people in the village talked about her. She could barely go beyond the doors. Grace's life was effectively over, Alexandra thought with a shudder.

Nat and Dennes worked. It was the best time of year for quarrying; it was, Nat thought, the only good time. Up here on the fell tops in the winter the frost affected the sand, the wet affected the sand, every bloody thing affected the sand but now the sand was dry, went easily through the mill and came out looking perfect to his now more experienced eyes. Up on the fell tops life was almost good if you could forget the rest.

It was late June, barely dark at any time, and quite often they didn't go home, they just lay down for a few hours in the tin-sheeted hut and went to sleep. It was best that way. You could work eighteen hours a day, seven days a week, and nothing could get in the way of hard, relentless toil. Taylor was there too, though he went home at night to stay with Dolly. They had found a woman to help her in the house. Dolly missed Grace and said so privately to Nat. Other than that no one spoke Grace's name. Alexandra Covington was to be married to the most eligible young man in the area. Nat tried not to think about her, too.

There were weeks of hot weather, and they had taken on an experienced quarryman who taught them a good deal that summer. He was called George Smith, a Sheffield man who had come to the area when his wife's father was taken ill, because she was from here. George was a cheerful sort and made them laugh, and in the warm weather there was a lot to smile about for quarrymen, it was so much easier.

Sometimes Shona walked up to the quarry at midday and brought them food, and occasionally on Sundays she and Dolly went up and they all had a picnic, and on those days Nat thought there was not a better place to be, with the wind down to a gentle breeze, the sheep grazing peacefully and the lapwings soaring overhead, the grouse making their strange noises in the heather, a deep purple colour as the summer continued, the bees droning there.

Nat went on making Dennes feel obliged to stay in that place every working hour, he made certain that they were both so worn out they couldn't think of anything else. As the days went on Nat thought how beautiful Alexandra would look in white with her dark hair and dark eyes.

Late one Sunday afternoon, when Shona had gone back to the farm and Dolly and Taylor had gone back to the village, he and Dennes sat down at teatime for a few minutes' rest. The sun was hot. Nat was just about to fall asleep when Dennes said suddenly, 'We didn't get an invitation to the wedding, Dolly said.'

'I heard.' They didn't talk much these days, there were too many delicate areas. 'I'd rather not go, thanks.'

'What do you think he's going to say to her on her wedding night?'

Nat opened his eyes and turned his head. 'What?'

'He's a doctor, Nat. Do you think he isn't going to notice?'

'You don't know—'

'I know. Are you going to let him marry her?'

'It was her choice.'

'So what was she doing with you?'

'Are we going to work, or are you going to carry on asking bloody stupid questions?' Nat said, getting up.

Dennes followed him and picked up a shovel.

The only trouble with quarrying in the summer, Nat thought, wiping his brow several minutes later, was that shovelling was such hard physical work, especially when it was the rock itself to be milled. The big pieces had to be broken down and then it all had to be shovelled by hand and it was exhausting. Nobody said anything else, but when it was dark they went home. Dolly had promised hot food and warm baths and it had been a long week.

When they got back there was a letter which had been hand-delivered. It was from Nicholas and asked quite simply if Nat would call at Esh House soon.

'Are you going?' Dolly said.

246

'No,' Nat said and went off down the yard and into the back lane.

It wasn't very dark out there. A dozen stars were lighting a pale sky. He heard the footsteps behind him.

'Do you have to follow me about? What are you, a bloody terrier?'

'I think you should go and see him,' Dennes said.

Nat turned around and glared at him. 'Did I ask you?'

'He's drinking himself senseless. He'll lose the foundry. When he loses it and Alex marries that fool, Peter, and has his bairns, you're going to feel like shite because you didn't do anything.'

'All right then, I'll make you a deal. I'll go and see Nicholas if you come with me.'

'I'm not going back there!'

'Fine. I'm not going either then.'

Dennes went back up the yard and into the house.

The next morning however, when Nat came downstairs to go to work, Dennes was waiting for him.

'I'll come with you to Esh House on condition that you go and see Alex.'

'No!'

'I'm not going with you then.'

'What could I say to her?'

Dennes looked patiently at him and glanced at the stairs for signs of Dolly before he said, 'When you've had a lass's knickers down it's the done thing around here among decent folk to ask her to wed you.'

'I couldn't.'

'Why the hell not?'

'I could hardly bring her back here, could I? He can give her everything.'

'If she'd cared about him, she would never have let you give her what for, would she? Well, would she?'

'It— it just happened.'

'I see. He's got education and manners and a nice family. The day she marries him you're going to want to die and the day she has his bairn you're going to wish you had.'

'I am not!'

247

'Aren't you?'

'I've got nothing!'

'You think he's going to make her happy when she wants you?'

'She doesn't want me.'

'You forced her, did you?'

'No.'

'Persuaded her then?'

'She was . . . she cried about her father and about the dog. It just happened.'

'Oh aye?' Dennes said sceptically.

'Peter can look after her. He can make her feel safe. He can give her a nice way of living . . .'

'What are we worrying about then? I'm going to work.'

Nat caught up with him halfway down the yard.

'Come to Esh House with me,' he said.

It was like a different place, Nat thought when they reached the gates. He had not been near since the day that Nicholas had had him beaten and thrown out, and it was a shock. The gates were partly open and there was no noise of any kind from inside. The garden had gone wild, the lawns were knee-deep in summer grass, the windows were dusty from rain and the front door gave as he tried to open it.

Coming back wasn't easy. He glanced at Dennes and thought that without him he would have turned and run, and he knew that Dennes was feeling the same because he kept his gaze frontwards and said nothing. He wondered how hard it was for Dennes to come back now, and as they walked into the front hall he half-expected to hear his mother's voice. Dennes hesitated there, glancing towards the stairs.

'You want to go back?' Nat asked him softly.

'No.'

The hall was thick with dust. There were dead flowers brown in a glass vase on the table there, ash was black in the grate and the summer sun played its light note over neglected furniture. Nat's mind showed him the day his mother had died, running up the stairs, seeing her body and then accurately once again the beating that the Irish boys

248

had given him, their laughter and the savage blows.

The study door was open. It took him all his courage to walk in. It was dark. He pushed back the thick velvet curtains and sunlight flooded the room. The air was dense with whisky fumes. Nat opened the windows. Nicholas was slumped forward across the desk, unconscious. He stank of spirit and himself. His clothes were filthy and on the desk were several empty glasses and on the floor were half a dozen whisky bottles. It should have been a triumph but somehow it was not; it was a defeat, a disappointment, it was like winning the race by default, like a cheat, a quick lay, a flat beer, a heavy cold so that you couldn't taste your food. Nat was ashamed. He waited for Dennes' reaction.

'Right, let's have him up,' Dennes said.

'What?'

'To bed. There's two of us, we'll manage.'

'Dennes—'

'Don't just stand there, get hold of him.'

'I thought you hated him.'

'I wouldn't leave a worm in this.'

They carried him upstairs. The bedroom wasn't much better but the linen cupboard had clean sheets so they stripped the bed and him and put him into bed.

Dennes stayed with him while Nat went home to get Dolly. She didn't want to go with him, but when she saw the state of Nicholas and of the house she set to with their help. By tea-time the house was much cleaner, the windows were all open to the summer warmth, the fire was on in the kitchen and when Nicholas awoke in the middle of the afternoon Nat was sitting by the bed.

'What the hell are you doing back here?' he growled.

'You sent for me.'

'I threw you out.'

'You wrote me a note.'

'I must have been drunk. You get out.'

Nat went over and poured water from a jug into a glass. Nicholas took the glass without a word and drank the water. Then he settled down and went back to sleep.

By evening when they had all worked, the house was much cleaner, and because it was they even tackled some of the garden. Dolly made a stew for when Nicholas awoke. He came downstairs in the middle of the evening, sober, shaved, clean and dressed. They were all in the kitchen by then.

'Get off my property.'

'Why, are you going to have us thrown off?' Nat said. 'You haven't got anybody to throw us off now, have you? Everybody's gone.'

'Get out of my house!'

As they left Nat looked back. 'Now look what we've done,' he said.

'He'll be drunk again by Monday,' Dennes prophesied.

The following day Dolly reported that Nicholas had gone to church, according to gossip. He had been sober and tidy and on the Monday morning he went to the foundry.

Alexandra had gone to Durham with Peter that spring to look for a house. She had convinced herself by then that she hated living up on the fell and wanted somewhere more civilised, and it was true that there were a number of pretty houses within the city itself, all of which seemed perfectly fine. She was excited and interested. Peter had friends in Durham who invited her to their houses. Some of them were married and had small children. They were all ready to welcome her. The women talked about clothes and children and their homes and their husbands, how much they liked Peter. They were all well-off, they had servants. Alexandra never got to see into their kitchens. She got to see their gardens and their dining-rooms and their sitting-rooms. She went on walks by the river with Peter, and they looked at various houses. They found the perfect house. It had a big, square garden, was within walking distance of the shops, was not too far from Peter's surgery and she would have all her new friends around her.

She went to see Grace often but she felt guilty in her happiness. Grace's father was gradually getting worse and Alexandra could not talk to Grace about Peter and the house and her friends and her future because Grace had nothing. Finding something to talk about was not easy. Often she made an excuse to leave early and went to see Peter's parents. Their house was a haven for her. She spent most of her time there. She hated going back to her own home. She hated the portrait on the wall of her beautiful mother, but most of all she hated the cold silence in the kitchen where she never cooked any more, and the old settee where Nat Seymour had taught her passion. Peter would have made love to her if she had let him, but Alexandra didn't want that, she wanted to be part of a family as she had never been, to be close and protected, looked after. She didn't want to be reminded of how Nat had treated her. There would be time enough for that when she and Peter were married.

One evening when she had been in Durham all day at the new house, she came back thinking about it. It was so light, the windows were big, the garden was pretty with flowers, the rooms were high and had decorated tiled fireplaces. She and Peter had bought furniture and she had chosen carpets and curtains. Her wedding dress was bought, the arrangements were made. Peter had driven her home then gone off and it was late now.

Each time she came back to it the house seemed more empty and less to do with her, almost as though it belonged to somebody else, whereas in fact nobody had wanted to buy it so far. She had taken from it the things which she liked to the new house and the rooms echoed. The summer night was clear and chilly now, so she lit the kitchen fire and intended sitting over it until it was time to go to bed, and then she heard the front door.

She ran, thinking that Peter must have forgotten something and there was Nat standing on her doorstep. Alexandra wished herself in Durham or at Peter's parents' house, anywhere but here. She let him in. She didn't want to take him into the kitchen but it was the only warm room in the house, and when she finally was obliged for politeness' sake to look at him and speak to him she was just so glad that she had agreed to marry Peter. Nat had both hands around the hat that he had taken off and they revealed him for a workman, they were rough and scarred. He was thin from working hard and he looked tired. His clothes were old and well-washed and worn. Alexandra thought of Peter, his neat hands, his expensive clothes, his educated voice and she saw herself through Nat's eyes. She was beautiful now, not as beautiful as Grace but happiness had made her so. She had fined down. She wore clothes which Peter's mother's dressmaker had made for her. She did no work now that she was to be Peter's wife and her hands were soft. On her left hand was the diamond ring which Peter had given her, one diamond and it flickered its colours, blue and gold dancing in the lamplight.

'I— I went to see Nicholas,' Nat said.

'Did you? How is he?'

'He was drunk.'

'So I hear.'

'He asked me to go and see him. I took Dennes. Alexandra, I— I wanted to ask you something.'

'Me? Well, ask away.'

He was standing with his back to the old settee but she was facing it. She wished that she wasn't. She wished with all her might that she had not given herself to him like that. She had excused herself a thousand times, remembering how hurt and upset she had been about her father and the little dog and her life. She told herself that Nat had known that, had taken her because she was vulnerable then. The trouble was that, faced with him and his cool blue eyes, she knew it wasn't true. She had wanted him and badly. She wondered why his mouth was so sweet. She had kissed Peter a dozen times and it was very nice and she liked the closeness, but Nat's presence was like a drug. It was as though he brought extra light in with him and gave the room a magic.

'Are you happy?' he said.

She laughed.

'Of course I am.' She was. Peter had made her happy by taking away the loneliness of her life, by giving her his family and friends, drawing her in, giving her a future.

'That's good. It's just that . . . when Ruffles died I . . . I don't want you to think that I . . .' Nat looked at her, straight at her for the first time. 'I don't want you to think I did that lightly, that it didn't mean anything to me. It was just that . . . I didn't have anything to offer you.'

Alexandra couldn't go on looking at him. She looked down at the diamond on her hand and began to turn the ring round and round on her finger. She wished more than anything now that she had not let him have her, it distorted everything, it made things seem important which she thought were never meant to be.

'I know that you care about Peter—'

'I do care about him.'

'Yes.'

'Nat . . . it was just that I was upset.'

'Is that all?'

'Well, I do like you. I always liked you, you know that.'

'And that's all?'

'That's all, yes. I shouldn't have— done that. I'm not proud of it.'

'Don't be sorry.'

'I'm not blaming you.'

'I don't mind taking the blame – if it's to be all there is. I love you.'

'No.' Alexandra remembered now. She remembered being small and her father struggling with the pits and how her mother had hated this place. Her father had been a man like Nat, beginning from nothing, working all the time, coming home exhausted and black with coaldust, with rough hands and her mother taunting him about how she had nothing worth having. They hadn't lived in this house then. He had worked so hard to get them to here and then her mother had died and her father was dead now too, worn out bringing black diamonds to the surface. That was what he had called the glittering coal which kept them and Alexandra hated it and she was not going to have it happen again with another man with another rock with her.

'No,' she said again. She looked at him. 'You can't come here and say that and expect anything. I'm going to marry Peter. You know I am. He's what I want.'

'He can give you everything.'

'Yes. Yes, he can.'

Nat had crushed the hat in his hands. Alexandra doubted that he would ever be able to wear it again. He wasn't even looking at her now. Alexandra could see how long his eyelashes were. She saw him out.

She saw how he straightened the hat as he walked away down the drive and then she shut the door firmly behind her and went back to the kitchen.

Twenty-Eight

Nicholas sent for Nat again in the end. It was one of those days which fool you into thinking it's early summer until the evening cuts it almost short. It was hot and made Nat want to go and put his feet in the stream up on the fell, but he had come home from work and got the message and after his tea had walked slowly over to Esh House where Nicholas was drinking whisky in the library. Nicholas was steady with the steadiness of somebody used to drink. Nat wondered whether the half-empty whisky bottle was only the first that day and concluded that it could not have been. Nicholas offered him a drink but Nat didn't like spirit anyway, and he thought that even if he had the sight of somebody putting it away so easily would have been off-putting.

'I waited for you to come back, you know,' Nicholas said confidingly.

'Come back?'

'Yes.' Nicholas laughed and waved the glass of golden liquid in the air. 'I pictured you pleading with me to let you back here. I thought you'd do it at least for the sake of your brother and sister.'

'We get by,' Nat said.

'I'm sure you do. I thought I had another ace up my sleeve. I thought you would come back for the foundry.'

'I couldn't. I let you down. It had to be either you or Dennes.'

'You love him like a brother, in fact.'

Nat wrinkled his nose. 'That's not quite how I'd put it, we're just there for each other, that's all.'

'How very touching.' Nicholas put down his empty glass and looked at it for a moment and then he looked at Nat. 'Did you know that Mr Hemingway is ill?'

'Grace went to see him.'

'Yes, of course. So you do know. I don't go to the works every day. I try to, but some days . . . some days I don't. I have responsible men there but I got to thinking lately about what it was like having you and Taylor there, and how well you worked and how good he was in the office and how fast you caught on to everything, and it seemed to me that if I had you there it would somehow be easier, that I might go to work every day, perhaps. Will you come back?'

Nat didn't know what to say. To work in Barmouth's Foundry was now his dearest wish but he was not Nicholas Barmouth's stepson any more in that respect. He had betrayed Nicholas for Dennes; the relationship could not go back to what it had been.

'I'd like to—'

'Good. Good. When will you move back in?'

Nat looked at him. 'No. I can't move back in or work for you.'

'I'll give Taylor work too and I'll look after Dolly—'

'Dolly is happy where she is and I couldn't do that. We're fine where we are.'

Nicholas looked regretfully at the whisky bottle.

'Are you sure you won't have a drink?' he said. 'I'm very lonely, Nat. I didn't know how difficult it could be. You added insult to injury when you went to Irish Back Street.'

'If I'd had somewhere else to go, I would have.'

'You're my stepson, Nat.'

'As far as I'm concerned that's all finished.'

Nicholas poured himself another whisky. 'You were a nice lad,' he said, 'once.'

Alexandra's wedding day was wet. Nat was glad of that. He couldn't have borne that it should be another of those rich deep days of which they had had so many lately, the heather so purple that it almost hurt your eyes and the sky so blue as if it would never rain any more. Up at the quarry it was dusty and he was glad of it.

He insisted on going to work that Saturday even though he knew that they had all pushed themselves far too hard for far too long. The others were having the day off, but Dennes went with him as usual even though Nat knew he would have given a lot for a lie-in and a day free. They set off early in warm rain which had settled the dust and put a gloss on the heather. Dennes walked silently but that wasn't because he didn't know what day it was. He had urged Nat to do a number of indecent things to Alexandra that week to convince her that she was doing the wrong thing and Nat had gone on working sometimes twenty hours a day to kill off the idea of her in his mind. Today she was to be married and after that he told himself things would be easier. She would belong to someone else and never to him again. She had never loved him, he told himself doggedly and it mustn't matter.

Dennes wasn't inclined to work, Nat knew, but once you were up there there was nothing else to do. The rain got worse until they were soaked and everything was turning thick under their feet. Dennes didn't suggest they should go home, take shelter or even stop, and the monotony of quarrying, Nat thought, was one of its pleasures. The reliability of drilling, blasting, milling, knowing where you were going right from the very beginning, seeing it all through until what you had was a pile of sand just the way it should be, as fine as it should be, the right texture, the right feel, it was in its own way satisfying. Even though it took all your strength to get it from the fell to the foundries he liked getting it there because it tried to defeat you every time, what with the weather and the people involved, the ponies and carts, the mill. It was a triumph to get it there and sometimes even then you weren't safe because if it wasn't right, if you had got a little bit of something, say, shale, into it, it made bad castings and there were complaints and you lost money and face and time and effort and energy and your temper usually, too, but it was work. It provided money and it staved off the cutting memories of Alexandra Covington's delicious body and the idea of wanting to kill a certain doctor who had never, as far as Nat knew, done anybody any harm other than possibly being too ignorant to save them from whatever disease their bodies had succumbed to.

It was the middle of the afternoon before Nat even paused. She would be married by now, he was safe to go back down the hill to the village. He couldn't run there, grab her out of the church and take her away and hide her. She was married now, she was somebody else's. When they needed a break he didn't go up to the hut where they usually sheltered, so Dennes didn't go either. They didn't even sit down, everything was so wet. Nat took a long drink of water and gave the bottle to Dennes and then he stood looking out across the moor which he loved and hated so much and then he would have gone to begin work again. Dennes lingered. Nat paused. 'Are you going to bloody help or are you going to stand there all day?'

Dennes ignored him, looking away through the rain with his eyes screwed up to see. 'There's somebody coming,' he said, 'a lass.'

'It's just Dolly. She said she might.'

'In this?'

'She worries. Women do, don't they? About food and things. Howay.'

'Shut your gob,' Dennes said gently.

Alexandra had worried that week about whether it would rain, about whether the food would be good, whether her dress would fit, whether her veil would stay on, whether she would hate having her family from Durham to stay. She didn't like them but she had nobody else and had had to ask her uncle to give her away. She didn't want to be given away, it was an awful term, as though she was an unwanted present. She fussed about the new house, she fussed about leaving her home and the old house seemed so reproachful. Everywhere she looked that week there were dust and cobwebs and the weather was hot so that the flowers in the garden drooped and wilted, and she went out into the cool of the evening in apology and watered them even though she knew that the following week when she was packed and gone she would give them no thought. Nobody had bought the house. Who in their right minds would want to live here with the dust and dirt from the quarries and foundries, the sleeting wind which brought winter across the fells, where the only pleasure was a fire eight months of the year round, and the rest of the time the windows rattled and the rugs lifted and the wind howled around the houses and the rain and wind battered defenceless gardens and turned soil to mud? The winter meant a foot or two of snow and months of hard frost and hot summers like this one were rare, usually it was just a few days here and there.

Peter worked hard that final week because he was having time off after they were married. He was so happy. Their new house was ready for them to go to. His parents had given them everything to make the house look good. They were going to have a holiday, just a few days at Whitley Bay, and after that they would come back to begin their new life. Alexandra was looking forward to it. She loved him so much. Late in the afternoon before the wedding she had gone into his arms and kissed him hard and he had kissed her back and smiled into her eyes and told her how much he loved her.

'This time tomorrow . . .' he said, and pulled her close.

They didn't spend the evening together. Alexandra was obliged to entertain her visitors as best she could considering that she never saw them and had nothing in common with them, but her aunt was pleased about her marriage and talked about Peter as if she knew him, though she didn't. How well people thought of him, what a lovely house they had chosen, how much time they would all be able to spend together. Alexandra sincerely hoped not. It was a very long evening and a still longer night and to Alexandra's horror it rained before dawn and went on raining. There was mist. The lovely weather was over.

As the morning progressed the rain poured down, and by the afternoon when they were due to leave for the church the garden paths were shiny with rain and her aunt for at least the fortieth time said what a pity it was that the weather had turned.

Alexandra was concerned for her white dress, she didn't want the bottom of it to get dirty before she got to the church. Her uncle made jokes on the way there, and then she was standing in the church doorway on his arm and she could hear the rain stotting off the roof.

She thought of all the food on long tables at the house, the house cleaner than it had ever been. She saw all the people waiting for her, mostly Peter's family and friends. She thought of how she would have liked her father there to give her away. The bouquet in her hands matched the flowers in the church, roses. The music began, her uncle urged her forward, they began to walk down the aisle. They were almost there and then she stopped. She didn't know why, just that she couldn't go any further, her feet wouldn't work. They worked backwards though, when she let go of her uncle's arm. She watched him staring at her. Retreat was all they knew. She backed several steps, and then she lifted up her skirts and ran and her feet worked well enough then.

She ran out of the church and into the rain, skidding on the wet stones of the path up to the church. She ran up the church lane, not towards the village but away towards the hill. The grass was long and wet and soaked her feet and then her legs and she kept tugging at her skirt which got wetter and wetter until it was soaked and heavy. The rain made her face cold and the tears made her cheeks warm. At some time she stopped and managed to get rid of the great long hated veil which was pinned to her hair with what seemed like a thousand pins all sticking into her scalp, and the stupid flowers which made up part of the headdress. She threw it off and her hair was all over by then because it came partly down with the lack of pins. It began to turn darker, curling with rain, and rivulets ran off it and down on to her shoulders. She was out of breath, had to keep stopping, it was such a long way up the hill, so steep and difficult to climb and road was a laughable name for the rutted track which made her stumble more than once and curse, and then finally she was beside the heather.

There was no mist but it was difficult to see through the rain. She saw the buildings of the quarry first, sitting up there right on the top of the fell, almost shameful they were so tatty, all tin sheets and make-do walls. And she had been right. The place was not deserted. Even though it was a Saturday afternoon, even though there was a wedding, even though the rain was coming down as though it had nothing better to do, she could see the two figures of the men as she made her way

260

across the top of the fell and down into the quarry. They were standing, not going back to work, not sheltering like any sensible person would. She walked on carefully in her new shoes over the uneven floor of the quarry, and when she got to the men she could make out Nat and Dennes, as wet as she was, dressed in working clothes, dirty, going on anyway just like her father had in the old days, not caring, determined. She had not realised until then that she was still carrying the stupid bouquet in one hand, holding up her skirt with the other. The white dress was inches deep in mud, her shoes were ruined, her hair was down.

'This is all because of you,' she said to Nat as he looked at her. 'You did this. I hate you!' She gulped over what was trying to be a sob and went to him and hit him with the bouquet.

Nat started to laugh. He took the bouquet from her and threw it away and then he pulled her into his arms.

'Don't you just look a mess,' he said.

Twenty-Nine

They went to live at Alexandra's house once she and Nat were married. Things weren't easy until then. For one thing, Peter Clifford came to the little house in Irish Back Street to sort Nat out. Luckily Nat wasn't there at the time, so Dennes took him into the yard and persuaded him that it wasn't a very good idea. This took some time and Peter had a black eye and a bleeding mouth when he went home. Dennes felt almost sorry for him. Alexandra's cousins went back to Durham declaring that they would never speak to her again, so that was no particular loss, and the white dress had to be washed, shrank badly and was fit for nothing but tearing into strips and putting over a hairbrush to increase the shine on your hair, so Dolly said.

Things improved a lot that autumn. For one thing Nat stopped going around looking like a wet fortnight, and living at Alexandra's house was wonderful. His mother, Dennes thought reluctantly, would have liked it. There was a piano, there were big gardens around the house, there were huge bedrooms so that everybody could have one each, apart from Nat and Alexandra who had a bad enough time being parted during the day, never mind the rest of the time. The bedrooms had views over the valley and over the gardens. The furniture was good, the beds were comfortable and Alexandra cooked meals with love. They were as good as Dennes had ever tasted. Alexandra wouldn't have anybody to help in the house; Dolly didn't like cooking and Alexandra didn't like housework so they both did what they wanted.

The autumn was fine, the quarry prospered. Nat kept sneaking off to the foundry. Sometimes Nicholas was sober and was there and would let him help. Sometimes he liked being there when Nicholas wasn't. Nat began to spend much more time at the foundry than at the quarry. Dennes envied him that.

In the late autumn at the house there were pears and plums and apples to be picked. The wasps ate a lot of the pears and Dennes got stung several times fighting with them for a share one Sunday in October. Alexandra made plum jam and bottled fruit and throughout the lower part of the house there was the smell of warm sugar and fruit from the kitchen stove. The jam was soon glistening in jars. Dennes got tired of it long before the job was finished and sneaked away to the garden. As he did so he saw Grace come in by the gate. She had come to see Alexandra from time to time since they had moved there but always when he and Nat and Taylor were at work. Taylor had gone off somewhere and Nat was in the house with Dolly and Alexandra, being supposedly helpful, kissing Alexandra on the neck from time to time and peering into pans. Dennes was sitting on an old seat by the wall at the top of the lawn. Grace had to come past him to get to the house, and when she did so he was astonished at how she looked. She was very thin indeed and no longer beautiful. There were shadows under her eyes and her eyes had lost their lustre. She didn't smile, her mouth was in a straight line and she was pale as though she had not been outside all the summer. She stopped when she saw him. 'Good afternoon.'

'Hello.' Dennes could not help but think of the last time they had been together, how hurt she had been. 'How's your dad?'

She looked down and he thought she was going to go on into the house without saying anything, but she didn't. She sat down on the nearest chair – there were several, old and rickety – and said steadily, 'He's much worse. They think it could be a disease which has just been discovered, called Alzheimer's. Have you heard of it?'

'No.'

'It's where people have symptoms like old people, when their minds go. He doesn't know me now, he doesn't know anything and the doctor doesn't think he will live very long.'

'I'm sorry,' Dennes said. 'It's awful for your mother.'

'Yes. I spend all my time with her. I thought you'd be at work.'

'Alex needed a hand picking the fruit and we haven't had a day off in a long time. Go in, she's in the kitchen making jam. We're thinking about getting her a stall on the market.'

Grace went on into the house. Dennes stayed where he was. He had no more desire to see her than she had to talk to him.

Grace went into the hall and through but she paused at the kitchen door. There was nobody in the room but Nat and Alexandra. He was standing behind her with his arms around her, kissing her neck in the hollow where her neck met her shoulder. As Grace stood there Alexandra flung back her head and turned slightly and he kissed her all down the column at the front of her throat, slow deep kisses. Alexandra had her eyes shut. Grace tiptoed back out of the front door and stood there for a few moments, her cheeks burning.

'They're not at it again, are they?' Dennes said mildly.

'I want to talk to him.'

'Just wait a minute or two. The jam'll boil over and then they'll move. How are things at the foundry?'

'Not good. Mr Barmouth wants Nat back there and so does my mother.'

'What, full time?'

'If he will.'

'He can't run it on his own, it's too much. Is Nicholas not there at all?'

'Oh yes, quite often I think, but my mother worries because she doesn't know what's going on and you can never tell when Nicholas will be drunk. I understand Nat goes there.'

'He tries to.'

'I thought you all hated him.'

'It's difficult to hate somebody who's given up.'

Nat appeared at the door. 'I thought I heard something,' he said.

'You were . . . you were busy,' Grace said, smiling.

Alexandra followed him out of the door, hanging on to him as though somebody was trying to run off with him. Dennes wondered, seeing her, how he had ever thought that Grace was the more beautiful of the two. Alexandra was so beautiful now he was surprised people didn't stop in the streets and stare at her.

'I came to tell Alexandra that I wanted to see you,' Grace said to Nat. 'I didn't think you'd be at home. Mr Barmouth and my mother want you to come back to the foundry, properly. He needs you there and my father is so ill and Mother is frightened. Mr Barmouth says that you know what you're doing and you can help.'

'I don't know that much and I certainly can't do it by myself.'

'He's there part of the time.'

'Grace, he doesn't know what he's doing mostly.'

'All the more reason. You can't prefer that wretched quarry.'

Nat glanced at Dennes. 'I can't leave.'

'Yes, you can,' Dennes said. 'George and I can run it, to say nothing of your blessed brother, wherever he is.'

'We'll need to take on more men.'

'We can do that. You know you want to be at the steelworks.'

Nat didn't say much more. Dennes got up and walked away into the orchard. The place looked so bare without its fruit. Nat followed him. 'I want you there too,' he said.

'Just take what you can get for now. Don't go making any trouble, they might change their minds.'

'I can't manage the place without you. Nicholas is useless and old man Hemingway's on his last legs by the sound of it.'

'There are plenty of good men. Just take what you're offered.'

'Dennes—'

'Nat, don't make problems. We're doing all right. Just leave it like that,' Dennes said and walked away.

Dennes had looked so right in the garden. Grace couldn't believe it when she saw him, so relaxed, so tanned, his fair hair bleached by the summer sun. She had thought that she hated him, had spent a lot of time that summer feeding that hate, remembering how disgusting she thought he was and then he was just sitting in the garden with a book closed on the lawn beside his chair. It was difficult to hate him when he looked like that, and then she had seen Nat kissing Alexandra in the kitchen and she was more envious than she had ever been in her life. Her own life was so tedious that she wanted to scream. Each day was almost the same. She sat with her father, sometimes she read to him. She rarely went beyond the house; her mother did not believe in sitting in the sun, she feared for Grace's complexion. Her mother was still telling her how lovely she was, though Grace knew that this was no longer true. Nobody would have looked at her now, not that she saw anybody, nobody bothered with a daughter who had disgraced herself so surely. There were few visitors to the house, none for her, and she went nowhere except to church with her mother, and even there people merely looked. In the afternoons she sewed and in the evenings she sewed again or read. Sometimes her mother went out for an hour or two for tea or to a friend, but Grace was never invited. It was as though she was invisible, as though she did not exist. She would have spent a great deal of time at Alexandra's house but she felt like an intruder now that Dennes and Nat lived there.

At first she had comforted herself, thinking that respectable people would have nothing more to do with Alexandra, but after a little while people accepted the marriage to Nat and Grace thought this was possibly because Alexandra didn't care. She was so happy. It was hard to watch that happiness. Nat's name was constantly on Alexandra's lips and her eyes shone when she talked about him.

That night when they went to bed, for once Alexandra was not smiling.
'Well,' she said when the door was shut, 'what are you going to do?'
'What do you think I should do?'
'I asked you first.'
'I'm not going without Dennes.'
'That's not a good idea and he doesn't think it is either.'
'I know what he thinks.'

'Nat, you cannot expect the Hemingways to accept Dennes into the foundry after the way that he treated Grace.'

'What do you know about it?'

'I know everything. She's my friend. It's too much of a gamble to insist that they take Dennes. You know it is. Why risk it?'

'Because he'd do that for me. He hates not being there, Lex, he was born to work in a foundry, same as me. I can't go off there every morning and leave him to flog like a horse at the quarry. He's very clever. He knows what he's doing. He got that quarry up and running—'

'So did you.'

'He's instinctively good with men. They work for him, they listen to him, he knows when things go wrong, he knows what to do, he knows how to sort problems.'

'And what do you know?'

'I can buy and sell. I know the customers and the needs. It's a good combination, Alex, but it only works together. I can't run it all, it's too much to do and Nicholas is not enough backing when things go wrong or I can't sort them or the men get fed up. I can't do it.'

'Grace's parents will not have Dennes there and neither will Nicholas, and you know it. Nicholas is the way that he is because Dennes put him there, because Dennes isn't capable of love. You saw the state of Grace today. He should be ashamed of himself. When I think of the men that she could have married, and she's stuck there with her wretched mother and her dying father and he's making civil conversation to her in the garden as though there's nothing the matter.' Alexandra marched off to the bathroom, taking a nightdress with her.

When she came back Nat was standing by the window. She went to him. 'Are you angry?'

'No.'

'Yes, you are.'

'All right then, I am.'

Alexandra went and got into bed and turned her back to him but when he got in beside her he turned her over.

'Come on, Lex, don't fight with me.'

'You asked me what I thought and when I told you you got angry, or is it just that you can't bear to hear Dennes criticised?'

'I don't want to go to the foundry without him.'

'You don't have any choice right now. Give it some time. Maybe after a while they'll accept him.'

Alexandra thought that with it not only being a new year but a new century, it should have been a complete new start and possibly even better, but it didn't happen. There was tension in the house because Nat had too much to do and would not ask Dennes for help. Dennes didn't ask him to discuss the problems and even between Nat and herself things were not the same.

It was, Alexandra thought later, as though Dennes was perfectly well aware that they were arguing about him. He took no more days off, even though the weather was savage, and as the nights cut in and he couldn't work up at the quarry he shut himself upstairs in his room and did paperwork; at least that was what he claimed.

Nat was at the foundry most of the time and when he came home he was in the study. On Sundays he went up to the quarry to help. Just before Christmas, Grace's father died. Nicholas rarely went to the foundry and Alexandra saw what a burden it became that winter. Nat left the house at seven, was rarely back before seven in the evening, and even then could concentrate on nothing else. Every night he fell asleep over the papers, and when she woke up in bed alone she had to go downstairs to find him and wake him.

Dennes was only there for the evening meal. Sometimes he went to the farm to see Shona and the rest of the time he went to his room like a lodger.

In the end, one night in February, Alexandra went upstairs and knocked on the door and when she heard his voice she went in.

It was a big room, all the bedrooms were, but she usually never went in it. Dolly went in there to clean and that was all. The fire burned brightly and the lamps were lit. It was all clean and neat and the oak furniture looked soft in the light. Alexandra had had a desk put in there

269

for him when he first moved in, and he was sitting there now with a
pen in his hand. He stopped writing when he saw her and got up with
the kind of politeness which halted Alexandra in the doorway.

'May I come in?'

Dennes smiled at her. It was, Alexandra thought ruefully, a
devastating smile, totally disarming, warm like a good bath. She
wanted to tell him *every* secret she'd ever had in her life. She closed
the door.

'I want you to help,' she said.

'With what?'

'He's drowning in it, Dennes.'

'You didn't want me there.'

'Did Nat tell you that?'

'He wouldn't.'

'Things have changed.'

'Got worse,' Dennes said.

'Yes, got worse. Will you help?'

'When he asks me to I will.'

'He asked you to before and you turned him down.'

'That was because at that stage there was too much to lose.'

'And now there isn't?'

'I don't know. Nat has to decide that.'

Alexandra got to the door before Dennes said, 'If I'd been a better
person I would have left.'

'You just about have,' she said. 'Why don't you come down to the
sitting-room occasionally, remind yourself what it's like,' and she
walked out.

It didn't happen all at once. What happened was that Dennes ventured
into the study one evening in February on the pretext of looking for a
book, and then stood leaning against the desk for a second or two
while Nat finished writing. When Nat looked up he said, 'Problems?'

'I can't be in the office *and* in the works, and however— however
good the men are they don't see the whole thing, just bits of the
process, you know, and not everybody works together, not everybody

works at the same pace and some don't want to be there and some don't work at all and some are slack and . . .'

'Bad castings?' Dennes said.

Nat sat back in his chair and looked up at him.

'Yes,' he said.

'Know why?'

'Not yet. There's so much work I don't know where to turn.'

'Does Nicholas come in?'

'Sometimes. And when he does he's fine but he's just so unreliable. He knows what he's doing, Dennes, he's so good when he's there, but with him not being there most of the time any more I get left with his instructions and things get mixed up and sometimes the men tell me differently if there are mistakes and . . . it's such a mess.'

'What's this?' Dennes asked, turning round the papers in front of Nat.

'Anchors for Wexford's.'

They stayed up all night. Nat didn't notice, he just felt the way that his shoulders eased as they talked. He didn't notice that Alexandra didn't come in to remind him that he ought to sleep. From time to time Dennes built up the fire and they sat down later in easy chairs while the winter wind howled around the house, and it was not until the dawn broke grey and cold that Nat realised this was what he had really wanted, to talk to somebody who knew what he was talking about.

While it was still fairly early he took Dennes down to the works and they walked around just as Nat did every morning, to make sure that everything was going as it should, that the furnaces were ready, that the men turned in for their shift, that the jobs were being done, that the office had no immediate problems, and when they had done this they walked back up the icy road to the house for breakfast, and Nat thought when he saw his beautiful wife ladling out big platefuls of ham and eggs that a man couldn't wish for more than he had then. He went into the kitchen and kissed her and said, 'I'm sorry I didn't come to bed.'

'Nat, you haven't been much use in bed for weeks. I didn't miss you.'

Nat brought his hand down on her bottom and she turned and swore at him and then he pulled her into his arms and she laughed and kissed him.

'Go and have your breakfast before it gets cold,' she advised him.

Nat didn't want Nicholas to find out that Dennes was at the foundry from other people, so that first evening he went across to Esh House to talk to him.

Nicholas had not been to work that day, but his behaviour was so irrational that he could turn up at any time. Nat wanted to be tactful but he was worried that Nicholas would be angry at the idea of having Dennes anywhere near the works.

Nicholas hadn't been to the foundry for nearly three weeks. At least he was sober, and then Nat wasn't sure whether he was glad of that. Nicholas was sometimes easier to deal with when he was drunk but things were much better these days at Nicholas's house and Nat had to be glad of that. There were servants, the place was clean and tidy, the drive was free of weeds.

Nicholas was sitting in the study. He welcomed Nat so enthusiastically that Nat was sure he knew nothing about Dennes being at the foundry.

'How are things?' he said genially. 'How's married life these days?'

'It's fine.'

Nicholas offered him a drink. Nat said he would have tea, and though Nicholas hesitated over this, they both had tea.

'How's the foundry?' Nicholas said.

Nat had been waiting for him to ask. 'I want to take on some new help.'

'What sort of new help?'

'Dennes.'

Nat waited for the explosion. He didn't have long to wait.

'I won't have that bastard in my foundry!'

'I need the help,' Nat said.

'You and him, you always were as thick as thieves,' Nicholas said as he got up. 'You expect me to have him there after what he did?'

'He's good. There's nobody around here better. Don't you want people who can do their jobs to run the foundry?'

'There are other men—'

'Who?'

'There must be. I won't have him there, Nat. You should think yourself lucky that you're there.'

Nat had been prepared for Nicholas's anger. He had not been prepared for his own.

'What do you expect me to do, run the whole place by myself? I can't do it. I won't do it. When was the last time you showed your face there? You treat it like a toy, something you can pick up and put down whenever you feel like it—'

'Nat—'

'And as far as anything else goes he's been about as good as anybody could be about this—'

'What does that mean?'

'He practically owns half of it!'

Nicholas said nothing.

'Have you thought about that?' Nat asked him.

'Oh yes, I've thought about it. Grace and her mother own it.'

'Are you never going to accept the fact that Grace married him?'

'She would have been better with me. Where is she now? Living with her mother, like some old— like some old maid.'

'That doesn't change the fact that he's entitled to be there. Even you can't deny that, and you should be glad of his help in the way of one foundryman to another even if you hate his guts. And if I were you I'd try to accept it.'

Nicholas was silent for a few moments and then he said softly, 'He's not a good man to cross. At least I've learned that much.'

'Couldn't we all try to work together?' Nat said.

'Would he want to do that?'

'I'm sure he would.'

'It would only be for the good of the foundry. He would know that, wouldn't he? I've got no time for him otherwise,' Nicholas said.

The men knew that Dennes was a good foundryman, they didn't care

273

about the rest of his life and he was good with people. He liked to be in the works, keeping things going, helping the men, organising, getting what he wanted without putting anybody's back up, ensuring that things ran smoothly. It left Nat free to sort out the orders and the work going out, to deal with the customers and the office and buying and selling.

Nat was not prepared for the summons from the Hemingway household and he didn't somehow realise until he got there that he would have to face Mrs Hemingway and Grace without the old man. It seemed strange to be there when Anthony Hemingway was dead.

They kept him waiting on a Monday morning when he had a good many things to do at work. He stood impatiently at the sitting-room window. The first spring flowers were struggling through the soil, bedraggled snowdrops.

Although Grace occasionally came to the house she was careful to make sure that she never came again when Nat and Dennes were there, and he wasn't very impressed when she walked into the room. She didn't smile at him or speak, her eyes had no sparkle and her dress was black and had no ornament because she was in deep mourning. Her mother looked even worse, her cheeks flushed a hectic purple and her dress, too, unrelieved in any way. In the harsh winter light they looked like two severe wax dolls.

Nat said good morning very politely, and wished that he hadn't bothered. Mrs Hemingway didn't return the greeting. She said immediately, 'I understand that you have taken Dennes Eliot on at the works.'

'That's not quite how I'd put it,' Nat said.

'How would you put it, Mr Seymour?'

'I asked him if he would come and help me to run the foundry.'

'Well, I should think he fell over himself. Don't you think it would have been polite to ask us first?'

'I didn't realise that you were an expert on steelmaking, Mrs Hemingway.'

Nat thought that the purple cheeks were going to burst.

'I'm not talking about steelmaking, young man, I'm talking about common courtesy. You know very well how that man treated my daughter.'

Nat looked at Grace. The whole village was under the impression that Dennes had bedded another woman, they had been ready to believe it and Grace had let them. She was respectable, she was pitied, her husband had made her life a misery. It was commonly thought that Dennes had beaten her, kept her short of money and gone with other women, that and more depending on how much people had to talk about. Grace was a wronged woman, she had the village's sympathy and because she was Anthony Hemingway's daughter nothing could possibly be her fault.

'We need him there,' Nat said.

'Somebody else would have done.'

'Dennes knows what he's doing as well as anybody I ever met. He's a foundryman first, just like the rest of us. It can hardly concern you as long as we show a good profit. He's not going to come to the house and play tea-parties.'

'I don't want him there.'

'I don't think you have the authority to do anything about it,' Nat said, 'but do by all means go ahead and try.'

Mrs Hemingway glared at him. 'I was going to offer you tea, Mr Seymour, but I won't.'

'I haven't time for tea,' Nat said.

'I think you should leave.'

Nat went, but Grace followed him into the hall and outside into the icy wind.

'I want to talk to you,' she said.

Nat looked hard at her. 'What lurid thing did you tell your mother he did to you?'

'That he broke my heart,' Grace said. It should have sounded stupid and dramatic, but it didn't because Nat knew very well that it was true. 'How could you bring him in like that? That foundry has belonged to my family since it was started.'

'Forgive me, Grace, but aren't you married to Dennes? How close do you have to get?'

'I'll be happy if I never see him again.'

'Yes, it must be difficult to forgive people things they can't help.'

'That's not very nice.'

'My mother is dead, Grace, even Dennes acknowledges it.'

'It ruined my marriage! He had no right to marry me feeling like that, and I don't want him at the works. If you don't do something about it, then I will.'

'You can try, but I don't think it will get you anywhere. Nicholas agreed to it—'

'He's always drunk!'

'He still agreed to it. I wouldn't waste your energy if I were you, Grace. You'd be better off doing a nice piece of embroidery.'

Grace said nothing for a few moments and then said softly, 'That's very insulting.'

'It is, isn't it? My patience isn't what it used to be.'

'Neither are your manners.'

'I have a lot of work to do, if you and your mother want to keep on living the way that you do. Think of it this way, Grace, Dennes is keeping you in the manner to which you are accustomed,' and Nat went off down the drive towards the foundry.

'Did you have to wipe the floor with her?' Dennes asked when the men had gone home at dinnertime and Nat related the incident. They could have gone home for dinner but they didn't. They sat in the quietness of the office and ate sandwiches and talked. Nat stared at him.

'You actually miss her, don't you?'

'Yes. There was a time – a very short time, admittedly – when I thought everything was going to be all right. Stupid. I thought I might have a wife and a bairn and some peace.'

'You could.'

'No.'

'My mother's dead.'

Dennes gave up on his sandwiches and went to the window. Nat couldn't see why. It was an awful view, the foundry yard with open sheds where the patterns were stacked high, and the yard itself thick with dust. Further over, though out of sight of the office, the young men played football in their three-quarters-of-an-hour dinner break. Nat could hear their shouts and the sound of the ball against their feet and against the wall which was the goal from time to time.

'When you don't say goodbye to people, you don't think they're dead, don't you find that? I see her everywhere I go. I know that she's dead but part of me won't accept it, thinks that she can't be, not while I'm alive, and sometimes I think maybe I'm the one that's dead and then all I know is that we're parted. I have to go on telling myself that I'll never ever see her again.'

'What about afterwards?'

'Everlasting life? Hell, Nat, isn't it enough without an afterwards? Who would want to go through any of this again?'

'People don't believe—'

'Oh, I know, I know. It's wonderful and there's ice-cream every day. That's a load of shite and you know it.'

'Have you thought about why you cared about her? I mean, I loved her but that's different.'

'It isn't so very different. She was the first person to ever hold me in her arms like that.'

'Like what?'

'Like a mother would. I didn't know until then that people have different capacities for loving and that your mother had a talent for it. She didn't love you less because she loved Taylor and Dolly. I couldn't believe that she might love me and it wasn't until I killed William Daniels that it changed. After that I didn't love her like you did. It wasn't a pure thing any more, it was all to do with selfishness and wanting and being jealous. It wasn't better for that but I couldn't help it.'

'You were just older.'

'Maybe. I can't get over the fact that it was apparently never meant to be, that she never accepted me like that because of what I was and the age I was. I used to think I'd wake up one morning and we'd be the same age and we could get married and things would be all right but they never were and now she's dead. She won't get old and be

277

around and be there for us to get impatient with. I wanted at least to watch her get old and to be there with her. I didn't really imagine that that wouldn't happen, at least that, even if I couldn't have her, just for her to be here so that I could see her.'

'Like it's somehow a cheat.'

'Don't you feel like that?'

'Yes, but I've got Lex now,' Nat said.

Nicholas began to come in to work every day. Nat had thought he might order Dennes out, order them both out but he didn't, and neither did he contradict anything they were doing. He came to work every day of one week until Friday and when Nat went to Esh House that evening he was drunk again. Nat threw out the whisky, sobered him up, stayed overnight and the following Monday Nicholas was back at work again. That week he was there every day, but on the Friday night he got drunk again because when Nat and Dennes went to the house after work at midday on Saturday he was in bed.

They spent the day there, going through what was now a routine, throwing out the whisky, sitting with Nicholas and when he awoke he shouted and swore and raged at them. While he slept they sat by the fire and had tea and homemade chocolate cake and by the evening he came downstairs.

'You can go home.'

'I don't think—' Nat began

Nicholas looked gently at him. 'I won't drink anything stronger than tea.'

'Why don't you come with me?'

'I don't need nursemaiding every minute. I said I wouldn't.'

'I just thought you might like the company, that's all.'

'When I need your company, Nat, I'll let you know,' he said and went out.

Dennes looked at the door. 'He's getting better,' he said.

'He's not like he was.'

'All he wanted was a son, you know.'

'Whatever for?'

278

'Don't you want a son?'

'All I want is a drink,' Nat said. 'Watching him sober up makes me thirsty. Are we going for a swift pint?'

'I don't think I could get one down after watching him.'

'Just think. You can sit in a horrible stuffy little room, with the sun showing every speck of dust, you can't hear yourself think for the din of foundrymen talking over the week's sweat. The old men are spitting and smoking and coughing, the young ones are yelling and laughing and drunk. Howay man, you couldn't ask for more.'

For a month everything they did was wrong at work. He shouted at them all day, he complained about the orders. He complained about how they treated the customers. He complained that the castings were no good, that the work wasn't being turned out fast enough, that there was no night shift. Then he complained about how the new night shift was organised and who would see to it. For a month all they seemed to say was 'Yes, sir' and 'No, sir' until finally one Friday afternoon Dennes lost his temper. Nat had seen it coming for a couple of days and finally Dennes told Nicholas to 'do it your bloody self then' and threw the papers at him and walked out.

Nat watched the papers fall to the floor, and he looked at Nicholas was who sitting behind his desk. 'You wanted that, didn't you?'

Nicholas paused before he answered. 'I thought I did, yes.'

'I think if you look closely at it,' Nat bent down and picked the papers up from the floor, 'you'll find he's right. He usually is.'

Nicholas got up and went out into the main office where he shouted at Dennes, 'Get your backside in here, I'm not finished with you yet! Are you listening to me, Eliot?'

Dennes went back into the office.

'Go and do some work, Nat,' Nicholas said, and when Nat closed the door after him Nicholas looked at Dennes. 'I didn't mean to push you so hard. I don't want you to leave, the figures are fine. I just wanted you to make a mistake, that's all.'

'I do, all the time.'

'Not that many. I'm never going to like you and you're never going to like me, too much has happened between us; but you're entitled to stay here and work because of who you are, so I'll try and be civil.'

'That would make a nice change,' Dennes said and walked out.

That night Dennes walked over to Esh House. It was raining hard and Nicholas was sitting over a fire.

'What the hell do you want?' he said lightly as the new housekeeper, Mrs Evans, showed Dennes into the sitting-room.

'I just wondered if you were all right.'

'You mean you thought I was drunk after this afternoon.'

'I thought you might be.'

'Do you want some tea? It's all there is in the house, thanks to you and that other interfering young bastard.'

Dennes stayed and had tea.

'Do you play chess?' Nicholas asked afterwards.

'A bit.'

They sat down over the fire and played while the rain spattered the windows, and it was very late when Nicholas finally conceded defeat. He eyed Dennes.

'So that's a bit, is it? Who taught you to play?'

'Nat. His dad showed him.'

'And is Nat as good as you?'

'He wins sometimes.'

Nicholas got up as Dennes started to leave. 'Tell me, why did you bother?'

'Sir?'

'You took everything, first Gwen, then Grace and afterwards the foundry – no, don't deny it. Anthony's dead, it's as good as yours and you know it. You may put up with Dorothy's moanings but you are married to her daughter. You must have known that I'd get in your way if you got me back to work, so why bother?'

'I admire you. Nat and me, we always did.'

Nicholas started to laugh. 'Whatever for?'

'Because you're a good foundryman. Because you started off at the bottom and because you can do everything. You made me think that people can get somewhere worth getting.'

'I don't have anything worth having now.'

'Yes, you have. You have ability, that's more important than anything in the world.'

Nicholas paused there by the fire and then he said, 'Do you have any idea why I don't like you?'

'Because of what I did, presumably.'

'No. I disliked you before you did anything. I remember when you were a child, seeing you in the back lane. It was difficult to tell what was bruises and what was dirt. I deliberately never went near if I could help it, you reminded me so much of what my life had been like when I was a child. I wanted to . . . pick you up and run away with you, your eyes were so hard. My childhood was just like that.'

'You gave me an apprenticeship.'

'I just knew that you were going to be good. You were so much brighter than everybody else, so much faster to understand and you loved it and that's something that people either have or haven't. I could go back to the bottle properly and leave you to get on with it.'

'I'd rather you didn't,' Dennes said.

Nicholas looked at him and smiled suddenly. 'Maybe I won't,' he said.

Thirty

During the spring and summer of that year Shona was often unwell. Taylor and George Smith had taken over the full running of the quarry and Dennes spent a lot of time at the foundry, but as Shona became worse he went daily to the farm. He found help for her but it was the company that Shona needed. He tried to persuade her to move in with them but she wouldn't leave her house or her animals. She had never been a great one for company, and when she could no longer go for her Sunday dinner they used to go over on a Sunday and Alexandra would make a meal, until Shona was so poorly that she couldn't do with a lot of company around her. After that Alexandra did her shopping and called in often and Dennes went there daily, ostensibly to milk Emerald and Bryan in the evening and lock up the hens and the ducks, but just to make sure that Shona was not left alone for too long. As the time went on he began staying overnight until it became every night.

The farm felt safe to Dennes, it felt like a big woman with a child. Each night the glow of its lamps in the old sitting-room beckoned as he walked home, the stones of the farm road hard under his feet. In the firelight, all else forgotten, he could sit with his eyes closed and just be. You could wipe the past, he had discovered. If you were careful and governed your mind you could live just for now, ask for nothing, accept the cold autumn dawns, the simple affection of the animals, be thankful for what had to be done each day and let the quietness grow up around you like summer grass.

He liked the crisp frost, going out to feed Shona's well-housed cows, talking to Emerald and Bryan, sitting in the byre while Bryan let down her frothy milk into the clean bucket, the warmth of her body, the patience of her stance. The fields were white and stiff and quite still and Shona would have him throw bread out for the birds each day as though she could take care of the whole animal kingdom.

Christmas came. Alexandra had lots of things planned at the house but Shona was too ill to go anywhere. She was quite content to sit over the fire and let Dennes do the outside jobs. She had good food, there was plenty of wine. They played board games and read and when the weather was fine Dennes walked along the cold roads quite alone.

Just after Christmas Shona had a stroke and died. The farm was willed to a nephew who came from Darlington to claim it. Grace went to the funeral just out of respect and she thought she had never seen anybody so silent or so still as Dennes was at Shona's funeral and afterwards at Esh House, where Nicholas had generously said they could have tea. He neither cried nor spoke and moved as though each step was an unaffordable luxury. He didn't look at her once and at the tea she didn't dare go to him. She felt petty, as though she had somehow betrayed him, and she left early and went home with her mother.

Nicholas asked Dennes into the library. There was snow beyond the window, several days old, rather dirty snow which was a nuisance because the paths were icy where the snow had been partially cleared, and a cold wind blew across from the fell.

'Are you staying at the farm?'

'Yes. Just until things are sorted. Philip – Shona's nephew – will see to everything.'

'Is he going to live there?'

'Yes. He has a wife and two children and he's worked on farms all his life. I'll have to show him how to go on with Bryan though.'

'Bryan?'

'Shona's cow. She's called Bryan. She likes you to talk to her when you milk her.'

'Really?'

Dennes was silent. He couldn't think why he had had to talk about Bryan. It made him feel so stupid. Every time he talked about her he wanted to cry and wanting to cry took him back to that night when Shona had been so comforting after his grieving of Gwen and he had not cried. He remembered reading something which said that when you cried, your tears were only for you. He didn't feel worth any tears, he wanted so much to run back to the farm and have it be normal there with Shona fussing over the chickens or stirring some delicious stew on the stove. He knew now that he could learn to hate the farm. Philip had been there with his pretty, gentle wife. They had a small boy of about two and she had a baby in her arms, a little girl with pudgy fists and huge blue eyes. The farm was fast becoming somebody else's. Soon he knew that even seeing it at a distance would hurt because of the memories.

'What are you going to do?'

'Do?'

Dennes thought about this room, he remembered pleading for Mary here. Nicholas didn't look any different, any older. He rarely got drunk now, he was clear-eyed and clear-headed. Dennes had learned to be glad of him at work, to respect his judgement. He didn't shout any more, he didn't argue, at least not on the same level. If Nicholas thought you were doing something wrong at work he called you into the office and questioned you tartly and minutely until he was satisfied everything was as it should be, and if it wasn't he fixed you with a very cold look and asked in bored tones if you were quite sure you had got that right.

'I'm going to stay at the farm until Philip takes it over, but I'll come to work every day. It shouldn't take too long. Apparently the will is quite clear, Philip gets everything, there's nobody else and he'll look after the farm, he knows what he's doing and he's good.'

'Dennes, things have changed. If I could go back and alter it, I would, but I can't. We've treated one another very badly in the past, but if there is anything I can do now to help I want to do it.'

Dennes looked at him and grinned suddenly and Nicholas smiled back at him.

'Thanks,' he said.

After her father died Grace's life got even smaller. She could have screamed with frustration. Her mother seemed reasonably content with a life which was only on the edge of other people's lives, and although Grace was gradually accepted as she was, nobody bothered with her at all. That winter it was even worse. The long dark nights, the short cold days sapped her energy until she would sit over the fire all day with a book in her hands. She badly wanted to go to Alexandra's house but she didn't, and by February when the world was full of slush and silence she had taken to getting up late, going to bed early, meeting no one, saying little and not wanting to do anything.

One day that month Alexandra came to the house, all red-cheeked and glowing from the walk, and invited Grace to go back with her. It was the first time in weeks Grace had felt lively. She went and sat in Alexandra's kitchen and ate a big bowl of broth and listened to Dolly's chatter, and then she helped Alexandra make cakes in the afternoon and a big stew for dinner.

Before darkness came she would have left, she didn't want to be there when the men came home, but she wanted so badly to be in company. Men were no longer of her world, she didn't know what to say to them, and especially she didn't want to see Dennes.

Taylor came back first from the quarry, and he was cheerful and open and treated her as though they saw one another every day, but the darkness had fallen for a couple of hours before Nat and Dennes came back. Grace couldn't help the way that she enjoyed the company. They all sat round the kitchen table and ate and the stew was just like it should have been, the beef falling apart, the vegetables cooked to perfection, the potatoes golden, the bread baked the day before, and there was still some apple wine which had been Shona's and after a glass of this Grace felt herself reluctant ever to go home.

She thought of the quietness of her house.

'So, Grace,' Nat said when they had finished eating, 'what are you doing these days?'

'Not much.'

'Have you ever thought about working?'

'Working? Doing what?'

'How about office work?'

Grace looked across the table at him. 'I can't do anything like that,' she said.

'Why not?'

'I don't know how to.'

'You could learn. There are typing courses to go to and you can add up, can't you?'

'Yes, but—'

'You're happy doing embroidery?' Nat said.

Grace looked hard at him. 'You're so rude to me. I don't do embroidery.'

'So what do you do?'

'I'm a lady, I don't have to do anything.'

'How very entertaining for you.'

Grace glanced quickly at Dennes. She didn't believe now that they had ever been married. He wasn't even looking at her, he was taking a keen interest in his empty plate.

'What would you like me to do, Nat?'

'Well, since you do partly own the steelworks it would be quite helpful if you did some work towards it, don't you think?'

'Why should I when you and Dennes do it?'

'We don't do the typing or open the letters or . . . well, I try to add up. I could do with some help. How about it?'

Grace glanced again at her husband. 'Have you talked about this?'

'I've only just thought of it.'

'Don't you think you might talk about it first?'

Nat looked at Dennes. 'Do you mind?' he said pointedly.

Dennes shrugged. 'Doesn't matter to me,' he said.

It was the worst thing he could have said, Grace thought. He didn't care, she didn't matter, he wasn't interested. It made her angry.

'All right then,' she said, 'I will.'

She regretted it afterwards; she didn't want to do it, she wasn't interested, she didn't like Nat, she didn't want to work, it was beneath her dignity. Ladies didn't work. Worse still, Dennes offered to see her home.

'I'm quite capable of going by myself.'

'I'm sure you are.'

'Come over tomorrow,' Alexandra called as they left, 'I'm going to sort out the attic. You can help if you like.'

Dennes didn't talk to her as they went. The air was bitter. She slipped once and he caught her, and Grace was so miserable looking into his green eyes and remembering how much she had loved him, but when she got home and he said goodnight briefly and went, she was happier than she had been in a long time, not least because he had said, 'You can start on Monday if you like. Half-past eight.'

'Isn't that awfully early?'

'Not really. If you were a furnaceman you'd be there at five. Think yourself lucky.'

The idea of herself as a furnaceman made Grace want to laugh when she thought about it later. She had thought too that her mother would be against the idea, but when she mentioned it her mother surprised her.

'You don't get out enough,' she said as though the foundry was a social outlet.

One of the things which frightened Grace was having to spend a lot of time with Dennes, but it didn't work like that, he was rarely in the office for long. It was Nat she dealt with mostly and that was easy by comparison. Firstly he showed her the filing system and then he set her to re-organising it. That took two or three days and during that time she got used to things. Being proud of her achievement in having the filing system perfect made Grace think back to the early days of her marriage when she had learned to bake and cook and sew and look after a house and be glad of doing something. She was so much happier. She had found a typewriting course and was studying that one evening a week. She even stopped starting and blushing every time Dennes walked into the office because he was always preoccupied and paid her little attention.

Grace went home for her midday meal. She would have liked to have stayed, because everybody else left and Dennes and Nat sat in the office and talked and she wanted to be involved and listen to the talk. Luckily one day in her second week it snowed so much that to get there and back and eat in three-quarters of an hour would have been folly, so they shared their sandwiches with her and she sat and watched the snow fall beyond the window.

She discovered that she was especially good at adding figures. At first the columns of figures were difficult, but they soon became much easier. It was not just the work, she liked the comings and goings of the men, the way people came in and out of the office, the problems, being there and knowing when the orders were good and when they weren't, what the shipbuilder had said about the latest castings, whether the idea of a shovel shop was a good earner. It was all of interest to Grace.

Every evening Dennes walked her home, since it was still dark when they left the office. She didn't grow used to him, but she managed to talk about work all the way home and that was safe ground. Even Nicholas was polite to her at work. And the best thing of all was her paypacket. Grace hadn't expected to be paid, had thought they wanted her to help because her family owned half of the company, but at the end of the week there was a little brown envelope on her desk. Her mother was horrified at the idea of working for money. Ladies didn't, but Grace had never tasted independence before and she liked it.

In the January of that year Queen Victoria died, and after the initial sorrow, the energy and ideas of the new King were quite inspiring. It made Grace feel energetic. Alexandra invited her over quite often then on Saturday afternoons, and Grace liked to go because once she finished work she had nothing else. One afternoon Dolly had been spring cleaning and Alexandra was baking when Grace got there. Taylor was out, he had begun courting a miner's daughter in the

289

village. Alexandra had told Grace privately that she thought Dolly had a young man too because she kept disappearing on Saturday evenings. Nat and Dennes were in the study. Grace sat down and sampled the freshly baked cake and had some tea, and thought how nice it was that some things had never changed. Alexandra's baking was just as good as it had always been. Nat and Dennes came into the kitchen to have tea and sponge cake with plum jam and they talked about the autumn and picking the pears and plums.

'It was harder work than Mr Templeton,' Dennes said, and Grace began to laugh because she knew Mr Templeton. He was their worst customer. He changed his orders often, he was always late with his payments and he complained about everything. Her eyes met Dennes' across the table and she remembered how much she had loved him and then she didn't want the rest of her cake. She said little more, she didn't stay. She began to walk slowly home and as she did so she heard him call her name, and she stopped while he caught up to her. Then she began to walk slowly again and Dennes went with her.

'We can do away with the marriage, you know,' he said.

'What?' Grace stopped again.

He didn't look at her. 'It can be got rid of. It was never real. I thought you might like that.'

Grace thought of the little house in Irish Back Street. She never went past the entrance if she could help it and she could not forget the good times. She thought how stupid it was considering how difficult everything had been, how she and Dennes had fought in so many different ways, how they had turned away from one another in bed, but her mind replayed over and over the way that he had tried to look after her. The truth was that if it had not been for him she would have been married to Mr Barmouth by now, and he seemed to her a thousand years old. Sometimes she took the amber ring from its tiny box.

'You mean divorced?' Such a dirty word it was, her mother would be scandalised.

'No, it's not like that, just as though it had never been.'

'I don't see how that could be.'

'Legally.'

'Legally? Is that all?'

'Grace, you might want to get married properly some time. Have you thought about that?'

'I never wanted to marry anybody except you—'

'You might want to.'

'What is this, Dennes, have you seen somebody you like? Has Gwen Seymour been reincarnated?'

He paused over that and Grace wished that she hadn't said it.

'I'm sorry,' she said desperately.

'No, I'm sorry. I should never have gone through with it. I just . . . I thought I could break free, you know, start over.'

'But you couldn't?'

'No, but I want you to be able to, if you want.'

Grace looked at him. 'You haven't thought very hard about this, have you?'

'What do you mean?'

'You lose everything that way.'

'Every what thing?'

'The foundry. Don't tell me you don't want it? I doubt you can breathe without it.'

'There's the quarry and I'll make my own way. I'll find something else.'

'Like what?'

'I don't know. You'll manage without me. Nicholas is there now and he seems a lot better. He and Nat won't cheat you.'

'You're going to go away, aren't you?'

'Yes, I think I probably will. I've spent my whole life here. It's not the world.'

'It's the best bit!' Grace said fiercely.

'You haven't seen the rest, Gracie, how do you know?' he said with a smile.

Grace had thought that she would never hear that softened version of her name on his lips again, she had thought that she would never want to, that she hated it, but it sounded so sweet now.

'I've seen London and that was nothing to get excited about,' Grace said and she set off walking at a furious pace, not looking back.

'People do come back, you know, Nat,' Dennes said, later that evening in the study, having suggested to Nat that he might leave.

'Do they?' Nat said in a hard strange voice.

'You've got Alex and the foundry and a future. You don't need me.'

Nat glared at him. 'I didn't ever need you. It was you. Where would you go?'

'I don't know. America maybe, Australia. There are lots of places. Nicholas will help you at the works and Taylor and George run the quarry much better without me.'

'And Grace?'

'She'll be free of me.'

'You think somebody else is going to take her, around here?'

'She could go to London, stay with her aunt.'

'Don't you think she's a bit old for that? And are you sure she wants to be free of you? That is the reason for all this, isn't it, your guilt over Grace?'

'What other reason could there possibly be?'

'The foundry. You feel guilty about the way that you got it.'

'I told you, I don't want the wretched foundry.'

'And you have to prove that to Grace?'

'It'll be hers then. She won't have any problem finding a husband.'

'She will when they find out that what she wants is you.'

'She doesn't, not any more.'

'Are you sure?'

'She never did want me, not me, somebody she thought I was.'

'And you never loved her?'

'No, I didn't.'

'But you do now?'

'No, I don't.'

Nat looked at him. 'So how come you spend so much time in the office when you're meant to be in the works, sitting on her desk talking to her?'

'I don't.'

'Yes, you do. Half a dozen times last week.'

'That was about work, Nat.'

'Dennes, you talked more to Grace last week than you did to me. What is she doing, running the place?'

'I didn't,' Dennes said. 'What are we talking about this for? I'm getting out, that's what I'm doing,' and he left the room.

On the Wednesday afternoon of that week he and Grace had the office to themselves and he stood against the front of her desk as he had taken to doing lately, Grace thought, and he said, 'Did you see your solicitor?'

'No.'

'I thought you were going to?'

Grace got up and put a file back into the filing cabinet. The wrong filing cabinet, the wrong place. She tried to remember for later, to move it, otherwise she would spend hours searching for it when she wanted it.

'I didn't say I was.'

'But we agreed.'

'No, we didn't.'

She didn't sit back down again, he was so very much in the way.

'We have to sort this out before I go.'

'Why?'

'Well, because.'

'Do you want to marry somebody else?'

'No.'

'Neither do I. So what's the problem?'

Grace did sit down again. She fixed a piece of paper into her typewriter. Her eyes told her that it wasn't straight but she didn't care. She consulted her notes and began typing faster than she should have, making mistakes.

'Could you get off the desk?' she said. 'We can talk about this some other time. I have a lot of work to do.'

'Don't you want me to go?'

'It was your idea.'

293

'I can't stay here like this, Grace.'

'Why not? I thought you were reasonably happy with things. You've got a nice place to live, the quarry, the foundry—'

'I gave you a way out—'

'There is no way out.' Grace looked at him. 'Nobody's ever going to marry me. I'm almost beneath their notice now. Can you imagine how they would treat me if you left me like that? You're my husband. If you walk out and leave me for good, nobody will marry me. I'll never have anything. I'm secondhand goods, that's what I am.'

'No, you're not. The law would prove that you're not.'

'Things like that don't mean anything to people around here, Dennes, it's appearances that do, and the fact of the matter is that you never wanted me. You married me for what it could get you and nothing more. You never loved me. You never loved anyone except Gwen Seymour, and I'm beginning to think that I never really loved you. I was just taken in by the way that you look. I thought there was something about you, something special. I didn't realise that you had given all the love you had to her. I thought there might have been crumbs left for other people.' To her horror Grace began to cry. There was no warning, no obstruction in her throat, no threat behind her eyes, no feeling of misery in her stomach.

She was quite well aware of the big window in the office, of people passing by, workmen, possible visitors, Nat or Nicholas. She was also aware of the papers which had scattered on to the floor around her desk. The 's' letter of her typewriter was stuck to the paper and would most likely make a black mark or a hole and it would all have to be done again.

He did nothing. He didn't move. He didn't walk out like most men would have done or try to take her into his arms or talk to her to try and stop the flow. Grace just wished that he would go away or that somehow she could get up and run out of the office but she couldn't. It was the most inappropriate place possible for them to have this kind of discussion, for her to cry. She was hot and uncomfortable and damp now and she couldn't look at him.

'You went to bed with her, didn't you?'

Some other very forward female said that, Grace felt sure that she couldn't have, not in a thousand years. The words were all cracked like old saucers, disjointed, but they came out anyway. He didn't say anything straight away but when Grace looked at him he looked straight back at her and said, 'No, I didn't.'

'I don't believe you.'

'I spent the night with her once, it was the night that she miscarried. She and Nicholas, he blamed her for what happened and after he'd gone I went into her room and held her in my arms until she went to sleep, but that was all.'

'I assumed that you had.'

'Why?'

'Because of the way that you treated me. I assumed that I was just . . . not good enough.'

'How could that possibly be true?' He had got down beside her now, down beside her chair. Grace hoped sincerely that nobody would come in.

'Then why didn't you want me?'

Dennes wasn't quite looking at her. 'I'm . . . not decent.'

'Dennes, I loved you.'

'That made it worse.'

'I don't understand. I've known you a long time, I know what you're like and what you've done. I can't see what difference it makes. Was there somebody else? Lily Hodgson or Mary at the house—'

'No.'

'What, then? Tell me.'

'All right, I'll tell you and after that I want you to go to your solicitor and sort it out.'

'I don't want to—'

'You will. I'm not going to come back into the office after this. I'm going to leave and your solicitor can deal with my solicitor and it'll be easier. I went . . . I went to bed with my mother. Not just once, lots of times, many many times, right from being a small child. I don't remember a time when I didn't, right up 'til she left me. I was almost a man by then. The last thing that she needed was another man. She liked me to tell her how much I loved her. She liked to pretend.' Dennes got to his feet.

While Joseph had slept on the rug on the kitchen floor she had taken Dennes into her bed. It was heaven after the rug, and there he could make her happy. She showed him how to please her. It was the only time that she was happy, and he could do it, like the magician he had seen that one time on the street, making things appear and disappear and change. It was like the book when you opened it. He could watch her eyes take on the blue brilliance they had once had all the time, watch her lips part, the pink tongue against her teeth. He thought then that she remembered being young, the feel of a pretty dress against her skin and the young man she had loved.

She confused them, the gin on her, she thought it was the days when she was young and played the piano. Her fingers were so fine and slender and pale against the dirty bedcovers and he could make the magic which other men could not, her eyes shining, widened, liquid, great starred pools. He could drown there in the darkness, slowly, slowly, going under again and then again until the little pit town was gone from his sight, the empty hunger was banished, even the bed was some miraculous island floating under them and he was the man that she had longed for all that time. It was his name on her lips and she was young again.

Grace stared at him. The sun had broken through the clouds and was edging its way into the office window, turning his hair to gold. She remembered now the child that he had been, she remembered people talking about the dirty house in Wesley Street. She remembered being told never to go near and knowing that other children were not allowed near, not to make friends with him.

Other children went about together, went to school, played football, went home to tea but the times that she had ever come close enough to Dennes and his younger brother in that small part of the back lane which they had designated theirs and where they spent nearly all their time she remembered well: those bright green eyes, hard just like they were now, the fair hair hidden under a dirty cap, the ill-fitting clothes. It was difficult to think of him like that. He was so big and intelligence had won in his face. Comfort had taken away the skinniness and good clothes had done the rest, but she could see that time had not rescued him from that back lane, and neither had Gwen Seymour because she didn't love him sufficiently or because the problems had seemed insurmountable.

He was on his feet now, ready to leave, waiting only for the disgust to take over her face before they were free of one another and he could walk away.

She remembered his mother, fair like he was, tall and slender and beautiful. Grace had seen her once, seen other women ignore her, cross the street away from her. She didn't know where Tammy Eliot had come from, but if it was true that she had spent her young life in a children's home, if she had been lonely and neglected and had had no way to survive other than by giving herself to men, then somehow it seemed understandable that she had broken her beautiful child over it.

Grace imagined Dennes as very small, very taking and she unable to provide the barest things which children needed. Perhaps she didn't know who the man had been. Perhaps he had treated her badly. Perhaps it had been nothing but a slight encounter before he went home to his wife, for a few pennies. Perhaps Tammy had hated Dennes for ruining her perfect figure with his very being and then needing all those things which a child needs, like a sponge soaking up all and giving little, the crying, the food, the love. Was it then that she had found the gin bottle? Was it the only refuge? And to take revenge in the most basic way possible, by making him provide pleasure such as men had done to her.

He was turning away, turning towards the door. Grace did the most unladylike thing she had ever done in her life. She got past him and turned around and stood back against the door. Dennes looked at her. He even smiled a little. 'Aren't you going to let me out?'

'No.'

'Why not?'

'Because.'

He misunderstood her. He thought she wanted the explanation.

'I'm not fit for anybody, Grace. I could go to bed with you and drive you out of your mind—'

'I don't want to be driven out of my mind!'

'Good. Are you going to let me go?'

'No.'

'You can't stand against the door forever. Somebody might want to come in.'

'Stop being so reasonable!'

'I liked going to bed with my mother.'

'No, you didn't. You couldn't have.'

'Why not? It was all there was. There was no food, not much anyway, there were no friends, there were no distractions like school or comfort. I wasn't even any good at football but oh, I'm bloody good in bed.'

Grace was starting to cry now. 'I love you, Dennes. Don't you care for me?'

'I told you. I'm not fit. I can't love you, Grace.'

'No? So all that time when we lived in Irish Street and you kept me, all those times when you didn't take me to you because— because I was so pure and you weren't, all that time when you were so kind to me – that isn't love? I think you're a liar of the biggest kind, Dennes Eliot, because I think you daren't love me because I was everything that you weren't. I think you're desperate to take me to bed, only you're a coward and you're going to run away because you're frightened that when you get me there I'm going to turn into your mother!'

Dennes was looking curiously at her but he didn't say anything.

'It's true, isn't it, Dennes? You're frightened because you hated her.'

He still didn't say anything for a few moments and he wasn't looking at her now. 'Men used to stay sometimes. At first I assumed that they were my father but I realised after a while that they weren't because they never stayed long. Joseph and me – we used to sleep on the floor. He was such an ugly little bugger, she never took him to bed. Do you know what the worst thing was?'

He stopped there. Grace waited for him to go on and when he didn't she said, 'What?'

298

'Saturdays. I hate Saturdays. There were parties on Saturdays and we never got invited. The other bairns they would— they would run down the back lane all done up with a present in their hands, you know. Our Joseph used to hang over the back gate, swinging on it a bit, you know? He used to hang over the back gate and watch them. I'd have given anything . . .'

Grace left the door to go to him. It was just as well, because moments later Nat came in. He didn't seem to notice at first, the silence, the fact that nobody was doing anything. He went to his desk and then he said into the silence, 'Templeton wants those castings today, Dennes. He didn't—'

'Oh, bugger Templeton,' Dennes said and walked out.

Grace went back to her desk, remembered the file she had put in the wrong place, spent several long moments finding it again and refiling it, and then she pulled the piece of paper out of her typewriter to start again.

'Where's he going?' Nat asked as Dennes walked away in the direction of the foundry gates.

'I don't know.'

'Do you have to fight in the office?'

'We didn't fight.' A tear splashed on to the typewriter.

Nat went over to her, and for the first time in her life Grace got up and put herself into a man's arms. Nat fastened both arms around her and held her tight.

'If he's hurt you I'll murder him.'

'It's worse than that. I don't think he's coming back.'

'There's nothing you can do about it, Grace.'

Grace moved away, eyeing the office window just in case Dennes was still there somehow. Then she sat down at the typewriter and began again.

Nat went home at six. Dennes was in the garden. It was almost dark out there. He walked across the soaking grass and Dennes, who was standing with his back to the house, either heard him or sensed him because he turned.

'I'm sorry,' he said. 'Did you manage to sort Templeton out?'

'Yes. Don't worry.' Nat hesitated but Dennes didn't go on, so he said, 'Grace cried all over me. My shoulder's still damp.'

Dennes smiled. 'Do you remember the first time we met?'

'You got me drunk. I was sick all over the back lane.'

'I never had a friend before then. It changed everything.'

Rain began to fall quite heavily in the gathering dusk. It made Nat think of all the conversations they had had in freezing back lanes in varying circumstances.

'Neither did I. We moved about too much. I was always fighting with everybody. We were always leaving. My father was always leaving. I don't ever want to do that again.'

'Do you know why this place is so clean?' Dennes said. 'It's because all the rubbish blows straight through it.'

'I love it. I found everything that's important to me here.'

Dennes touched him on the shoulder.

'I'll see you later,' he said.

Nat watched him cross the lawn, go out of the side gate and then he was lost from sight.

Grace had walked home in the rain and her mother had insisted that she should go upstairs and change before she took cold. The fire was burning cosily in her room and so was the lamp, but she didn't change, she stood by the fire. She went to the window after a little while and listened to the rain falling and looked out into the dark garden. Light from the downstairs rooms spilled out on to the lawns. She pulled the curtains across and went back to the fire. She didn't even want to cry any more. She felt cried out, empty. Her mother would expect her downstairs soon, changed and ready to eat. Grace didn't think she was ever going to eat again.

She heard a noise behind her like somebody knocking on the window. She stared and then jumped after it stopped and started again, and she went over and opened the curtains. Dennes was standing on the flat porch roof outside her window. She drew back the curtains and opened the window.

300

'We do have a front door you know,' she said as he eased himself inside.

'I saw the light. Anyroad, I don't want to talk to your mother.'

'You're soaking.'

Dennes took off his hat and pushed back his hair. 'So are you.'

'I walked home late. I thought you'd have gone,' Grace said, and went over to the fire and stretched out her hands to the blaze.

'How could I leave here?'

'I keep telling you. It's the best place in the world.'

He followed her over to the fire and turned her to him.

'Will you have me, Grace?'

'Of course I will. I love you.'

Dennes went over and turned the key in the lock. He had the awful feeling that when he did so the room would change, and he would be fourteen again in that dark room in Back Wesley Street from where he had heard so often the sounds of other children playing in the lane. He had even known some of their names, though they had never spoken to him except to shout obscenities from safely across the street. They had long since stopped fighting with him unless there were more than two of them. Occasionally a gang of them got him down into the dirt and kicked him and thumped him and forced him to say that his mother was a whore, but they grew tired of that after a while and left him alone.

When Joseph had been younger he was frightened to be left in the kitchen alone at night. Dennes had found him a special blanket for these times and promised him stories later. She would be calling him, it might be late, the children would have gone inside. Her breath was gin-sweet. He could pretend, just like Joseph did over the stories, eyes closed, mind freed, outside, sunshine, the wind in the heather and he like a bird flying low over the purple sea.

Dennes locked the door and turned around. The room hadn't changed at all. The fire was burning so brightly, the room was well-furnished and neat. Rain ran down the window and the girl was standing, her fair hair dark with rain. She didn't know anything about this, she didn't know how it could be, so awful, so sweaty, so low. His instincts told him to run, all geared for flight.

She was perfect. He didn't want to spoil her. She was debating with herself whether to go to him, he could see, but she didn't, she stayed where she was and let him walk all the way back to her. He cupped her face in his hands and kissed her. He could taste the desperation on her and the fear, the way that she was holding herself back in case he might think that she was bold, that she might want him too much and he would back off. He kissed her and then he eased away the fear by talking to her until her eyes were shining and she was laughing and breathless and confident.

Somebody knocked sharply on the door to remind her of dinner. Dennes picked her up and carried her over and put her down on to the bed and she bit her lip over the deception as she called out that she didn't want anything to eat, she had a headache and was going to rest. The footsteps went away.

Her neck smelled faintly of the eau de cologne that she had put on that morning, her hair smelled of rain and her clothes smelled of foundries and sharp wet dust and the office papers and the cigars which Nicholas smoked. She took down her hair and it was long and luxuriant and curling damply.

He thought that she would be shy and awkward but she was only sufficiently so to remind him that this was new. Her body was young and creamy, smooth and soft and so eager. She tried to hold back but Dennes didn't let her. He coaxed her into forgetting all the ladylike submissive things she had spent her life learning until she was naked in his arms and smiling into his eyes.

It was a wonderful bed, the sheets were clean, the pillows were white, and yet at the back of his mind he thought that he could hear Joseph crying faintly from downstairs. He tried to remember that Grace knew nothing about this, she didn't want or need sophistication, tricks, the cleverness that jaded bodies demanded. The slightest touch was enough. Short of clumsiness nothing mattered now. He had created the fire in her eyes, could see the way that her body drew bravely nearer. He didn't have to say anything beyond a few soft words. She was not frightened, she was not pleasured out of her mind so that she was the receiver rather than a participant. She was fully in her senses and totally in his arms, her blue eyes bright with love and her hands cool on his skin. He had considered gentleness in case she was hurt but it was not like that either, it was a complete and total meeting of two fully willing people and Dennes had never experienced anything like that before in his life. She was not spoiled, she was not injured, she was his. She was his wife.

The fire burned low in the grate. The room was quite dark beyond the pool of light which the lamp gave. Grace thought that she loved him more now than she had ever done, and though he hadn't said so she thought that the feeling was returned. She smiled at him across the pillows and then leaned over and kissed him. He drew her down and prolonged the kiss and then he said, 'Will you come and live with me? I want you in my bed every night.'

'As well as in your office every day?'

'I'll try to keep my hands to myself in the office.'

'We have to tell my mother.'

'I'll see her tomorrow night,' Dennes said and fastened his arms around her.

Luckily Dennes was out of the office nearly all the following day or Grace knew she would have got nothing done. She made mistakes and had to double-check everything. Nat and Nicholas had gone to Sunderland to do business and it was an unusually quiet day.

Grace went home and ate with her mother and afterwards Dennes arrived. She took him in where her mother was sitting by the fire, for once not doing anything. Dorothy looked up when they walked in but she didn't seem surprised to see Dennes. Grace had thought that her mother would object, perhaps even shout, but she did neither and when Dennes had been polite and said good evening and how fine the day had been and enquired after her health, he paused and then he said, 'I want Grace to come and live with me.'

Dorothy Hemingway looked down. 'I thought that might happen. It isn't what I wanted for my daughter,' she said.

303

'I know that.'

'When I was young all I wanted was to get away from here but I didn't, and I swore to myself that I would make sure that my daughter did, that she married well and had everything. She's so beautiful that I knew I couldn't fail. I sent her to London, spent money on beautiful clothes and it happened. One of the most eligible young men in England offered to marry her and because of you she didn't accept him. You of all people. You were the lowest—'

'Mother—'

Dennes tightened his fingers on hers.

'You were the lowest, commonest boy in the whole place. In my worst nightmares I never dreamed that this could happen.'

Grace let go of his hand and moved in front of him.

'The business is partly yours now, Grace, I know,' her mother said, 'but this house is mine and I won't have him here.'

'Go and get your things, Grace,' Dennes said.

'But—'

'Go on,' he urged her gently.

Grace left the room. Her mother looked at him.

'You did this for the business, didn't you?' she said.

'Yes.'

'You and that Seymour boy, you think you're going to own everything, don't you?'

'Yes, I think we are. We have the quarry, Nat's talking about opening up the pits again and Mr Barmouth will give his stepsons his half of the foundry, I think. It's always a gamble of course, but when you have nothing, you have nothing to lose, whereas your husband and Mr Barmouth had everything. If you don't let us live here you'll lose Grace now.'

'Does that mean that you want to live here?'

'No, but she does, I think. I'd be civil. I don't get drunk and I don't go with other women and I make good money. You could teach me to play the piano—'

'I don't believe that you want to play the piano.'

'I do. Do you play chess?'

'No.'

'I could show you. Let us stay,' Dennes pleaded. 'I won't speak with my mouth full or sing before breakfast or talk about the foundry at mealtimes.'

'We always used to talk about the foundry at mealtimes, before Anthony became ill,' she said wistfully.

'Do you know about Mr Templeton?'

'He was the bane of our lives,' Dorothy said and a faint smile started along her mouth.

'He still is. Do you know what he did last week?'

Grace paused halfway down the stairs with a bag in either hand. It was the sound of her mother laughing, not the kind of laughter which ladies were given to, which she had been taught was the only kind of laughter which ladies were allowed, softly, with a hand up to the mouth so that they did not show teeth or (God forbid) the inside of their mouths. Her mother was really laughing, the kind of infectious laughter which Grace dimly remembered from her childhood, openly and wholeheartedly.

Grace sat down on the stairs, and when the laughter stopped there was the sound of her mother's animated voice, the one that she used when she was telling some gossip to her friends, the tone she rarely used in her daughter's presence. Grace left her baggage on the stairs and went into the sitting-room, and there were Dennes and her mother sitting in front of the fire, drinking sherry together. Dorothy's eyes were bright and her cheeks were flushed and she was smiling at him.

'Your mother says that if we behave we can come and live here,' Dennes said.

Grace looked at her mother for confirmation.

'You don't really want us here,' she said. 'You let him talk you into it.'

Dorothy looked down into her sherry. 'I'm rather afraid I did,' she said.

'He's like that,' Grace said.

'It's very lonely here without your father.'

'I know.'

'It would be even worse without you.'

Grace sat down on the arm of the chair where her mother was sitting, something she had never been allowed to do before. Her mother always said that it would damage the chair, but now she didn't say that or anything else, and when she looked up Grace hugged her.

They had another sherry and then Dennes and Grace went for a walk in the garden. It was such a lovely night, still and fresh and warm like full summer. Through the open window they could hear Dorothy playing the piano.

'On a clear night you can see Yorkshire from here,' Grace said, and she put her hand through his arm and walked him to the bottom of the garden where lilac trees grew so that she could lean over the wall and look past the little paddock and beyond the railway line and the houses to where, in the distance, there were trees and tiny square fields. 'Do you see?'

Dennes turned her so that she was facing him and he said, 'I see you. That's all I want.'

Grace watched the garden behind him, the big rockery at the top by the far wall, the various flowerbeds and formal lawns and the wrought-iron furniture beneath the porch window. He drew her into his arms and kissed her, and the sound of the piano music was soft in her ears, and the breeze which had seconds ago brushed the heather was gentle against her hair.